"Wildwitch . . . 'Tis Madness, the Feelings You Loose in Me."

He reached for her then, his fingers tangling in the curling tresses at the nape of her neck. "Tessa, God help me, I—" Fire flared in Rafe's eyes, his touch . . . his kiss . . .

Instinctively her hands swept up, her palms bracketing his stubborn, beard-roughened jaw, her fingertips skimming the silky midnight richness of his hair. At that instant she realized he was trembling, this bold seafarer who had hurled defiance at England's cruelest nobleman.

Rafe's whole body was shaking with need. And she wanted to give him all he asked, wanted to take the very essence of his soul inside herself and make it hers . . .

Wildwitch

KIMBERLEIGH CAITLIN

B
BERKLEY BOOKS, NEW YORK

WILDWITCH

A Berkley Book/published by arrangement with
the author

PRINTING HISTORY
Berkley edition/May 1991

ISBN: 0-425-12725-7

A BERKLEY BOOK® TM 757,375
Berkley Books are published by The Berkley Publishing Group,
200 Madison Avenue, New York, New York 10016.
The name "Berkley" and the "B" logo
are trademarks belonging to Berkley Publishing Corporation.

PRINTED IN THE UNITED STATES OF AMERICA

10   9   8   7   6   5   4   3   2   1

To Evelyn Witter, Max Collins, David Collins, and everyone involved in the Mississippi Valley Writer's Conference and the Writer's Studio— Thank you.

Prologue

THE fairies danced upon the sea, sprinkling the waves with stars. Tempted by the sight, Tessa skipped to the edge of the shore, reaching out her small dimpled hand to catch one of the tiny creatures, but they darted away with laughter she alone could hear. And Tessa was left with wet rivulets of silver sifting through her fingers.

More determinedly, she plunged deeper, even as the cold water lapped at her chubby knees, then her round, bare belly as she toddled toward the bits of light, unafraid.

A rush of a wave tumbled over her, splashing her face, filling her mouth and nose with salty water, but she didn't tumble down beneath it, and despite her age she didn't shriek or wail. She laughed as her face broke through the water, blinking her dark-lashed eyes, and shoving the thick mass of riotous curls away from her gypsy-sweet face.

Her feet were scarcely touching the pebbly bottom now, the sea spray filling her as if it were alive and wonderful, beckoning her. She wanted to fling herself into its arms, wanted to delve into its magic, its mystery. Beneath the deep, she knew, there were the fairy castles and fairy folk that had ever peopled her father's delicious fireside tales.

Once again she rushed into the water, pushing off with her toes, and she felt a strange, wonderful sensation of being suspended in the water, as if she were flying.

The sea filled her senses, making her head whirl in a maze of colors bright as jewels and three times as rare.

Then suddenly, someone grabbed her, whooshing her out of the water's arms and then she was safely in the strong arms of her father.

"Nay, nay, little one," he said teasingly. "The fairy folk cannot have you yet."

"Play," Tessa cried, her bottom lip thrusting out as if robbed of some sweet meat. "Want me to come play. Heard them, Papa. Singed to me."

William of Ravenscroft cradled his tiny daughter in his arms, his eyes glowing with tenderness. "Come now, poppet, the fairies must not be so greedy," he told her. "It has only been three summers since your mama and I plucked you from the waves. Surely you don't think the fairies would steal you back so soon."

Tessa squirmed as her father's arms tightened fiercely about her. His eyes darkened as if he were afraid some mystical being truly would snatch her from his grasp.

"Story, Papa. Tell me story 'bout me an' the fairies an' the ghosts from the sea."

"But you've heard that tale a hundred times," he teased her, "surely you cannot wish me to tell it again."

"Please! Please, Papa!" Tessa begged, knowing

the question and the answer was a game between them.

With a sigh, William crossed to the stone where he'd sat with his wood carving, and sank down among the yellow curled shavings, perching Tessa on his knee.

"Once upon a time, there was a man named—" He paused, waiting.

"Will'am," she lisped.

"And a beautiful woman called—"

"Hagar."

"They loved each other very much, so much that their love spilled over and filled the tiny cottage where they lived. They needed someone else to help soak up all this loving, and they thought that a child—a little girl—would be the perfect one to do so. But though they prayed and prayed to be blessed with a child, none came to brighten their days.

"They were very, very sad as time dragged on, and sometimes William would awake at night to find Hagar weeping."

Tessa stilled, subdued by the thought of her mother's sorrow, even though she knew the joy that was coming.

"One night, after William had found Hagar weeping, he felt he could not bear his wife's sorrow any longer. He left the little cottage and wandered along the cliffs to the sea. A storm had come the night before, and everything was washed clean from it, but though William usually loved the sea and its magic, tonight he found no comfort in watching the sea-sprites dance about upon the moon path in the waves.

" 'How dare you gallivant so joyfully when my

wife is in such pain?' William railed at the fairy folk, shaking his fist at them. And he threw a shell into the water to shatter the moon path. The fairy folk, their dance ruined, circled around William and threatened to plunge him deep into the sea where the great fanged monsters wait."

"Monsters," Tessa repeated with childish glee. "What next, Papa? What's next?"

"William faced the fairies unafraid. He knew he'd spoiled their dance, and they were right to be angry. But the image of Hagar, in the cottage for years and years to come, with no husband, and no baby for her to love, made him strong. William straightened tall and stared into the fairy king's eyes. 'I'll go to the monsters and gladly,' said William, 'if you will but grant me one wish. Give my poor wife a babe to love.'

"The fairy king scratched his diamond beard, his sea-green eyes dark with thought. 'Never have the fairies met a human who has not deafened us pleading for his own life,' the fairy king said. 'Mayhap we can help you. There was a ship from France we charmed into a reef a night past, and among the treasures was a child of such beauty and such courage, we carried her off in a magic cradle to our castle beneath the sea.'

"William's heart was thundering so hard, he could scarce speak. 'May my wife have this child? In exchange for my life?'

" 'Nay, this child is special, marked by the stars,' the fairy king told him. 'She is far too wonderful for mere humans to keep forever. Already the seers of the fairy kingdom have peered into her future and divined that she will be carried off some day by the lord of the sea, a bold sea ghost who will come for her. But mayhap we could entrust her into your keeping for a little while—until she is grown. Then you must give her back to us.' "

Tessa snuggled closer, the story and her father's warmth making her drowsy from her afternoon of play along the shores. "What happened then, Papa?" she asked, trying to stifle a yawn.

"Why, then, William agreed, and the fairy king took him to that tiny cove, where the waves lap quietly, and there, in a fairy cradle, was a tiny baby girl, more beautiful than anything William had ever seen." Hands, callused from work and care, smoothed over Tessa's soft cheek.

"So you taked the baby," Tessa said, leaning into his caress.

"William took the baby to Hagar, fully intending to give himself over to the fairy king, afterward. But when the king saw how much Hagar and William loved each other, he could not bear to part them. So, with the fairy king's blessing, William and Hagar kept the fairy child, bound only by the promise that when the lord of the sea comes to claim her, they will let her go."

Tessa gave a sated sigh, burying her face in her father's strong chest. Her lashes drooped, closed. "Tired, Papa," she whispered, and felt the answering rumble of her father's soft laugh.

"Then sleep, Tessa, babe," he whispered, kissing her tumbled curls. "Sleep, little love, and dream away of the sea phantom who will make you his bride someday."

Chapter One

THE roar of cannons thundered across the English Channel as flame spewed from scores of huge guns embedded in the bellies of the ships engaged in a deadly battle on the roiling sea. The English fleet coiled about the slower Spanish vessels like a great fanged serpent, striking at will, then skidding out of the grasp of the armada's massive galleons.

For days Queen Elizabeth's seamen had taunted their Spanish rivals, daring the hot-tempered captains to break away from the battle formation strictly commanded by the lord high admiral. The smug arrogance of the northern seamen ate like poison into the hearts of the Spaniards, searing deep into the pride that was more precious to them than life, until the threat of hell itself could not have leashed the fury in Captain Rafael Santadar's broad chest.

He braced his lean legs against the pitching quarterdeck, sickeningly aware that the rest of the Spanish fleet had fallen far behind him, agonizingly certain that he had been duped by a deadly gambit: Sir Francis Drake had lured him toward disaster. One of Rafe's hands clenched in white-hot frustration about the hilt of his saber as his helmsman battled to bring the *Lady of Hidden Sorrows* closer

to Drake's *Revenge*—a prize that would bring to its
captor not only glory, but mayhap enough magic to
put heart back into the sick, half-starved crewmen
who manned the armada's ships. But there would
be no laurels at the end of this foray, Rafe thought,
sensing imminent defeat. There would be naught
but a noose crushing his throat and the hope that
his crew would not share his fate.

He seethed with frustration, the taste of helplessness bitter on his tongue. He had no choice
except . . . except what? To turn from Drake's attack? To flee? The very thought seared him like a
flaming brand. Never once had a ship under his
command turned from battle. But if the *Lady* held
her course, these men who trusted him so blindly
would soon sleep with the serpents of the deep,
their death the price of Rafael Santadar's pride.

And if they rejoined the rest of the Spanish
fleet? Rafe jammed his fingers back through the
unruly mass of ebony waves that tumbled about
the chiseled perfection of his features, his gaze
sweeping over the battered, beloved hull of his
gallant *Lady*. If they returned without Sir Francis
Drake as their prize, a hangman's noose would
dangle from every spar, the punishment for dis-
obeying the lord high admiral's express orders.
Rafael's knuckles whitened as his hands clenched
into fists.

God forbid that a man with sea spray in his blood
should use the instincts gained in a lifetime of
roving stone-scoured decks. Saints forbid that any
mere ship's captain should disobey the bumbling
commands of the dull-witted king or object to the
misguided notions of a nobleman who grew seasick

at the sight of water. Spain would have had a better chance of invading England if Philip had sent the *Lady* alone, free under my command, Rafe thought grimly. But nay—

"Rafe, beware!" The cry shattered his bitter musings just before all sound was drowned out by the crash of a cannonball into the mast above Rafe's head.

Rafe dove from beneath the mast, the horrible sound of cracking wood wrenching through him as though his flesh had been torn. He braced his free hand against the pitching deck, the layer of salt cast across the boards to absorb the gore of battle grinding into his palm.

Oblivious to the pain, he leapt to his feet a heartbeat before the main yard crashed down, the shattered wood hurling thick, deadly splinters at the men battling to reposition the cannon. Rafe winced as he felt something slice his cheek. He brushed it away, his hand warm with blood, and had scarce regained his balance when the roar of another cannonball pierced the wind.

The second deadly ball cracked into the ship, smashing the block on which one of the massive cannons stood mounted. Rafe cried out as a hideous scream split the powder-hazed air, and the cannon's wooden supports shattered as the huge barrel crashed down onto a scrawny powder boy.

Rafe lunged across the blood-washed deck toward the lad, but felt a hand clamp around his arm to halt him. He wheeled in fury, desperation, nauseated by the death surrounding him.

" 'Tis too late." Bastion's ebony gaze locked with Rafe's, holding the soul-deep empathy that had

bound the two men in unbreachable friendship for
five long years.

"Sweet Christ, Bastion—"

" 'Tis too late for all of us." The tall nobleman
wiped his arm across his sweat-sheened brow, his
handsome features taut with defeat.

A sound grated from Rafe's throat, half curse, half
plea, harsh with despair. Too late . . . The English
had named him Phantom of the Midnight Sea, weaving tales about his courage and cunning nigh as
fantastical as those the Spaniards whispered about
Drake. The English sailors whispered of pacts with
the devil's bride, a winsome, poisonous spirit who
would wrap Rafe's ship in her midnight hair at his
command.

If only he *could* call upon some dark spirit as the
English sailors claimed, to carry him away along
with his beleaguered countrymen. But this was no
game of seek-and-dare. There would be no escape
for the *Lady* this time, nor for Philip's great armada. The arrogant, aristocratic planes of Rafe's face
contorted in anguish; his sensual lips tightened in
helpless rage. This was all a hideous waste—every
ball that pierced the ship's side, every man who
screamed in agony at the loss of arm, leg, or life.

If only he had heeded his first impulse when
Philip had summoned the *Lady* under Rafe's command to join the ill-fated fleet, Rafe thought desperately. If only he had lost himself in the maze of
islands that lay, treasure-rich and passion-hot, in
the far-flung seas an eternity away from avaricious
monarchs, scheming noblemen, and fanatical priests
thirsting for the blood of innocents. For all that he
loved Spain itself, he loathed the religious plague

scourging his country. He had sought to escape it through countless voyages to distant shores, but his quest to elude the Inquisition and Philip's hunger for England's throne had been hopeless from the start. Rafe had known it.

But he had ever been a warrior, battling the enemies of his country. From the moment he had stepped upon his first pitching deck, he had recognized the vital importance of recognizing the chain of command—on his own ship and in a vast kingdom as well.

Rafe's gaze flashed to the Spanish ships, then back to Drake's *Revenge*, the savage pride that burned soul-deep within him warring with his love of his men and his ship. He would no longer hurl them into this fools' cause. It was time to make an end. "Come about!" Rafe shouted. "Rejoin the fleet."

Smoke-darkened faces turned to him with a mixture of shock, disappointment, anger, and relief. Then murmurs worked through the mass of soldiers and sailors crowded together on the deck. "Retreat? Nay! Captain, don't—" The protests welled from the battle-grimed men like the swell of the waves.

"Get this goddamn ship back to the fleet!" Rafe roared, the sound of his voice turning the bravest of his men into cowards.

"Aye, sir."

"Whatever you say, sir."

Rafe wheeled, barking out commands, hacking at the fallen rigging with his saber in an attempt to cut free the fallen mast. Bastion labored beside him, as always Rafe's second pair of hands, almost his second self since that long-ago day when Rafe had saved him from the clutches of a band of English cutthroats.

"C-Captain."

Rafe looked up at the sound of a choked voice and saw the wide, frightened eyes of his cabin boy.

"Th-the ship is taking some water," Enrique stammered. "Lopez says we—we'd best go about. He vows the leak is not enough to sink her, but there's so much damage—"

"Lopez struck his first sail before your father was born. If he says she can stay afloat, she can stay afloat."

"Aye, sir."

Rafe's gaze swept to where a bone-thin sail maker wrestled with torn, flapping canvas. "Get de Leon to brace that accursed spar before it falls and crushes what firepower we yet hold," Rafe roared, "and—" Rafe felt timid fingers tap his arm. He wheeled to find Rique chewing nervously at his pale lips. "What in the name of the devil—"

"Y-your pardon, Captain, sir, but Lopez . . . he said to—to tell you a shell hit an arm's breadth from the powder magazine. Told me to assure you that no—no stray spark—"

Bastion's laugh rang out, and for a moment Rafe felt an urge to pummel any man fool enough to jest, yet the sound of Bastion's chuckle seemed to lift the fearful Enrique's flagging spirits.

"Rique, *mi querido niño*," Bastion said as he swung his arm around the boy's thin shoulders, "if a spark had touched that magazine, I promise you the captain here would be in no need of assurance, except mayhap that of final absolution. It seems that God hasn't deserted us after all, eh, Rafael?" Rafe caught the wry twist to Bastion's lips; his friend's face was awash with distaste as he peered across the deck.

"But betimes, *mi compañero*, I wish some of his servants *would*."

The acid humor in Bastion's muttered words made Rafe follow the young nobleman's gaze to where a figure seemed to materialize out of the haze that hung over the deck, pristine robes of the dread Inquisition wreathing his tall figure. Rafe could not stifle the sudden trickle of foreboding that slid down his spine.

"Encina. What the devil is that fool doing out here?" Rafe spat as loathing mixed with fierce resentment washed through him at the sight of the passenger. He had been forced to give the man berth on his ship, though for some strange reason Encina despised him. His jaw clenching, Rafe cast a scathing glare toward the man he knew to be his enemy. "I ordered that bastard to stay in my quarters during the bombardment," Rafe ground out.

"Perhaps the good father is on a mission of mercy," Bastion said with a wicked blandness, "to, shall we say, ease the plight of the dying."

Rafe snorted in disgust. "The only death Encina wants to see is my own, though God alone knows why."

Rafe's fingers rose to the powder-grimed collarbone exposed by his torn doublet, touching the aged scar that bisected a birthmark arcing across his flesh in the shape of a scimitar. Had Encina been able to open the faded scar with a slash of his ebony gaze, Rafe was certain he would even now be spilling his lifeblood on the salt-coated deck.

He felt the deck shift beneath him as the ship heeled leeward, its bow easing toward the Spanish galleons clustered on the distant sea, but his eyes stayed locked on the Inquisitor's enigmatic countenance. Thin as the blade of a stiletto, Encina's nose slashed between the sharp angles of his cheekbones, his full, carnal lips curled in a mysterious half-smile. It was as if in that slight curving of the Inquisitor's lips there lurked all the ugliness inherent in the religious fanaticism infesting Rafe's homeland—the blackest of curses, the most hideous of mysteries, the darkest of terrors.

Rafe stared at Encina, transfixed for endless seconds that seemed to fade into eternity. His nostrils filled with the remembered stench of human flesh roasting over burning faggots, and his eyes and ears were singed by the memory of terror-stricken faces, of men and women screaming, as the flames of the auto-da-fé ate away sanity, then life itself.

A stab of pain raked Rafe as he remembered the ever-gentle Brother Ambrose, the holy man who had taken in an orphaned boy and then, years later, had died rather than betray a fugitive Jewess to the Inquisition's crucible of death. In that instant Ambrose's beloved countenance blurred, bleeding into delicate, angelic features drowning in horror.

Rafe's mother . . .

He shuddered at the hazy memory, the sharp tang of danger from the Inquisitor sweeping through him more fiercely than even Drake's grave threat. His gut lurched as he saw Encina cross himself and turn his eyes, glittering with a strange kind of triumph, heavenward. Then the blinding haze of gunpowder closed its skeletal fingers about the Inquisitor, hiding him once more in a swirl of mist.

Berating himself silently, Rafe spun again to his

task, battling along with a dozen of his men to rid the *Lady* of her crippled mast. But he had scarce driven his blade through a single length of the stubborn cord when a cry rang out from below the deck, a cry that drove all color from the face of every man who heard it.

"*Fire!*"

Rafe staggered a step back, feeling as if a cannonball had slammed into his gut, his eyes battling desperately to pierce the pall of gunpowder that all but obscured the deck from his view.

Cries of terror erupted from the soldiers, and Rafe's own sailors turned to him, their eyes wide with horror. Fire . . . that most dreaded of all calamities on the sea. Fire, the disaster that would most likely kill them all.

Enrique's ghastly white face swirled before Rafe's eyes in a whirl of smoke that already bore the sharp tang of burning pitch and would soon bear the stench of death.

"The wounded!" Rafe bellowed. "Go below and get the wounded. Then abandon ship, each whole man carrying one who is injured. Manolo, prepare the boats!"

Rafe's eyes swept in an agonized path across the *Lady*'s hull, the one home that had ever really been his, the only place he had truly belonged. His jaw clenched as if each lap of the flames consumed a piece of his soul.

Bastion's face was white as he aided Manolo and the terrified cabin boy in settling a groaning soldier into one of the longboats.

"How . . . how did the blaze start?" the wounded man moaned.

"Cannonfire," Rafe bit out. "Drake's cursed cannons."

"Nay, sir." Rique's voice quavered with fear and confusion.

"What?" Rafe's hands closed on Enrique's spindly arms.

" 'Twas—'twas not cannonfire. Could not have been. Lopez . . . Lopez said the fire started among the dry stores, below—below the waterline."

"Below the waterline? Then how the hell—" Rafe felt the slash of talons in his chest, his stomach twisting as the stark certainty drove itself deep into his heart. Among the dry stores below the waterline . . . No man should have been near the storage hold. Every lantern and fire had been extinguished long before the *Lady* had first engaged Drake. Then how . . . ?

A soft splash at the side of the ship made Rafe turn, startled, to where the first of the longboats was being launched. Nay, impossible, Rafe thought as his gaze suddenly caught a wisp of oaken gold on the cresting waves. Even in the throes of panic the men could not have launched the craft so swiftly. Yet there was the longboat, cutting cleanly through the swells.

Rafe stared, his eyes struggling to pierce the engulfing haze. Though he could see only the outlines of the figures who manned the craft's oars, the person who stood in the small vessel's prow was illuminated as if by some hell-born flame, his graceful hands folded in prayer, his lean face turned toward the heavens.

Encina.

"Rafe!" Bastion's voice was raspy with smoke. The

billowing clouds were choking and searing the lungs of the men as smoke poured from the hatches. "The last boat lies ready. We have to abandon ship before she goes down."

The fury that had been building in Rafe through the endless weeks at sea, through the grating necessity of bowing to those less skilled than he, through frustration and helplessness, roiled through him. "I'll not consign her to the sea for naught, Bastion," Rafe said. "Drake will pay the price for the *Lady*'s death and for the death of my men."

"Dammit, Rafe—"

"I'm going to sail her into the *Revenge*, Bastion, and pray God I reach Drake before the powder magazine explodes."

"Sweet Christ, you can't mean—" Bastion's mouth hardened, and Rafe could see understanding flit across the young nobleman's face. "So, we take that bastard Drake down with us, eh, *compañero*?"

"*I* take Drake down with *me*. You join the others."

"You can't sail this hulk alone, crippled as she is," Bastion bit out. "We'll finish this together, Rafe, as we started it."

Rafe saw the stubborn set to Bastion's jaw and acknowledged the bitter truth to his words. He couldn't see to maneuver the *Lady* and steer her toward Drake at the same time. A hot fist seemed to crush his throat. He raised one hand and gripped Bastion's shoulder. Their eyes held for an instant. "Friend." The single, choked word from Rafe's throat brought a reckless smile to Bastion's face.

"You would do well not to spread such ugly rumors, *amigo*, else—"

"Captain, sir?"

Bastion's words were cut off by a quavery voice, and Rafe wheeled to where the gangly Enrique now stood.

"I—I'd like to stay, too." The boy raised his dark eyes to Rafe, gazing up at him with the worshipful expression Rafe had ever tried to quell. "Manolo and I could man the sails well enough so that you'd have a better chance."

Rafe drove his fingers back through his hair, his mouth twisting in pain. "Rique, this ship is going to be blasted into bits. You can't—"

As if to mock him, the tattered sails flapped in the wind, slowing down the *Lady*'s already waning speed.

"Damn Philip! Damn me!" Rafe felt a sickness roiling in his chest. "Manolo, Rique, set the topgallant to leeward. Bastion—"

"I'll take the helm. The others will need you on deck." He spun and bolted toward the hatch.

"Bastion!" Rafe called. The man paused and turned. "Ease toward Drake with the greatest of care, lest he be alerted that there is fire aboard. We have to dupe him into thinking the *Lady* is sinking—and lure the greedy bastard close."

Bastion gave a short nod, then plunged into the veil of smoke. "Cast off!" Rafe bellowed to the men waiting to lower the last of the longboats. A horrible sensation shot through him as his last hope of survival was blotted out. Death. He had courted it a thousand times and had even laughed at it.

But now, as he met the Reaper's stare, he knew it was no longer some rakehell adventure to be embraced with the same heedlessness as a courtesan. Death's face was hideous and haunting, the face of a phantom born of a nightmare twenty-eight years past.

With an oath Rafe shook himself as the sound of Rique's reedy voice babbling prayers and Manolo's grunting and cursing snapped him back to the present. His eyes stung, and his lungs burned. Heat burned through the soles of his boots from the inferno blazing below as he yelled directions to Bastion, but Rafe could not banish his mother's beautiful, horrifying face from his memory.

Features, once beautiful, savaged nigh beyond recognition, were lost in a tangle of honey-colored hair, deep blue eyes fierce with love for him, yet devastated by terror and loss, pleading. 'Twas too late, too late to delve into the desperation in those memory-shrouded eyes, too late to do aught but confront his own mortality. The image of her face hung in the haze as Rafe gripped the gunwale, his eyes straining, his mouth cursing, desperate as the ship inched toward Drake's own . . . closer . . . closer.

The English artillery roared, and the sound that had filled him with anger and bitterness moments before now twisted his mouth with a savage joy, because it assured him that Drake was not yet aware of the flames eating through the *Lady* from within.

"Windward, Bastion, a sword's breadth windward," Rafe directed in a hoarse voice all but lost in the choked coughs of Bastion. "If we can but hold for a minute more—"

"Captain!"

"Holy Mary!"

Rafe wheeled at the sound of Rique's sob, glimpsing in that instant a burst of flame roaring through the *Lady*'s pitch-encrusted deck. Rafe's hand flashed up instinctively to cross himself, and then he froze as the world exploded into a thousand shards of pain.

Chapter Two

THE sea was crying again, low and mournful, in tones that Tessa alone could hear. She turned her face into the wind sweeping the jagged stretch of coastline, wishing the gusts could dash away the pain clenched about her heart. But the long fingers of melancholy only bit deeper within her, raking more cruelly than the sting of the salty spray or the sharp tang of gunpowder rolling in with the tide.

Hagar was dying.

Tessa struggled to still her quivering lips, her perfect teeth catching at the fullness a dozen swains had dreamed of tasting. Though she willed the burning tears from her onyx-bright eyes, she could not keep her gaze from straying to the withered figure curled up on a boulder at the sea's edge.

Though she was wracked with pain, Hagar's whole being seemed strained with impatience. Her wide, childlike eyes roved out across the waves; her face, shrunken and sweet as a dried apple, was alive with the eagerness of a maiden awaiting her lover. Even the wreath of heather spray fastened askew in her pure silver hair looked like an ornament fit for a bridal bower, while gnarled fingers that could be infinitely gentle tossed purple blossoms into the lacings of foam cresting the swells.

She was waiting for him, Tessa knew. The husband Hagar had lost to those wild, relentless waves nearly a decade before. Tessa could see it in the old woman's smile—that beautiful, innocent smile that bold William Ravenscroft had carried in his heart across the sea—the smile that could warm even the chill touching the mists.

"Are you coming for her, Papa? Will you come again to bring her treasures?" Tessa whispered softly, memories of the man who had loved her like his own daughter tugging, bittersweet, at her heart. She swallowed hard, picturing Ravenscroft's gray eyes, the corners crinkled from squinting out across the glimmering waves, his salt-toughened features echoing the strength of a sea cliff and the gentleness of the safest of harbors.

The image her mind had conjured smiled, rope-scarred fingers reaching out as if to offer comfort, and she could almost hear that much-loved gravelly voice saying "Quit yer stewin' about, Tessa girl. 'Twill all come right in the end."

Despite her anguish, Tessa felt her own lips curve upward in an answering smile, and the burning sense of loss she had endured in the month past eased at the strange certainty that soon the long dead sailor would again carry off his own beloved.

Peace would be the gift brave William would offer his Hagar this time. And Tessa knew it would be the most welcome gift of all.

Her fingers clenched into fists, the bitter memories and fears that had eaten at her these past weeks intruding once more as she turned her gaze again to the figure beside the sea. In truth, peace had been scarce in the gentle Hagar's life since the night the kind Tarrant, Earl of Renfrew, had summoned them to his castle and told them that the *Mistress Gallant* had met her doom. Silhouetted against the crimson backdrop of a banner bearing the Renfrew device of a stag *courant*—a running deer—the earl had solemnly informed the assembled families of the sailors that all hands had been lost.

The anguish of that moment had been seared into Tessa's memory forever, and she had wanted to hate the nobleman who had owned the ship on which her father had served. But she could not, even in the first rush of grief. For despite the mighty earl's majesty and grandeur, the child Tessa knew he had once experienced a sorrow as great as her own.

Murder's blood-hued shadow dripped over the walls of Renfrew Castle, casting a dark pall over what had once been the most glittering of structures, leaving the earl hopeless.

How well Tessa could remember lying on her pallet in the darkness, listening as her father whispered to Hagar of the tragedy that had befallen his master, the earl. It had happened in that distant, fear-inspiring land called Spain—the disaster that had robbed the earl of his cherished only daughter and the little grandson he had hoped would succeed him. A band of cutthroats, William said, had descended upon the delicate Anne Renfrew, her bold Spanish grandee husband, and their young son, killing them and scattering their bones in an attempt to hide the hellish deed, so that the desperate earl had not even been given the solace of laying his loved ones to rest in the vast Renfrew crypt.

Grief? Aye, Tarrant Renfrew had borne it in plenty. But that emotion had been a luxury Hagar and Tessa could ill afford as they were forced to fend for themselves outside of the safe haven offered them as William Ravenscroft's own. A gawky girl, Tessa had been. Useless. Her head stuffed with fantasies fed by dreamy William's rich store of wondrous tales. While Hagar . . . no skill had she, no strength, except the beauty that had once turned men's loins to flame.

Flame, in truth the desperate woman had been consumed by the fires of hell after William's death. Rage swept through Tessa, as fierce as though she were again confronting the vicious brute Hagar had been forced to wed in order that she and Tessa might survive.

Jervis Keegan had taken all the wonders William Ravenscroft had given his wife and daughter and had sold those symbols of the sailor's abiding love, destroying Hagar's sanity. Even years after Keegan had met his end, people guarded against the evil eye whenever the old woman passed.

Witch. How many times had Tessa heard the superstitious villagers of Gnarlymeade whisper that dreaded word as they pointed surreptitiously to the aged woman who clung so fiercely to her love of the sea. They loathed Hagar, thought her touched by the Dark One. Yet neither their fear nor the old woman's increasing frailty had stopped them from seeking her out, to beg for love potions or possets to cure fever or far more sinister brews Hagar had always refused to make.

Even that morning while Tessa was on the beach gathering mussels for breakfast, an ebony-masked woman had stolen up to bedevil Hagar, demanding a deadly mixture destined, no doubt, for some faithless lover's flagon of malmsey.

Hagar had cackled with glee over the woman's fury at her refusal, telling Tessa of the incident with childlike relish. Tessa had seen no humor in the situation. She had felt only the thickening of the deadly cloak of mystery the villagers were weaving around them, a superstitious dread that would one day destroy them both.

No, Tessa thought fiercely, the blood-thirsting dolts would have no time to vent their hatred upon Hagar, or on Tessa. For soon death's white hand would scoop the old woman from their midst. And then Tessa would leave this place forever.

She swallowed the knot of grief that rose in her throat, shielding her face from Hagar's eyes with her own rippling raven tresses. Anguish beset her every time she thought of the deadly mass swelling on Hagar's breast. For months Tessa had watched the lump grow, burning hot and painful, as she had gently bathed the old woman. And now, the end must surely be near.

"Child?" The reedy voice held the petulant tone of a fractious babe. Tessa shoved back her curls and her sorrow, still clutching the roots she had been grubbing to brew a heartening tea.

" 'Tis all well, Mama. I'm here."

"Nay, you must come! Call William at once, so—"

"Papa is away, Mama," Tessa interrupted, trying to keep the tremor from her voice as she thought longingly of the man who had taught her to use wood-carving tools, the man who had shown her what wonder dreams could hold.

The tiniest twinge of resentment nipped at her consciousness at Hagar's blissful oblivion. But Tessa crushed even that slight annoyance, ashamed. She should be well used to deflecting her foster mother's questions about the husband the aged woman had adored. Yet Hagar's innocent words, spoken in gentle madness, always slashed open old wounds, old grief, preventing William Ravenscroft from sleeping in peace, even in Tessa's own heart.

"Remember, Mama? Papa is off at sea," Tessa said evenly, levering herself to her feet and thrusting the roots into the leather pouch tied to her waist. "But perhaps I can help until . . . until he comes." Brushing the dirt from her fingers, she hastened over to where Hagar sat. The blue eyes that were ever misted now reflected a clarity Tessa had not seen for years. A mingling of outrage, anger, and fear was trapped beneath the sparse lashes.

"Someone be trying to catch the fairies," Hagar said. "Ropes. They be trying to bind them."

Tessa followed the direction of the old woman's palsied hand as it pointed out over the waves to where coils of torn rigging and charred lengths of timber had washed in from the day's fierce battle. Though the whole of England had held its breath awaiting the outcome of the clash in the Channel, even the approach of Spain's great armada had held no power to penetrate the shroud of sorrow wrapped about Tessa.

Tessa forced a smile to her lips and knelt beside her foster mother, wrapping one arm around the bent shoulders. "Whist, now, all is well."

"But we must warn them—William's fairies. We must—"

."Papa's fairies are far too canny to be trapped by mere ropes. Most likely they will knot the cords up into flower petals and weave a charm about them."

"A charm? William would like that." Hagar's face brightened a little; then the brief light faded. "But mayhap they'll work a charm on you," the woman said softly. "Mayhap they'll send their sea ghost to wed you."

Bittersweet memories tugged at Tessa as Hagar spoke. William Ravenscroft had so loved to spin the tale of the sea sprites for Tessa when she was a child. He claimed the sprites had given Tessa to him and Hagar, exacting from them the vow that when it was time for the girl to wed, they would release her to a phantom born of the waves.

It had seemed the most mystical of stories, and Tessa had embraced it eagerly, clinging to it until the harsh realities of death, despair, and life with Jervis Keegan had driven the dream dust from her eyes.

Tessa smoothed her callused palm over Hagar's wrinkled cheek and pressed a kiss on her silver hair. "I'll not hie off with any sea ghost this day," Tessa said softly. "Nor any other, so long as you have need of me." She took Hagar's fragile hand in her own, carefully drawing the old woman to her feet. "Come now. 'Tis time we got back to the cottage. The stew is most likely done, and I'll brew you some tea."

"Tea?" Hagar turned to Tessa, lips parting, eager. "Will you put honey in it?"

"Aye, I'll put honey in it if you promise to lie down after you drink it. Papa would want you to sleep a little."

" 'Tis hard for me to sleep. Hurts."

"I know," Tessa said soothingly, attempting to guide Hagar toward the wattle and daub cottage clinging to the sea cliff's edge. "But I'll show you the new marionette I carved. 'Tis King Philip of Spain with knobby knees and a most prodigious belly."

"You needn't try to play ring-a-rosy with me, miss," Hagar said. "I know what you be about."

"And what is that, Mama?" Tessa managed a weak smile.

"Never you mind." Hagar pulled against Tessa's grasp, and the mischief twinkling in her vague eyes warmed Tessa's heart. "You be a stubborn child, even for a fairy." With a laugh tinged with a tightness born of pain, Hagar hooked her frail fingers in her heather crown and sent it sailing upon the sea gusts whisking past the rim of jagged stone.

" 'Tis a crown to trap the evil ones, my poppet!" Hagar cried out to something she alone could see. "To drag them down with their ropes and their timbers."

Tessa gently urged her foster mother forward, her lips curved in a half-smile. "You would have our noble Drake drown, Mama?"

The woman's lips curved with pleasure. "Not to be drowned," Hagar whispered conspiratorially. "But to be carried down to the castle beneath the sea. The one in the waves, all carved of crystal."

The tightness about Tessa's heart lessened, and she forced herself to release her dread of the future and the specter of death and soul-deep emptiness it would bring. She laughed as Hagar continued weaving a tapestry of the fantasy world her William had peopled with wraiths and fairies, to whom the old woman now added Sir Francis Drake.

Tessa laughed until she caught a glimpse of a grizzled, dull-witted face half hidden in the brush—a face that was yellow with fear and had a blind cruelty that chilled her blood.

She started to call out, recognizing the smith from the village below. But the filthy man was already hastening down the path to Gnarlymeade, leaving behind only the sound of the sea.

Yet now the sea whispered a warning.

Like a jealous lover the sea raged, hurling silver-crested waves against Rafe's battered body. Desperately, he clung to the splintered plank that held him afloat in the whirling madness, chill waters filling his nose and mouth, brine stinging his eyes, already raw from powder smoke, exhaustion, and despair.

With every shifting of muscle, pain ground through his thigh where some fragment of mast or hull or metal had been driven into his flesh by the force of the explosion. But even the wound that plagued him held little power to dull the torture that ran far deeper.

Armageddon.

Rafe closed his gritty eyelids, heedless of the burning, wanting only to shut out the scenes that tormented him even now, endless hours after the clashing ships' guns had fallen silent. But the sea flung the horrific images back at him as though to taunt him with its betrayal, tormenting him with the hideous sound of shattering hulls, the screams of sailors torn by cannon fire or being sucked down into the sea's dark belly.

Yet most merciless of all—the sea's final, most crushing betrayal—lay in the shifting patterns of the waves and the shadows of the enemy ships, now scattered in the distance like a child's toy fleet. For amid those blurred images, the sea-spawned enchantress painted agonizing images of Bastion's laughing face and Rique's wide-eyed innocence.

Dead, both dead, the sea reminded Rafe, *as much by your hand as if you had pierced their hearts with your saber.*

Guilt twisted in Rafe's gut, a shudder of self-loathing rocking through him as a wave swept him high, the force of the water nigh ripping the plank from his grasp.

She was right to blame him, his sea witch, Rafe thought bitterly. For it had been his choice to lead his men into disaster. And he alone should pay the forfeit unyielding fate demanded.

A choked sound, akin to a sob, was wrenched from him; the hot dampness of tears burned his chilled cheeks. It would be so easy, he thought numbly, his fingers loosening on the mangled length of wood, so simple to let go . . . of pain, of life. Without the *Lady,* without Bastion, without the crew Rafe had fashioned from a mass of raw adventurers, he had nothing, *was* nothing. It was the most bitter of ironies, was it not, that he alone should live? The one man with naught to lose, with no one, not even Bastion, left alive to lament his passing.

So many of the others, from the bumbling gunner lad to the crotchety old Basque sail maker, had had families—wives or mothers, at least—who would grieve for them. Yet they had died, while only Rafe had lived.

But no—at least one other had evaded death's claws. The thought burned Rafe like a poisoned brand. A breaker crashed, icy, over his face, but he scarce felt its chilling force as a fleeting image of blade-sharp features and disturbing opaque eyes flashed across his memory—the grand inquisitor, gliding away from hell upon sea-borne wings.

Encina. Lucero Encina. The man who despised Rafe. The man who sought to destroy him. But had the hatred roiling within the inquisitor's soul burned so deep that he had been willing to cast Rafe to the devil at any price? Even at the cost of the armada's defeat? Even at the cost of a hundred other lives?

It seemed impossible, absurd, that a man who had never even looked upon Rafe's face before the armada left port should go to such lengths to destroy him. Yet why, then, were the instincts honed in countless battles now clamoring inside Rafe? The memory of Encina's triumphant, satanic smile gnawed within Rafe.

He would live. Rafe gritted his teeth and dug deep into himself, dredging up his last reserves of strength. He *must* live to find the man who had sent his ship to the bottom of the sea and murdered his men. Vengeance. The *Lady* cried out for it from her tomb in the sea, and Rafe would give her rest if it cost him his own soul.

As if in challenge, the sea witch whirled her mighty current against him, taunting him with the relentless tug of her silvery, deadly skirts.

His stomach lurched as she bore him aloft, then dragged him down, carrying him ever farther from the vanishing fleet.

Vengeance? her voice jeered within him. *You are wounded, weak as a babe, and I have broken the strongest of men.*

A wild, soaring laugh burst, raw, from Rafe's lips. "Ah, but don't you know?" he sneered. "You are my lover, my only lover, and capricious bitch that you are, 'twill please you more to torment me than to grant me peace."

A smile split his parched lips as he clung to that thought, his feverish indigo eyes fastened upon the distant hazy line of gray that bordered the glittering sea. England. Land of heretics. Pirates. The bastard queen who had brought mighty Spain to its knees. He would have to gain those hostile shores if he were to survive.

His eyes narrowed against the glare of sunlight glinting off the sea. Despite her wiliness, Elizabeth Tudor had failed to crush from her subjects all loyalty to the Catholic faith. If he could but gain the shore and find some Englishmen with such religious leanings, mayhap they would dare to aid him, find a way to help him escape to Spain. At best, 'twould be like searching for the tiniest of uncharted isles within a vast sea, or a single, minute star in all the heavens. And he'd be slowed by his wound as well. No, he had suffered a score of injuries more daunting in years past and had battled, caroused, even wooed ladies afterward. He would grasp his only chance.

As if in answer a mighty wave swept him high, the water rippling against his stubbled cheek. A fierce, feral smile slashed across Rafe's lips, and his voice was harsh with determination. "Let me live, you cursed temptress, yet another day. And I vow I'll prove constant. I will give you my very soul if you'll but grant me life this one last time."

Passion and resolve pulsed through him as he locked the full force of his will upon gaining that elusive shore. Grinding his teeth against the exhaustion, the pain, he kicked against the pull of the waves, driving himself closer, ever closer to his destiny.

Tessa shifted restlessly on her pallet, her eyes open wide against the darkness that pressed in all around her. For hours she had struggled to sleep, to gain some small store of rest to build the reserve of strength she would need on the morrow. But it was as if a bevy of Hagar's sprites darted about the cottage's corners, pricking at Tessa with arrows wrought of dread. And even the haunting presence of her father, which had soothed her on the cliff, now whispered soft reproach: *The pain was worse this night, worse. Your blasted tea can do nothing. Your stores of food be almost empty, and your coin is gone.*

Tessa tried to blot out the voice, her hands knotting in the faded coverlet. It was just that she had not been able to peddle her wares. The chest was full of new-worked ruffs, if she could but go to the castles to sell them. And her marionettes . . . If she could gather a crowd at some crossroads and perform, there would be coin aplenty. But she dared not leave Hagar.

Not even long enough to steal down to the village? her father's voice challenged.

Tessa shoved herself upright, fighting the bitter taste that ever beset her tongue at the thought of a sojourn to the cluster of dank hovels three miles east of the cottage. Especially not to the village, Tessa thought fiercely, throwing back the meager coverlet she allowed herself, all the others being mounded over Hagar's easily chilled form. Most likely Tate McKenna is still angry over my refusal to bed him, and Alisette is still raging over the dolt's faithlessness. Aye, and they all no doubt be conjuring devils upon King Philip's ships.

I trusted you to take care of her, the voice railed at her.

"I have, Papa!" She shut her eyes for a moment, furious with herself for having fallen prey to Hagar's madness, for sobbing to some spirit that most likely had little use for the mortals it had once loved.

"You don't understand how hard it is. The people here, they make my skin crawl." She crushed the urge to continue pleading with her father's ephemeral spirit as a far more menacing vision rose in her mind— that of the village smithy, his eyes glowing, cruel.

Nay, she did not have the fortitude to endure the dull stares, the sly murmur as she passed. She did not have the patience to listen to their idiotic rambling about sin and sorcerers and Satan.

A scrap of memory flitted across Tessa's mind, and a smile dimpled the corner of her mouth as she recalled the last time she had walked Gnarlymeade's rutted streets. She had seen a spindly cooper's apprentice make the sign to guard against the evil eye as she passed, and she had not been able to resist sashaying over to him like some Siren and brushing his cheek with a kiss.

The lad had fled, wild-eyed, as though he could feel the flames of hell licking at his heels, and Tessa had not been able to quell her laughter until she was halfway home.

A wistful smile curved her lips. William Ravenscroft would have roared with glee had he seen the boy's rabbitlike flight. But even now she could not fully enjoy the incident. For it had taken her precious little time to see the subtle danger in her jest, and she knew she had to rein in her mischievous nature.

"If a thunderbolt ripped open the heavens and split a blasted tree, that lot of fools in Gnarlymeade would need to find someone to shackle with the blame," Tessa muttered to herself. "And if there is anyone on this coast they would take joy in accusing it would be me."

Forcing herself to her feet, Tessa shook out the skirts she had worn to bed to ward off the biting drafts. Nay, it was better thus. Better that she and Hagar stay close to the cottage while Spain reached greedy fingers toward English shores, for fear could make the most gentle hound savage its own master. And as for anyone who might be seen as an enemy . . .

Bare feet chilled by the earthen floor, Tessa made her way to Hagar's pallet to reassure herself of her foster-mother's safety. Her strong, supple fingers, in aching contrast to the withered ones curled upon the old woman's cheek, brushed back the tangle of moon-colored hair strewn across the crumpled, worn bedding. Though Tessa had scrubbed the bedcovers that very morning, the coarse homespun was already taking on the smell of the sweat that beaded the old woman's brow. She leaned down, laying her cheek against Hagar's shrunken one. "I love you, Mama," she whispered, her eyes stinging. "I'm doing my best to take care of—"

Tessa straightened suddenly, dashing away the

teardrops stinging her eyelids. Drawing her hands away from her face, she turned, suddenly aware that the orange and red lights dancing upon the darkness were not caused by the throbbing of eyes strained with crying. Rather, the lights were coming in through the cracks in the oak shutters.

She padded across the tiny room and pushed one of the shutters open. Her eyes fought to identify the eerily torchlit shapes upon the cliffs. They seemed like a seething mass boiling up the path from the village, and for a heartbeat Tessa was certain that the Spanish legions she had so impatiently dismissed from her mind had landed to lay waste to all within their path.

She started to spin around, intending to rouse Hagar and carry her into hiding in one of the caves that riddled the cliffs. But she froze as she glimpsed features that were disturbingly familiar—Tate McKenna's saffron hair glowing amid the crowd, Alisette's ivory cloak, the smith's hulking form. Tessa stared as though seeing them all for the first time. Moon rays splashed shadows across the mass of Gnarlymeade villagers, and the torchlight stripped their faces of all decency, leaving naught but stark, primal viciousness.

Tessa gaped for an instant. The sounds from the nearing crowd were clearer and more frightening by far than any threats couched in Spanish.

The voices railed in English, lashing out a single word that chilled Tessa's blood: *"Witch!"*

"Child?"

The thin, thready voice made Tessa wheel to where Hagar now sat upright upon her pallet, her lips parted in a drowsy smile.

"Be that William coming?"

Wild fear bounded in Tessa's breast as she stared into Hagar's sweet, innocent face, a face soon to be savaged by the mob storming along the cliffs. When Hagar saw them, suspected the evil they intended, there was no telling what would happen to the fragile thread of sanity she still possessed. Unless Tessa could hasten Hagar to safety without the old woman suspecting . . .

Biting her lip, Tessa grasped at Hagar's tremulous question. "Aye, Papa is come," Tessa said, dashing to the pallet. "Let's hasten to meet him near the caves."

"Meet him?"

Tessa winced at the joy that sprang into Hagar's soft blue eyes. "Aye, Mama." She draped a coverlet around the old woman's shoulders and drew Hagar to her feet. "We'll run down the path and surprise him."

"But—but nay! I cannot!" Hagar's gnarled fingers reached up to her tangled silver tresses, her eyes sweeping the worn fabric of her nightdress. " 'Tis a sight I look! A fright." A laugh gurgled in the old woman's throat, and Tessa felt panic race within her. "Tessa child, find my blue gown. I have to make ready."

"Nay, Mama! There is no time!" Tessa lunged to catch hold of the old woman's arm, but Hagar evaded her with stunning agility, whirling on her shaky legs with the rapturous aura of a new-bloomed maiden.

"William. My William!"

The screams of the crowd outside the little cottage swelled, seeming to swallow the tiny room and engulf the whole world. Desperate, Tessa clamped her fingers about Hagar's thin arms, and she shook the mother she had ever loved. "Mama, you have to come with me! Now!" Tessa yelled into Hagar's face, loathing herself for the pain that flashed across the old woman's features. "Papa is not coming. Never coming. But, Mama, the villagers are."

"William . . . " The aching, empty little whisper tore at Tessa's heart. "He's not coming?"

"Mama, do you want to die? Do you want them to murder us?" Tessa cursed, her fingers clenched tight around Hagar's frail wrist as she half dragged the woman toward the door. She heard Hagar sniffling and felt the chill night air dampen her face as she threw open the oaken door. It was as though cannon fire had split the night, the sound setting the mob to shrieking in fury. Their faces blended in a whirl of macabre horror. Tessa knew nothing but blind terror, the primal need to flee, to survive. She wrapped her arm around Hagar's waist, the old woman's cry of pain mingling with the crowd's roars as Tessa struggled to drag her from their path.

"Burn the witches! They'll not escape us!" The shrill cry grated against Tessa's ears, filling her mouth with the taste of raw panic. Stones sliced, knife-sharp, into Tessa's bare feet, and thorns raked savagely at her skin and hair as she plunged toward the cliffs as though she could feel death's chill breath upon her neck.

But the old woman beside her had none of Tessa's lithe strength, and even Tessa's arm urging her forward could not bring fleetness into Hagar's limbs.

Desperation pulsed deep in Tessa, the sound of

the charging crowd behind her swelling ever louder, becoming more menacing. A cry broke from her lips as she felt Hagar stumble, and Tessa heard the old woman shriek as she stubbed her toe on a jagged stone.

"Hurry, Mama!" Tessa urged. Summoning every wisp of her fast-waning strength, Tessa struggled to bear the old woman's weight as they battled onward. Yet Hagar's frail form was stunningly heavy, dragging at Tessa, slowing her as she forced herself to keep running.

We'll never reach the cliff, Tessa thought wildly, heedless of everything except the precious weight of her mother against her and the vital need to escape the jaws of the ravening mob.

"William . . . Will. I knew you'd come."

Tessa started from her own fear-crazed thoughts at her mother's raspy whisper. Hagar's voice was filled with a haunting serenity, but her already flagging steps grew even more awkward.

"Mama, help me. You have to try," Tessa begged brokenly, her eyes, her will, fixed upon the sea cliff's edge. It beckoned, dangling a chance of salvation with its twisted pathway winding down to the sea and its tangled web of crannies and caves that Tessa knew as well as she knew Hagar's tiny cottage. If she could gain that perilous path, it would carry her and Hagar to safety, and one misstep would send the villagers catapulting into the embrace of death.

Brands seemed to have been thrust into Tessa's shoulders, shooting flames through her exhausted arms, while twin demons burned her lungs with white-hot lances. A ragged sob raked her chest as she struggled to breathe, fought to keep on running.

But as she neared the outcropping of stone, her battered endurance crumbled.

Familiar as she was with the cliff, she knew she would need all her strength and steadiness to negotiate the twisted paths. If only she could stop for a moment, catch her breath for a heartbeat before she plunged downward, she could carry them both over the brink of the cliff and down the path to safety. She cast a glance over her shoulder at the crowd surging behind them, still terrifying, although their pace, too, had slowed as they crossed the rugged terrain.

A moment, Tessa thought desperately. Just one moment. She staggered to a halt, and sucked in a fiery, steadying breath, her shoulder raking against the coarse bark of a tree that clung to the rim of stone. Hagar sagged, limp, against her.

"Mama, 'twill be all right," she choked out. "We're nigh there." Her toes bit into the ground as she prepared to lunge the final steps over the top of the cliff. But at that instant the moon bathed Hagar's withered face in silvery light, revealing wide, glassy eyes staring at nothing and pale, shrunken lips curved into the ghost of Hagar's babelike smile.

"Nay!" The denial was ripped from deep inside her, the cry of a tortured child. "Mama!"

Dead. Sweet Christ, she was dead.

The certainty slammed into Tessa's stomach like the fiercest of blows, draining away all hope, all will. Her legs gave way beneath her, the coarse tree bark scraping her back and arms as she crumpled to the chill, damp earth.

Grief, hideous, racking grief, slashed through her as she clutched her mother's limp body. A sob clawed at her throat. Wild relief mingled with a

stunning sorrow that drove all thought from her
mind. She reeled from the pain, nearly drowning
in it, wishing that she would drown. Even the loss
of her own life would have been a fair price to pay
for an end to this anguish.

The pounding of footfalls seemed to engulf her,
swallow her. The stench of hate and brutality roiled
about her. But she cared not. The bellowing of the
crowd seemed like a macabre fantasy, a child's night
terror.

"Mama." She clutched the birdlike fingers of
Hagar's hand, stroked the tangled mass of silver
hair. "Mama . . . "

"There the witches be!" The triumphant cry penetrated the haze of Tessa's grief. Her broken crooning was lost in a gasp of pain as her tresses were
yanked in a brutal grasp.

Her head snapped back against a beefy male
shoulder, and Tessa cried out as she saw the leering,
blood-lusting faces. Their enemies, the savages who
had driven her and her mother to desperate flight,
and Hagar ultimately to death.

Tessa struggled against the hands that held her,
still clinging to the old woman's limp form. Feral
protectiveness surged through her as she battled to
shield her mother's body from the pack of savage,
circling beasts.

"Murderers!" Tessa screamed. "Leave her alone!
She's dead. Dead!"

A meaty fist slammed into Tessa's jaw with bone-
shattering force. "Shut yer yap, Satan's daughter."
Her attacker turned. "McKenna, get the cursed hag
away from her!"

Tears burned Tessa's cheeks; hysteria ran wild in

her chest as hands locked upon the old woman's frail body, ripping her from Tessa's grasp.

With a cry of anguish, she fought in vain to grab hold of her mother's limp arm as Hagar was hurled to the rocky ground. "Nay!" she screamed. "Mama!" Tessa tried to free herself, but her captor's sinewy muscles only coiled more tightly around her, the stench of the forge making her certain it was the filthy smith who held her. "Let her go!" she shouted. "God curse you!"

" 'Tis not God who honors yer curses, is it, witch? Aye, but he'll watch wi' a whore's own pleasure as ye roast upon a stake! Cursin' brave Sir Francis, feedin' poison to the waves."

"You're mad, the lot of you!" Tessa cried. "Hagar!"

"Did you not hurl nightshade into the sea and call out incantations?" The hated Alisette's pointed features appeared near Tessa, the eyes that had once sparked with jealousy taking on a glimmer of righteous satisfaction.

" 'Twas naught but a wreath of heather!" Tessa kicked and tore at her assailant. Anguish ripped through her like a jagged-edged sword as a heavy boot slammed into Hagar's fragile ribs. "Stop, for Christ's sake! She's dead, damn you!"

"Think you that matters?" someone cackled. A coarse hand turned Hagar's slack body face up so that the torchlight painted her death-glazed features the hue of blood. "She'll soon feed the flames. And you, her child, devil-spawned—"

"We'll see you both cooked on Satan's spit." The smith's breath was hot in Tessa's ear. "An' God will rejoice in yer screaming!"

"There'll be no screaming from Hagar, you bastard! You can't hurt her now." A hysterical laugh rose in Tessa's throat, her eyes raking the night-shrouded sea as Hagar's last joy-choked whisper echoed in her mind. "Papa came for her," she said.

But the smith heard nothing, deafened by his thirst for her pain. "Drag the witches down to the place where they worked their evil magic." He licked away the saliva pooling at the corners of his eager lips. "Take them nigh the sea."

Tessa saw three men jerk Hagar's body upright, blood lust glittering in their eyes. Spittle flew into the old woman's glazed eyes. But it was the slight curve that still softened Hagar's mouth that tore out Tessa's soul—the ghost of her mother's sweet smile.

The thought of that innocent face being consumed in flame, even shielded by the oblivion of death, was an agony too great for Tessa to bear.

With all of her strength, she drove her elbow into her captor's groin, then broke free the instant she heard his bellow of rage.

"Beware! Catch her!" the cries rang out in warning. But Tessa was like a wild thing, her fists flailing, teeth tearing at any who would try to stay her from reaching her mother.

She drove toward the old woman, crazed with the need to wrench her from the cruel mob's grasp. But at that instant hands flashed out, slamming with bone-cracking force into Tessa's back.

The rim of the cliff spun before her eyes, the loosened stone giving way sickeningly beneath her as she hurtled toward the edge.

Then Tessa was falling, plummeting into stygian blackness. She screamed, grasping desperately for the jagged stone wall of the cliff, the certainty that she was crashing to her death an icy knot in her breast. Suddenly a giant fist seemed to smash into her body, driving the air from her lungs in a rush of stark agony as a maze of blinding colors swirled before her eyes.

Sweet Savior, it hurt so much she must be dying, Tessa thought, fighting to claw her way through the pain to the peace that awaited her.

"Mama," she croaked, reaching out for Hagar's hand, wanting the old woman to draw her into the shimmering serenity beyond the pain. But other hands closed about Tessa, warm hands, tender hands, their strength seeming to seep into her very soul.

"Nay," Tessa choked out, "I . . . have to find her."

"*Chitón, chica.* Hush."

The deep velvet tones enveloped her, wrapping her in a soothing cocoon of warmth.

Tessa's fogged mind struggled with confusion. "Please," she groaned. "Please help me."

"*Sí, ángel.* You're safe now."

Tessa opened her eyes, but jabs of pain pierced her, blinding her, sickening her. She caught but a glimpse of the presence bending over her—the hair dark as midnight over the sea, the face rugged, tender.

"Who—who are . . . " Her faint voice trailed off.

Hagar's voice seemed to whisper upon the wind: "Mayhap they'll work a charm on you . . . send their sea ghost to wed you."

"Sea ghost," Tessa murmured without knowing she spoke aloud. "Mama warned me . . . "

Tessa's lips curved in a faint smile as she drifted into the haven of the bold sea phantom's arms and away. Away from the beach and the mob and the horror and into a world of crystal castles beneath the ocean waves, and fairy sprites who blessed her with Hagar's sweet smile.

Chapter Three

HOW long had he lain there, cradled within the crook of stone? Rafe did not know. He knew only that he had crawled ashore what seemed an eternity past. Half dead with fatigue, he had ripped strips of linen from the hem of his shirt and bound them about the jagged wound in his thigh. He had been too exhausted to attempt to dislodge whatever was embedded in his flesh and had promised himself that he would tend to the task when he awoke. But now the wound scarce even oozed blood, and opening it would start the flow afresh, weakening him. He could ill afford weakness now.

Weakness? He was cursed lucky not to be dead! He cast a grateful glance toward the cold waves. They had numbed his pain and slowed the flow of his blood, most likely saving his life. Yet now he longed for some heat to drive back the ice that seemed to chill the very marrow of his bones.

The sunrise would be a mixed blessing, for while it wrapped him in golden warmth it would also strip away the cloak of darkness secreting him from the prying eyes of any who might happen along this godforsaken strip of beach.

A grim laugh breached his lips as he reached down to tighten the bandage on his leg. Only a madman would choose this rugged wasteland as home. Daunting cliffs soared above the ledge on which Rafe sat, and the stone face fell away beneath him before plunging into waters studded with huge boulders, like the fangs of a ravenous beast that would tear open the hull of a ship and devour it, as they had nearly devoured Rafe as he battled his way through that deadly maze.

Rafe had no idea what lay above him, obscured by the rim of earth. The lushest valley, perhaps, or the most verdant farmland, he thought with a stirring of wry amusement. Or some vast city or bustling village. But of a certainty, whoever dwelt above would likely be discomfited to find an enemy Spaniard upon their shore and would more likely still be eager to capture him.

Rafe's fingers closed around the dagger still encased in his soft leather belt. Even though he lay wounded, it would prove difficult indeed for one of Elizabeth's subjects to chain *this* Spaniard and display him like a dancing bear in a player troupe. Already he had endured a hell far worse than any English heretic might serve him. The will to survive that had ebbed away as the *Lady* disappeared into the sea now surged into his limbs anew with his thirst for vengeance.

" 'Tis not what you would have wished for me, is it, Brother Ambrose? This thirst for another's blood," Rafe murmured, leaning his head back against the rough plane of rock behind him. He closed his eyes as the beloved hermit's face rose in his memory. Ever the peace weaver Ambrose had been, truly forgiving any wrong done him, infinitely patient, with a tolerance rarely seen among the Spanish. Rafe could still smell the musty, familiar scent of herbs and leather and ink that clung to his clothing as he bent over his young charge, teaching, always teaching.

The holy man's hermitage had been chill and bare, yet within that tiny hut the hermit had flung wide the gates of the world to Rafe—showing him a tapestry embroidered with blazing deserts, raging oceans, and jungles heavy with foliage. Ambrose had taught him French, Italian, Latin, and English, languages the hermit had treasured; and he had woven among them bright-hued skeins of history glittering with threads of intrigue and adventure.

Enraptured, Rafe had listened to his mentor, drinking in all the knowledge the brilliant man had to offer. Yet never had Rafe suspected what other, subtle lessons he'd been taught—a respect for true wisdom, empathy for the suffering of others, and a sense of justice, honor, and courage that had little to do with flashing swords and blazing pistols.

Now Ambrose's carefully mastered lessons, combined with Rafe's own battle-honed instincts, would prove his most valuable weapon in effecting his escape. It would be enough. It had to be, Rafe thought, his memories melting away, carried off by the sound of the waves.

Ever attuned to his mistress's capricious moods, Rafe raised his head, a tiny smile playing about the corners of his mouth as he listened. Even without opening his eyes he could hear the subtle shift, sense that the sea's formidable temper was rising. Yet though he could hear the gathering storm in the distance, the wild, sweet tang in the air that ever accompanied the sea's fury was strangely absent.

Bemused, he drew in a deep breath, trying to smell the storm. But there was nothing, nothing but the slightest hint that something was very wrong. His eyes snapped open, his weary muscles tensing.

But though the breakers still displayed their formidable magnificence, he could detect no tempest rising.

The hair at the nape of his neck prickled as he listened, alert. The sounds he had heard seemed closer, sharper. Voices. He could hear them on the wind now, high above him, and he could see an eerie orange glow staining the rim of the cliff. A fire? No, there wasn't the thick stench of land being consumed by a blaze. The glow was something more perilous for him—torchlight.

The wickedly curved blade of his dagger hissed as he pulled it free of its scabbard. Madre de Dios, had they come for him? Had he somehow been discovered? No. No one could have guessed he had found haven on this shore. Why, then, the shouts? The shrieks of outrage splitting the night?

"Burn the witches! Take them!"

Rafe's flesh crawled at the blood lust in the man's voice and could sense the hot eagerness in the unseen face, an eagerness Rafe had been forced to confront far too many times upon the countenances of his countrymen as they reveled in the Inquisition's awesome spectacle of auto-da-fé. San Savior, the English heretics were putting some poor wretch to the flame!

'Tis none of your concern, Santadar, Rafe told himself grimly. The Inglés are hungry for blood,

and it would please them no end to add you to
their pyre. It would be suicide to interfere. It would
be mad.

But at that moment a woman's cry—desperate,
shattered with grief—tore at him.

"She's dead! Leave her alone!"

He could feel the woman's anguish as though
it were inside his own skin. Mad? Rafe thought,
casting caution to the winds. It would not be the
first time he had been labeled thus.

With an oath, he slipped from his hiding place
and began to climb, his hands grasping at the
steep cliff face, his leg throbbing as he fought to
reach her.

"*Perdición*!" Rafe's scraped fingers bled as he
struggled to gain a handhold. Then suddenly his
heart lurched and he froze as he looked up.

"Por Cristo! She is going to fall! Don't let her!"
He gasped the words, a desperate prayer, as a sil-
houette broke the line of orange rimming the cliff.
Skirts whirled like a phantom's robes, and hair flew
wildly about a lithe body as the woman clawed at
the emptiness beyond the edge of the cliff.

"Mama!" It was a hopeless, agonized cry. Instinctively, Rafe stretched out his arms, as if his will
alone could break her fall, but the figure plunged
onward, plummeting down, down.

Rafe heard the mob's angry roar at being robbed
of their prize, felt his own stomach roil at the sickening thud as the delicate figure crashed into an
outcropping a stable's length from where he clung.
Heedless of his own safety, he crept across the space
that separated them, his feet skidding on the rocks.

"Sweet Mary, don't let her be dead!" Rafe said the

words over and over, as though to weave a charm to
hold the girl's spirit in a body that must have been
crushed by so great a fall.

He flung himself to his knees beside her, his
stomach knotting as moonglow limned death-pale
features obscured by a lush tangle of ebony hair.
She was tiny and so delicate, Rafe thought wildly.
She could not possibly have survived the fall. Yet
he clung to hope, remembering the courage he had
heard in her voice as she confronted the mob.

He reached out and touched her ivory skin,
which was still as warm, soft, and smooth as a babe's.
He pressed his fingers to the delicate arch of her
neck, finding the hollow where her pulse should
have throbbed. Nothing.

"Blast it, *chica*," Rafe said through gritted teeth,
scooping her up into his arms. "Don't let those savages do this to you!"

The shouts of the mob above sent outrage and
fear for the girl shooting through Rafe's lean form.
He cast a furious glance at the cliff's edge, its once
clean line now sullied by the silhouettes of the cruel,
screeching townspeople.

"The witches! They both be dead now, an' we'll be
gettin' no screamin' to pleasure us!" a feminine voice
cried in the tone of a child robbed of a sweet.

"Stop yer caterwaulin'!" someone else snarled.
"We have the old hag here, an' Tessa she be among
the crags at the bottom of the cliff. We'll drag 'er
to the stake even if she already be dancin' with
Satan."

Tessa? Rafe cursed the vicious wench above for
giving the girl in his arms a name, a name that made
the fallen waif even more painfully real to Rafe.

"What if she flew away?" The whining cry set Rafe's blood to boiling. "What if she escaped?"

"Look you, Alisette. I'll throw my torch down, an' ye'll see."

Rafe's heart lurched as he saw a flaming brand arch through the night sky. How many times had Ambrose, a healer, warned him about the danger of moving someone who had taken a fall? Yet scarce thinking, Rafe hauled the girl into a hollow the harsh waters and winds had carved into the stone.

His eyes locked upon the torch streaking in a blur of light down the crags. In a shower of embers, it landed on the ledge an arm's length away from Rafe's boot. Gritting his teeth against the pulsing pain in his thigh, he scrambled deeper into the hollow, holding his breath, afraid even that the slight rasping sound would betray them. He held the girl closer, as if his body could shield her from the mob.

Sweet God, could the townspeople see the two of them? If the cursed murderers descended upon Rafe and the girl, there would be small chance of escape. Hampered by his injured leg, he had barely been able to climb the jagged cliff himself. To attempt it with the girl as well would be impossible.

And beneath them stretched the beach, studded with boulders that gave way to the implacable sea. They were trapped as surely as though they lay chained in the hollow of stone.

Suddenly Rafe's racing thoughts were stilled by an odd silence from above, a silence heavy with fear. He could sense it. He wished desperately that he could see the crowd, but the outcropping that shielded him and Tessa blocked his view.

He strained to hear some sound, gain some clue as to what was happening, but there was naught but the ominous silence. "By God's wounds," he heard someone say at last. "The witch be gone."

There was a shriek. Then a voice he recognized as that of the bloodthirsty wench of moments ago babbled, "But—but she cannot be gone! She—Tate, tell me she did not fly away!" There was real fear in the woman's voice now and none of the eagerness that had laced it before. Rafe rejoiced in it, praying the mob would succumb to terror and not search for the girl further.

"Tate." The wench's voice was choked. "She could not have flown unless she really was a witch."

"Of course she was a witch!" the harsh voice interrupted, and in those masculine tones Rafe could hear a warning. "Remember? The fine lady who came to the village. She said—"

The voices of the man and woman were lost in fearful gasps and uncertain babblings.

"Don't be fools," a gruff voice broke in. "Even if she do be a witch, even if she do be flown, we still have the hag, and she, after all, be the one we wanted."

"You cannot mean to burn old Hagar," someone said. "She be dead. An' Tessa, she loved 'er sorely. Mayhap she'll do us evil."

"Evil?" the gruff voice bellowed. "I'll do ye evil if ye be soft on Satan's daughter! Damn yer hides, we snared at least one of the birds we set our nets for. An' I intend to see this old whore roast."

Rafe's stomach churned, and he gritted his teeth against his fury and helplessness. Whoever still lay in their clutches was dead—they had said so, and the girl had cried it out in her anguish. But the girl might yet live. Rafe's fingers tightened about her delicate frame, willing life into her as he listened to the shouts of the crowd.

"Rannal is right," came a cry. "I rousted meself from me bed fer a burnin'!"

"I did the same! An' I'll be damned if I'll be cheated."

The cries above swelled. The crowd was eager again, hungry. Shouts of triumph rang out, and Rafe could almost see the murderers falling upon their prey. He felt a stirring of relief as he heard the crowd recede from the ledge above, but he couldn't banish from his mind thoughts of the poor woman they still held, and the gruesome rite that awaited her. There was naught Rafe could do for her, but the girl . . .

The still-burning torch cast a faint light into their tiny lair. Gently, Rafe stroked the hair away from Tessa's features, feeling for any sign, any thread of life, but before his probing fingers could complete their task, they stilled upon the girl's face, his breath catching in his throat.

A sea sprite. Madre de Dios, the girl had the face of a sea sprite. A delicate nose, upswept dark brows, a mouth seemingly molded to tease and torment, and crescents of sooty lashes that fell rich upon high cheekbones. Yet 'twas her chin that caused hope to surge anew through Rafe. It was the most wondrously stubborn chin he had ever seen on a woman. It revealed a stubbornness that would not be defeated by the hatred of a cursed mob or by a tumble from a mere cliff.

"Wildwitch." Rafe felt his heart slam against his rib cage. "Don't let them win!"

He caught his breath, stunned as he detected the tiniest of sounds, the merest of whimpers.

The anguished whimpers pierced Rafe's very soul, as the delicate fingers pressed against his chest, clutching his tattered shirt in a desperate grasp. "Mama . . . "

Rafe cradled her tightly against him.

"Nay, want to . . . have to find her." The girl's voice trailed off as she sank back into the void of unconsciousness, but her fingers stayed clamped, iron-tight, about Rafe's shirt, as though she fought to cling to life. A jolt of joy and protectiveness shot through Rafe, driving back even the pain burning in his leg.

Mayhap it was that he had seen so many die upon his ship, mayhap it was that he had nearly drowned himself, but life suddenly seemed the most wondrous of gifts.

"Alive! Damn them all to hell, you're still alive!" he repeated, his voice harsh with victory. "And I vow you'll remain so, if it costs me my very soul."

The phantom was calling, snaring Tessa in a gossamer web of sea foam and salt spray. She struggled against him, wanting desperately to follow the rough-velvet voice that lured her, yet knowing there was some reason she must not.

"Wildwitch," the wine-dark tones urged her, fingers woven of mist caressing her cheek. "Come away."

Yet though her whole body ached to touch the sea phantom's hair, longed to kiss the arrogant curve of lips obscured by diamond-bright haze, she could not keep her dread at bay.

"Promised . . . " She forced the word through stiff lips. "Promised Hagar I wouldn't."

But the mystical world Tessa was floating in only threw back at her a dozen images of Hagar, no longer broken by life, but young and alive and laughing.

"Hurry along, Tessa babe," her mother bade her, tugging one of the girl's dark curls. "We ever knew you would away with him."

Tessa hung back, hating the stark vulnerability sluicing through her, feeling it deepen into unaccustomed fear. "Nay, Mama, I cannot . . . cannot leave you. Jervis—"

"Do you not know, poppet?" Hagar's laugh rippled out.

"Jervis cannot touch me now. And in truth, the love I shared with William was worth the pain I suffered under Jervis's heel."

Tessa reached out toward her mother, picturing again the horrible bruises discoloring Hagar's fragile jaw during the time with Jervis, hearing Hagar's cries. "Nothing . . . nothing could be worth risking—"

" 'Tis worth risking anything, Tessa babe. Worth risking everything."

"Wildwitch."

The phantom's voice throbbed with longing, tugging at something deep inside Tessa, something even her fear could not make her deny. As she ran toward him, his cloak of midnight whirled about his broad shoulders and his lips parted in welcome. He stretched out sinewy arms to embrace her, but as she flung herself against him, he melted away. She cried out, feeling herself hurtle through the mist. Yet it was no longer spun of rainbows and light, but rather of suffocating darkness.

"Nay!" Tessa cried, clawing at the blackness where the images had vanished.

But her fingers only bared hideous scenes of Jervis Keegan's brutal face, his huge fists pummeling Hagar's slight body, and of flames licking hungrily at flesh.

Burning her . . . Jervis was burning her!

Tessa cried out, wrenching at the bonds wrapped around her, but 'twas no longer the mist that chained her, rather 'twas the folds of a midnight-dark cape.

"Let me go!" she cried to the ghostly figure. "I have to help her."

But the phantom only clutched her tighter, his voice oddly rasping, tinged with sorrow.

"I wish to God we could."

There was anguish in that dark, silky voice, anguish that drizzled foreboding through Tessa's veins like icy water.

Desperately she fought to wade through the suffocating numbness besetting her senses, but the crashing pain in her head blinded her, leaving her adrift in a sea of darkness.

Darkness haunted by a phantom? Nay, 'twas not his voice, not some misty sound born of dreams. Those deep tones were painfully real, sweeping away her fantasies and leaving behind a reality far more hideous.

"Witch!" The cry ripped through Tessa's mind, raking wide her terror.

She shook her head in an effort to clear it, white-hot spikes seeming to ϸierce her skull. But hands, infinitely gentle, held her firm.

"Hush, *chica*, hush. You'll do yourself harm."

"Mama . . . they're burning her."

"There is naught you can do, wildwitch, naught you can give her now but your prayers, your love, and your determination to stay alive yourself."

"Nay!" Tessa shoved at what seemed a solid wall of iron, yet warmer, smooth. She opened her eyes and saw a dark, mystically handsome face whirling above her in circles. Pulse racing, she clutched at the arms that held her as the crash of the waves and the sound of the screams snapped into focus. 'Twas real, she thought wildly. Her horrible dream was real. She was by the sea, and Hagar . . .

Thrusting herself upright, Tessa screamed a denial, her eyes fixing upon the hellish scene painted red and orange upon the beach below—villagers shrieking with glee, drowned in the light of flames, writhing about a blaze even now consuming a huge stake . . . a stake to which was bound a limp figure, its once silver tresses afire.

"Don't, wildwitch." The deep voice of her captor seemed filled with pain. His large hand cupped the base of her skull, pulling her face against his broad, muscled chest. "For God's sake, don't look."

A horrible animal sound rose in Tessa's throat.

She drove her balled fist into her captor's chest, heard the man let out a grunt of pain. Breath hissed between his bared teeth, but his grasp upon her loosened for only an instant. With all the strength she possessed Tessa wrenched free, nigh hurling herself from the ledge in her desperation to reach Hagar.

"Stop, blast it!" Rafe called after her, gritting his

teeth against the pain lancing through his bruised ribs. "They'll kill you!"

Kill her? Rafe thought grimly. The mob would get no chance to work their evil upon her. The girl was flinging her own life away, dashing madly down the crags in a crazed rush certain to send her crashing to her death.

Rafe grasped the hilt of his dagger, his scalp prickling as he heard the crowd roar when they saw her—a wolf pack, blood-maddened, turning upon its next prey. He launched himself after Tessa, stones jabbing at him, the wound in his thigh, scarce noticed before, raking him now with razor-sharp claws.

He saw the girl slam to a halt, facing the mob, and even from a distance Rafe could sense her courage and the mob's . . . what was it? Fear?

A chill rippled down Rafe's spine, but he kept on bolting downward, toward her.

"It's Tessa!" he heard someone within the mob cry out. "She be alive!"

"Impossible! 'Tis impossible!" Gasps rippled through the crowd. "We saw her fall from the cliffs!"

"God save us, she do be a witch."

'Twas as though the girl held them all in a mystical spell, the sea winds lashing her hair, her face pristine white against the twisting flames.

"A curse upon all of you!" Tessa's hysteria-tinged voice trailed chill fingers down Rafe's spine. "I wish to God I *could* sell my soul to the devil! Then I would hurl you all into hell!"

The strength in her voice held the mob at bay. Their pinched gray faces told Rafe that in truth they expected the earth to split open and swallow them at her command.

But the next instant Rafe sensed something crumbling within the girl. He knew not whether it was because the wind shifted, carrying with it the stench of charred flesh, or because the breeze rolling in upon the waves now had a soft, mournful sound.

A hopeless sob rent Tessa's breast, and she crumpled to her knees in the white sand.

A murmur rippled through the mob, her show of weakness feeding again the fires of their cruelty and superstition.

"Seize her!" a bull of a man bellowed. "We'll make an end to her as we did the old hag!"

Rafe saw several cruel-faced figures step toward Tessa, but he sensed in them some hesitation. In that instant he saw his only possible chance to save the girl, aye, and to save his own cursed skin.

Despite the danger, a grim amusement stole through him, and his teeth flashed white in a feral smile. In a dozen different courts—in Spain, France, and countless exotic islands lost in the great seas— beautiful women had told him he was as handsome as *el diablo* and thrice as tempting. Mayhap if he could play the part for these cowardly English dogs . . . Madre de Dios forgive him.

Driving back the tide of pain in his thigh by force of will, he closed the distance between himself and Tessa, then thrust his dagger into its scabbard and planted his hands on his narrow hips. " 'Tis folly to threaten the devil's bride." His voice was velvet over steel, resonating through the night, dark, mysterious. "You cannot know what demons she might summon."

A rustle went through the crowd, and he could

see the women clutching at their men's arms, could see the bull of a man who had seemed to be the mob's leader sink back against the dark shadows of his minions, his smithy's apron stained where it covered his quivering belly.

"Who—who are you?" The bravado in the hulking smithy's face was shot through with fear, fear the man was obviously fighting to conceal.

Rafe saw Tessa straighten and turn her face toward him, but he wrenched his gaze away, loosing upon the sea winds a sinister chuckle. "*You* know me right well, do you not, smith? Have we not met in the flames of your forge a dozen times?"

"The flames? I—I know you not."

Rafe let a terrifying laugh rake the night. "You lie."

"Nay, I— Jemmie, Tate, grab the murderous bastard."

"Ah, but they know me, too. I crawl into their souls at night, listen to their lust, their lies." Rafe took another step toward them, his lips curling in a sneer as they shrank back. "You have already done enough this night, burning the old woman. Before you pluck away yet another life, I shall steal one of you for my own, to replace—"

A sharp surge of triumph pulsed through Rafe as he saw a good portion of the crowd skitter away and disappear into the night. He dared to cast a glance at Tessa, meaning only to make certain that she was still all right. But this time it was he who felt a sudden urge to step back—from the tempest raging behind the girl's perfect features.

Her face gleamed like bleached ivory, her flawless skin drawn tight across the dainty curve of cheekbone and chin. Her eyes glittered onyx: her berry-red lips trembled not with fear but with fury, indignation. 'Twas the face of a savaged Madonna, or was it the face of the devil's own angel?

With one graceful sweep Tessa got to her feet and moved toward him, regal as an empress, despite her rags.

"My mother was no witch." Crystal clear, Tessa's voice lashed the night, her gaze locked upon Rafe's face. "I will not let her lie in her grave with that legacy."

Rafe felt an odd tingling of embarrassment heat his cheekbones; then it flamed into anger. What was she doing? He was trying to save her cursed life.

His hand shot out and closed in a bruising grip upon Tessa's arm. "Don't be a fool," he whispered. "They'll burn you."

The girl choked out a wild little laugh, tears welling up on her lashes. "Think you I care?"

"Your mother would have!"

Tessa flinched beneath the weight of his words, and Rafe saw her catch her lip between her teeth. The gesture was achingly childlike, and he felt a sudden urge to pull her into his arms, comfort her. He could almost see the gaping wound in her soul.

He heard the rumble of the crowd and cursed himself. He had become lost in Tessa's eyes for only a heartbeat. But that heartbeat might well be his last.

The superstitious fear that had rippled through the mob moments before had vanished, leaving the blind rage of men who had been made to look like fools.

The light of the torches still gripped in the villagers' grimy hands glittered red in their sunken eyes, and Rafe could smell the stench of blood lust upon them.

His hand closed on the hilt of his dagger. He was but one man—one man who knew well when Dame Fortune had cast her dice against him.

"He be a murderin' Spaniard!" a voice called out. "A devil-spawned Spaniard shielding the witch!"

The men at the front of the mob surged forward a step. Rafe forced Tessa behind him and drew his weapon.

"Kill them!" a feminine voice shrilled.

The smith lunged toward him, wielding a flaming torch as though it were a sword. The makeshift weapon hissed toward Rafe. He leapt back, evading the full force of the blow, a burning pain searing his forearm as the flames licked at his skin. He heeded it not, lunging toward the hulking smith with pantherish grace, his blade biting flesh. But the swift movement cost Rafe dearly; a hot, sticky flow of blood dampened the bandage on his leg. The mob roared, scenting his blood.

Hopeless. Rafe knew 'twas hopeless. He spun toward the girl, meaning to give her a quick, merciful death away from the stake. But at that moment he saw one of the other villagers dive toward him. Rafe prepared to meet his charge, but something pale, the size of grapeshot whizzed past him. With a horrible crack, the object slammed into Rafe's assailant's face, and blood burst from the man's bulbous nose as he fell, half conscious, to the sand.

Rafe's eyes flashed back to see Tessa scoop something up from the shore. A stone! The little witch had hurled a stone!

Rafe felt a sudden wrenching in his chest at the girl's courage, courage as pure, innocent, and moving as that of the cabin boy Rique who had perished on Rafe's ship. Pain lashed through him as he poised his dagger, ready to plunge it into her breast.

But at the last instant something stayed his hand—a sound in the distance, which made the mob fall silent, listening. Hoofbeats. A dozen riders, at least, crashed through the gnarled brush at the end of the beach. Rafe glimpsed bright silver armor and destriers dripping with velvet and steel.

"Warburton."

The name was whispered among the crowd, and that single word seemed to hold more power than the threat of the devil. Even in Spain Rafe had heard rumors of Neville, Lord Warburton, a man who would suffer anything to lay before his queen the head of a hated Spaniard.

Rafe stiffened, his gaze flashing to the stony cliffs that beckoned to him like the islands sailors' eyes conjured after voyaging too long—mirages, untouchable, impossible. And yet if he could grasp Tessa's hand and bolt for the stone rim—

"Hasten!" He caught her wrist and started to run. "The cliffs. Head for the rocks."

Suddenly the earth before him seemed to erupt in a mass of sweat-sheened sorrels and bays, their massive hooves slicing the turf all around him.

" 'Tis a Spaniard, milord!" one of the armored men bellowed. The others sent up a cry of triumph.

Before the soldiers could fall upon him, Rafe gouged deep into his soul, dredging up all the strength and daring remaining within him. With a guttural roar, he flung himself through the mass of horsemen and maneuvered Tessa into the crowd of fleeing townspeople.

Eager cries rang out behind them from men-at-arms hungering for their Spanish prey. Rafe heard the villagers' screams as the horsemen plunged heedlessly among the crowd, trampling anyone in their path. He cursed as the terrified mob engulfed the two of them, blocking the narrow trail that was the only access to the cliffs above and escape.

Escape? Nay. He and Tessa would never reach the top of the cliffs before the English riders overtook them.

"This way! Run!" Tessa's voice cut through the panicked shrieks of the crowd. Rafe's eyes caught hers for a heartbeat; then she tugged him through the crush of villagers toward a wall of solid stone.

Rafe started to pull away from her. But suddenly the moonlight glinted on a break in the jagged rock. A break too small to admit a destrier—in truth, almost too narrow for Rafe himself. An amusing thought flashed into his mind: He, the grand adventurer, the bold seafarer, was being rescued by this slip of a girl.

The thought vanished as vicious cries slashed the night like a blade.

Rafe saw Tessa fling a glance over her shoulder, caught a glimpse of her beautiful, tormented features. Then they plunged into a maze of darkness lit only by the faintest of hopes.

Chapter Four

THE barren hollow lay in a tangle of brambles as though God himself had scorned it. Tessa moved closer to the meager flames. Soreness drummed dully through the score of scrapes and bruises she had suffered in her fall, but she scarce felt the pain.

She only stared blankly into the maze of thorns and stone, glad somehow that she was lost among them, wishing she could lose herself in their midst forever. For never did she think she could bear to look upon sapphire summer skies and heather and feel joy again.

A movement a cart's length away caught her eye, and Tessa gazed at the stranger, who was hunkering down beside a pile of twigs, driftwood, and grasses. The flowing seafarer's shirt clung to the rippling muscles of his back, covering the broad shoulders that tapered down to a narrow waist and hips encased in breeches of blue-gray. Hair, dark as sin and thrice as tempting, fell in disarray over his collar. The clean, sharp lines of his face were half hidden by the silken waves.

"That fire will bring Warburton down upon us,"

she bit out. "You might as well raise up a banner and be done with it."

But the Spaniard only turned, regarding her with enigmatic indigo eyes before he bent to coax bigger flames among the bits of kindling. "Are you warm yet?"

She started at the soft-spoken words, stunned to find that the fire now blazed hot and bright. How long had she been lost in grief? Minutes? Hours? Her gaze locked with the dark-haired man's, and she she sensed that he had been watching her for some time.

God how she hated him for seeing her thus vulnerable, hated the soul-deep understanding in his eyes, the tenderness carved in his features—features whose masculine beauty far surpassed even that which she had conjured for the visage of her phantom. Pity had ever made her angry, chafing her with the knowledge that someone else knew how helpless she felt. To shield herself from that stinging pain, she sent him a fulminating glare.

"Oh, aye, I'm warm. 'Twill give me the greatest of comfort when they hurl us both into Warburton's dungeons."

"Come, now, 'tis scarce a bonfire. And 'tis hidden in this crook of stone."

He strode toward her, the long-legged grace of a man wed to the sea somehow made all the more dauntingly masculine by the slightest limp. Tessa's gaze flashed down to his sinewed thigh, her eyes locking on the linen bandage stained dark with blood.

"Your leg . . . " Tessa started. "For God's sake—"

" 'Tis nothing." He shrugged, one corner of his

mouth tipping in a half-smile. "Scarce a scratch."

She gritted her teeth at his dismissive tone.

" 'Tis you, wildwitch, who concerns me." One large hand reached out to brush her cheek. "I wish I had some food to offer you, or at least a cloak."

She shrank away from his gentle touch, grief and bitterness welling up inside her. "Don't trouble yourself, milord Spaniard. No doubt there was passing little space for such amenities upon your ship, what with it being stuffed with inquisitors and torture devices and vicious, murdering soldiers."

She wanted to goad him to anger, drive him away. But she was stunned to see anguish dart in quicksilver flashes across his features, torment nigh deep as her own.

He levered himself to his feet, half turning away from her, and in the moonshine she could see the rippling muscles that spanned his broad back knot in pain.

"I think after this day you'll have small cause to worry about 'murdering' Spaniards, milady," he said bitterly, and despite her own misery Tessa felt a brief sting for having baited him.

"Of course"—the Spaniard turned toward her, his dark brows low over narrowed eyes—"you'll still be forced to shield yourself from chivalrous, honorable Englishmen such as those we encountered."

His words pierced Tessa's armor of anger like a masterfully aimed lance, and she faltered beneath the nightmarish images that rose inside her. She suddenly felt chilled. The tiny flames but an arm's length from where she sat seemed to jeer at her. She leapt to her feet as though to escape her hideous memories but they only coiled tighter about her,

choking her. Nay, she thought wildly, she could
not, must not, let her anguish break free before this
man. To do so would cleave the single fragile thread
she still held upon her sanity.

She heard a soft curse, then a weary sigh as he
raked his fingers through his hair. "Tessa . . . "

She was stunned to hear her name upon the lips
of the stranger, stunned further still as he went on.

"I didn't mean to . . . " He hesitated, those mes-
merizing indigo eyes regarding her with solemn
apology. "Remind you of those men, remind you of
your mother. But 'tis not weakness to show grief,
chica. There is no shame in it."

"Don't tell me about grief, you pompous Spanish
bastard! Nay, nor shame! You've played the honorable knight, whatever purpose it served you. Now
get the hell away from me." Tessa spun away from
him. "Just leave me alone."

The words were a whisper, a plea, and she loathed
herself for having uttered them. But there was no
strength left in her. Nothing but an empty void that
ached for Hagar's winsome smile and the childlike innocence that had allowed the old woman to
fling her thin arms about Tessa, long after girlhood
had flown, and comfort her with kisses and loving
embraces. "Tessa babe, Mama loves you." Every
night before Hagar drifted to sleep she had whispered those words, her affection giving peace and
security to Tessa's restless spirit.

Tessa raised shaking fingers to her face and covered her eyes with her hands as she sank down on
the cold earth, and it was as though the flames that
had consumed her mother now consumed Tessa's
soul as well.

"I should have protected her, saved her," Tessa choked out. "She trusted me."

She heard muffled footsteps approaching from behind her, and she could sense the tall Spaniard scarce a hand's breadth away from her. Yet she had not even the will to muster shame at this show of weakness.

"You did all you could, wildwitch."

She felt the soft wool of his sleeve brush her shoulder as he lowered himself beside her.

" 'Twas not enough! She was like a babe. Helpless. And I let them . . . let them burn her."

A jagged sob tore through her, and she lowered her hands from her cheeks to see the face of the Spaniard taut with compassion, his eyes bright with tears. He was but a stranger hurled up on an enemy shore, a man whose own life was in jeopardy. How, then, could he ache for a nameless old woman and for her, a girl who had slashed him with brutal words?

She winced as she felt his rope-toughened palms cup her face, thumbs gliding over her cheeks, brushing away her tears. "They didn't burn *her*, wildwitch." His voice touched her, breath-soft as his hands. "Her spirit had long since flown."

"Her hair was aflame . . . and her face—"

"I assure you, they could not touch her."

A strange ripple of warmth soothed her as he echoed Hagar's own words from her dream.

"There was a hermit I knew when I was a child." Pain and love touched the man's voice. "He always said that God scooped innocents up in the palm of his hand before the flames could touch them."

"Nay, not God. Papa. Papa came for her."

Tessa shut her eyes against the agony of loss, the horrible aching emptiness of being alone. She grieved for herself, abandoned by the only two people she had ever dared love. "Why . . . why didn't he come for me as well? Why didn't he take me, too?"

Arms flashed about her, strong arms tempered with tenderness. They crushed her against the broad wall of the Spaniard's chest, his heart thrumming against her ear as he cradled her against him.

"Cry, wildwitch, cry," he urged her, his breath warm against her temple, his lips soft as they rested upon her tousled hair. "I promise you that even this grief will pass."

And she did cry. Hideous, racking sobs that rent her very soul. Tears soaked the man's torn shirt, burned her cheeks raw. She could scarce breathe, the pain ran so deep. How long she wept, she knew not, knew only that the Spaniard held her, comforted her, crooning soft endearments in a language rich and sultry as the darkest wine.

"*Sí, ángel*, little one." His murmurs soothed her as exhaustion weighed her eyelids. "Pour it all out."

Tessa curled even tighter against him as she quieted, her face buried against his half-open shirt, his hair-roughened skin radiating warmth through her numbness. She whimpered as the smooth metal of a ring heated from his skin pressed against her cheek. But she nudged the small circlet away, burying herself against the man's welcoming strength.

Drained. She felt so drained. This Spaniard's tenderness was like a safe harbor in a storm. She sank deeper into the haven he offered.

"I don't even know your name," she breathed.

She could sense the warmth of his smile. " 'Tis Santadar, milady," he said, the words a caress. "Captain Rafael Santadar. I am called Rafe."

"Santadar?" Tessa hiccuped, nuzzling her tear-streaked face against his bronze, satin-smooth skin as tales of the sea unfurled like silk ribbons in her exhaustion-numbed mind. Stories of a sea phantom had seeped into her own dreams, a bold captain whose single flaw was that he was an enemy Spaniard.

"I heard a story of a man named Santadar," she breathed. "They called him the phantom."

"The Phantom of the Midnight Sea." There was pain in Rafael's voice. Tessa felt a sudden urge to comfort him as he had eased her anguish, but her weariness was too heavy, sucking her down into darkness.

"Sorry," she managed to whisper. "I'm sorry I hurt you. My temper is . . ."

"I've faced far worse, wildwitch," his voice drifted to her. "'Tis forgotten."

"And your wound . . ."

"Just sleep now."

"Sleep." Tessa echoed. Her eyelids fluttered, the lashes coming to rest upon pale cheeks.

Rafe stared down at her for long moments, more moved by her sorrow, her trust, than he would have believed possible. He trailed his fingertips across rose-kissed lips, then down over the chin that filled him with such rare delight.

Rafe raised his eyes to where the dawn-blushed horizon fell away into what he knew was the sea.

"She is like you, this woman," he said to the distant waves. "My wildwitch." He turned his gaze again upon Tessa's face, still in what he sensed was unaccustomed repose.

Shifting his position, he felt a dull thrust of pain in his leg, knew full well he should check beneath the bandage, cleanse the wound, remove whatever was embedded within. But Tessa was so soft and warm against him—and he was suddenly so blasted tired.

He smiled inwardly. Once he had known an ancient sailor who had carried a musket ball in his leg for forty years without troubling to extract it. The aged sea wolf had sworn the chunk of lead enabled him to predict storms on the ocean and foretell hurricanes.

Rafe sighed, burying his face deeper in Tessa's heather-scented hair. The ability to foresee disaster—'twould be a gift worth having when he returned to the sea. Amused tenderness stole through him as he drowsed. The sailor had boasted that he had predicted every storm that blustered his way. Would the musket ball have warned him of the tempest even now cuddled within Rafe's arms? A sea storm of ebony curls, blazing dark eyes, and soft lips that tempted him.

He felt himself drifting deeper into sleep, and was glad . . . glad for now, at least, to abandon himself to the storm.

Pain exploded in Rafe's side, hurling him from dreams of midnight-hued hair and flashing eyes the color of ebony. He cursed, rolling away from whatever had struck him, fighting desperately to remember where in God's name he was as he grabbed for his dagger. But webs of sleep dulled his senses and the blazing sun rising in the east blinded him as he struggled to focus on a maze of plunging horses and savage faces.

"Dog! Spanish bastard!" The words lashed out at him, snapping him to awareness and bringing back to him the events of the day before, a day filled with death and danger and Tessa's raw courage.

But these men were no wild mob armed with scythes. Rich armor and caparisoned destriers flashed before Rafe's eyes.

Warburton. The name was branded in Rafe's consciousness as he bolted to his feet, battle-ready. He caught but a glimpse of Tessa's fear-whitened face as he lunged past her, hurling himself toward the man nearest him—too late. A flash of gleaming metal arched toward him. The flat side of a broadsword slammed with bone-shattering force against his wounded thigh. Agony exploded in his leg as the chunk of metal embedded in his flesh clawed deeper into the muscle.

A guttural cry was ripped from his lips, and a red haze drowned him as the pain drove him to his knees. Cool hands, Tessa's hands, fought to break his fall, and the smooth, sea-scented folds of her skirts pooled beneath him as he crumpled to the ground.

"Rafe . . . sweet God!" Her voice drifted to him, and there were tears in her agitated tones.

Then rough hands grasped Rafe's arms, nigh wrenching them from the sockets as two of the lord's minions yanked him from Tessa's embrace, jerking him upright.

"Did ye think ye could escape us, ye accursed papist scum?" Dull yellow eyes gleamed through the slit of one man's rusted visor, and fetid breath turned Rafe's stomach.

He fought to clear his blurred vision as an elegantly appointed figure urged his mount forward, the hooves of the plunging black stallion slicing the turf inches from where Rafe stood. Trappings scarlet as blood dripped from the majestic beast; the rider's chest was emblazoned with the raging boar crest of the Warburton lords.

"Look you, men!" A voice like stones grating across iron rang out. "Did I not tell you we would find the puling Spaniard crawling like a maggot upon the belly of the cliff? Yet I had not imagined that he would already have found some traitorous whore's skirts to hide behind."

White-hot rage lanced through Rafe, mingled with blind terror at the name Warburton had flung at Tessa—traitorous whore. In the space of a heartbeat the consequences for her part in his flight struck Rafe, and he wrenched at the arms of his captors, desperate to be free. "The woman is no traitor! I took her hostage—held her against her will!"

"I see no chains about those pretty wrists, and you, milord Spaniard, are as weak as a suckling rat. If she had chosen to flee, you would have been helpless to stop her."

"Damn you, she is innocent!"

"Silence! Her guilt and her punishment are for me to decide." Warburton's eyes blazed with hatred. "You I arrest in the name of the queen!"

Rafe struggled against his captors, desperation firing his next words as he strove to turn Warburton's wrath away from Tessa and bring it down upon himself. "Queen? You have no queen—only lecherous

Henry's bastard, got off the bitch Boleyn."

He heard Tessa's faint gasp, relished the deadly silence of Warburton's men-at-arms. Then something slashed toward him, and the English lord's iron-toed boot crashed savagely into his jaw. Rafe's head snapped back, the salty sweetness of blood filling his mouth as he sagged against the men who held him, only their brutal grip keeping him on his feet.

"Spanish scum!"

Rafe heard Warburton's roar as though through some hell-deep tunnel, saw him slam back the visor that had obscured his face, a face now purple with rage. There was the menacing hiss of a steel sword being stripped from its scabbard before the noble man's weapon flashed high. In that instant Rafe knew he had pushed the cruel lord too far. He would die. And by dying, he would abandon Tessa to the clutches of this monster.

"Nay!"

He started at Tessa's scream, then was stunned as she leapt between him and Warburton's naked blade.

"Tessa—" He cried out her name, but his plea was lost in the nobleman's dark curse.

"What the hell—"

"You must not kill him, my lord." The girl's voice held not a tremor; her hair rippled back from that pristine enchantress's face. "Else you will face Her Majesty's wrath."

"Wrath? The man is a bloody Spaniard. I'll gift good Queen Bess with his head upon a pike—"

"And end up with your own adorning London Bridge for your efforts."

Rafe gaped at the girl, sensed all surrounding them staring as well.

"How dare you—" Warburton rumbled.

" 'Tis for your own sake I dare speak, my lord. He is an enemy captain washed up on our shores, a man of considerable importance."

Rafe had seen battle-hardened sailors face cannon fire with less courage, and he marveled at Tessa's cool words.

"If you kill him before Her Majesty's councillors can question him . . . " Her face waxed pale, her jet-hued eyes catching at Rafe's for but an instant. "The queen's lack of patience with mistakes is nigh as legend as her father's."

Warburton shifted in his saddle, discomfort evident in every line of his body, despite its shield of armor. "Insolent wench! 'Twould serve you well if I cleaved you in twain."

"As you wish, my lord." The girl who had blazed with defiance earlier was now such a picture of humility that Rafe would have laughed aloud had the danger not been so thick around them. "I meant no disrespect. I was but trying to spare you—"

"You, a rag-clad guttersnipe, were trying to spare the lord of Warvaliant Castle from the queen's wrath?" His sword dropped slowly to his side. "Who the devil do you think you are?"

"Naught but a weary peddler, my lord. Tessa of Ravenscroft." She took a step forward, the sunlight washing over her features. "You probably remember me not, but I've ofttimes come to Warvaliant Castle."

"To drive me mad, I warrant! Tessa, you say?"

Rafe felt a stirring of betrayal as he heard the tentative recognition in Warburton's tones.

"Aye, my lord. I am the girl who works the ruffs."

One of Warburton's gauntleted hands rose to his gorget, as though he were fingering one of the intricate starched ruffs that usually bedecked his velvet doublets. "The wench with the puppets," Warburton mused. "Aye, I know you now. A most diverting visitor at the castle's gates, as I recall." The nobleman paused, his silence lying heavy on the air. Rafe sensed Tessa's shoulders stiffen beneath the coarse fabric of her gown. Something in Warburton's tone made Rafe's skin crawl.

"You left Warvaliant in much haste last time you visited, seller of ruffs. I . . . er, my mother, Lady Morgause, was most disappointed."

"No more, sir, than I. My own mother, she is ailing." Tessa's voice dropped low. "*Was* ailing."

"She had the good sense to die, then?" The cruelty of the question made Rafe want to strike the arrogant nobleman.

Rafe clenched his fists. "Your savages burned her mother," he grated.

"*My* savages, you say, Spaniard? Is it not true that your King Philip loaded the armada with inquisitors and with instruments of torture to use on the English people? 'Tis even rumored the holds of your vessels are filled with wet nurses to suckle the babes orphaned after you slaughter every Protestant on this island."

"There were no women on any Spanish ship. And the inquisitors . . . " The words died on Rafe's tongue, his lips stiff with loathing at the memory of the white-robed figure of Lucero Encina gliding like an evil specter across the waves, after he had turned the *Lady of Hidden Sorrows* into a hell.

The chuckle that rumbled from Warburton's chest

made Rafe clench his jaw. "Well, it matters not what your monkey of a king sent to ravage English shores in any case, does it, Spaniard? 'Twill all lie at the bottom of the sea before the week is out. Yet 'twill not be without a high toll in English lives. Aye, and a high price from the purse of our good queen. And there is naught Elizabeth Tudor loathes more than an empty treasury—unless it is one of the men who helped to drain it."

"You and your queen can go to hell," Rafe snapped. A shadow fell across Neville Warburton's features, and Rafe felt the cold fingers of death trail down his spine.

"You'll *wish* you were there, papist scum. Aye, wish it when our 'heretic queen' flays your skin from your body with white-hot knives. But the wench is right: You must be alive to afford Queen Bess that amusement."

Rafe had faced death a score of times, faced it and laughed, but in this man, this Warburton, there lurked something spawned by Satan himself.

"Take me, then, to your queen," Rafe said. "Let her witness Spanish courage. But the girl, Tessa—"

"You can wager that we'll take you to the queen, captain, as soon as you heal enough to survive the journey. And Tessa—" Warburton's tongue caressed the soft syllables.

"Release her, curse you. I took her captive, held her against her will."

"Did you, now, milord Spaniard?" Warburton leaned down from his mount, his gauntleted hand snarling in Tessa's dark hair. "Then I shall be forced to rescue our poor little puppet mistress from your clutches—and draw her into my own."

Chapter Five

WARVALIANT. Like a huge gargoyle, the mighty castle rose from the sea cliffs, its ugly claws digging deep into the stone, its turrets tearing at the sky. It had dominated these lands since the glittering Plantagenets possessed England's throne, and it was as though the very ashlar within those ancient walls had soaked up both the madness and the majesty that had graced the reigns of Lion Heart, and evil John.

Inside the fortress's daunting walls Tessa shuddered, the meager folds of her gown little shield against the drafts that swept the dank corridors. Thick, musty air clogged her lungs; dust from the bones of nameless prisoners centuries past seemed to sift over her skin as Neville Warburton and his men led her deeper, ever deeper, into the great beast's belly.

She had always hated the huge edifices where she sold her wares, preferring the wild, windswept sea and the meadows, sweet-smelling with blossoms. Even the hovel she and Hagar had shared had an openness about it. Through countless tiny cracks the winds could whisper to her, call to her. Here, buried deep in stone, it was like death—cold, still, empty.

Death . . .

Tessa swallowed hard, squinting into the dimness that cloaked the passageway despite the torches of Lord Warburton's men. Her gaze fixed yet again upon the slumped form of Rafael Santadar, slung carelessly over the shoulder of a massive man-at-arms. His midnight hair fell in rough-satin waves about his face; his sinewy arms dangled limp as a rag doll's, while his leg . . .

Tessa felt her stomach lurch as her eyes flicked to the armor of the man who carried the unconscious Spaniard. Beneath Rafe's thigh, the polished steel breastplate was dulled with blood. And with each step the careless oaf took, he ground sharp metal deeper into torn flesh.

She knew not where Warburton was taking them, had no idea how long it would be before they reached whatever destination he had planned. But she did know that with every drop of blood that flowed from the gaping wound, Santadar's meager chance of surviving diminished further.

'Twas a miracle the man had managed to live this long, what with the reckless dash Warburton had made across the wilds to reach Warvaliant. Blood drunk the nobleman had been, like a lunatic child rushing home with his prize.

Warburton had been oblivious to Santadar's suffering, and Tessa had wished to God she could be as well. But she had felt every twist of agony, felt the pain as though red-hot pincers tore at her own flesh as she watched Rafe clench his teeth in stoic silence.

Twice she had dared call out to Warburton, remind him that he would need his prisoner alive to remain in the good graces of the queen. She had prayed the cruel lord would not detect the threads of desperation in her voice, knowing that the slightest betrayal of weakness would bring Warburton down upon her like a shark upon blood. But the nobleman had been too busy gloating over his triumph to take note of her tone. Only Santadar had seen through her, and he had shot her a reproving glare.

Infuriated, she had hardened herself against him, vowing to yield no more to his idiotic pride. But when finally he slumped in the saddle, only his bonds holding him on his mount's back, Tessa had not been able to stifle a surge of relief that he was at last out of pain.

A lump in the floor caught at her foot, and she stumbled, the pain in her shoulder as it grated against rough stone jolting her from her musing. The walls of Warvaliant Castle suffocated her once again as her eyes focused on Rafe.

She had vowed to interfere no more, resolved not to place herself in peril for a man who only chafed at her efforts in his behalf. But she could not stop remembering the gentleness with which he had held her, comforted her.

So lost in her anguish had he become that he had never once acknowledged his own pain, both from the wound in his leg and from the bitter defeat he had suffered. Her gaze darted to the massive shoulders of the English nobleman, then back to the helpless Spaniard.

'Twould be madness to cast her lot with an enemy of the Crown, she thought grimly. She was crazed to feel loyalty to a man she had met but a few hours ago. Why, then, did she have this insane urge to fling herself betwixt Rafael Santadar and Warburton, to defend the Spaniard like a lioness guarding her wounded mate?

Mayhap it was true what the villagers had said. Mayhap her wits were as addled as poor Hagar's had been. But Tessa knew she could do naught but aid Rafe, no matter what the cost. 'Twould serve her right if they strung her up at Tyburn, she thought.

With an inward bow to her own recklessness, she swept up the torn hem of her gown and ripped a strip of fabric free.

"My lord?" Her voice echoed back to her from the darkened passage, strong and clear. Yet she almost faltered when Warburton paused, his wide, rough-hewn face angled toward her.

Bushy rust-hued brows met over his hawk-like nose. "You must be patient, my dove," he said. "I'll attend to you when our brave sea captain lies chained."

"Chained?" Tessa echoed. "You need no chains to bind a dead man. Unless you allow me to stanch Captain Santadar's wound, you'll need a grave digger instead of a jailer."

Warburton spun around, his scowl making Tessa's heart lurch. "Aye, and then, as you keep reminding me, my own head might be forfeit. But I am no longer convinced our sovereign would be so wroth if the rogue were to die. Santadar is a scurvy Spaniard, a rabid dog to be slaughtered, either by Queen Bess's retainers or by mine. While you, my little puppet mistress, would do well to remember that upon this island we have a name for those who give succor to an enemy, and that name is *traitor*."

Tessa glanced at the man carrying Rafe, who had stopped in the wake of his master. She felt as though Warburton had cast before her an invisible gauntlet. Never, even as a child, had she been wise enough to ignore a direct challenge. It had cost her countless sprained ankles, bumped heads, blackened eyes. Yet now the stakes were far greater. She gritted her teeth, arching her neck proudly.

Boldly, defiantly, yet cursing herself for twelve-times the fool, she stomped over toward the man and thrust the wad of cloth between Santadar's torn flesh and the merciless point of armor.

"So that is the way the winds blow, wench." Warburton's sneer seemed to clench invisible fingers about Tessa's throat, but though her arms dropped again to her sides, her eyes glinted with a veiled defiance that was more infuriating to the nobleman than open belligerence.

She felt Warburton's gaze flick down over the bodice of her dress, lingering on the full curve of breast, the narrow dip of waist. His lips split into an ugly leer. "By God's blood, I vow you shall pay for that, mistress. Aye, in the only coin you possess."

"My fate is the queen's to decide, as is Captain Santadar's." Her insolent words cut through the corridor. She saw a flash of fury darken Warburton's cheeks, heard the choked gasps of his men. Yet despite the fact that her words had shored up her battered pride, Tessa already wished them back.

It was a fatal error to bait a man like Neville Warburton. Scores of times she had heard tales told about the red-haired giant's cruelties. She had ever been careful to keep herself from the nobleman's piercing eyes, and yet here she stood, like a cursed lunatic baiting the monster. And why? Because of some honor-crazed Galahad who had stumbled across her path but the night before.

"My—my lord." The words were thick in her throat. "I—" But she was stunned to find that the apology her mind had formed would not pass her lips. Her chin jutted out stubbornly despite the fact that she knew her actions were dangerous.

"Aye, I am your lord, doxy. And here at Warvaliant, that is akin to God." With that, Warburton stalked into the winding darkness, his men-at-arms hastening behind him. For a moment Tessa stood frozen, staring after them. Then the gauntleted hand of one of Warburton's men urged her on.

"That was foolish, wench." The strange voice emanating from beneath the man's visor dripped warning. "If you want any beauty left in that face of yours, you'll keep your mouth shut and serve my lord in any fashion he desires."

"I—"

"*Any* fashion. I have seen what he is capable of." His words sent chills racing down Tessa's spine. "And the Spaniard," the man said quietly, "forget him. He will soon be dead, either at the hand of Lord Warburton, or that of the queen." Was there a gentleness in his hushed voice?

Tessa glanced up, but the man's features were hidden, his visor making him a faceless entity.

"Nay," the man said. "You needn't look at me like that. Your eyes could steal a man's soul, but mine has already been bartered to this castle and to this lord."

Tessa jumped at the sound of a heavy door slamming against stone, and she felt the man's arm steady her an instant; then it was gone.

One of those who had been leading the procession entered the chamber, and Tessa watched as he thrust his torch into an iron sconce inside. Light dribbled in macabre patterns upon the dank cell walls, and the mound of hay in one slime-encrusted corner.

"Chain the Spaniard within," Warburton's voice rang out. His eyes, cold and merciless, regarded Tessa with twisted pleasure as his man lugged Rafe into the cell and dumped his limp form onto the soiled straw.

Santadar gave a weak groan as the wad of cloth Tessa had used to stanch his wound fell to the dirty floor. Instinctively, Tessa took a step forward, meaning to replace the crude bandage, but the cell walls seemed to close in upon her. Warvaliant's dungeons held a hundred secrets, whispers of death, torture. At that moment she could almost see ancient specters pushing their bony fingers against her chest.

She froze, her nails digging deep into the palms of her hands as her eyes darted to Warburton. He was smiling as if he sensed her rising fear. Tessa's heart plunged to her toes.

" 'Tis a most unpleasant prospect, milady, is it not? Even for one well used to crawling about in a filthy hovel. Of course, your accommodations will be much more pleasant." He turned to the man nearest him. "Smythe, you will have the honor of escorting our lady guest to my chamber."

"Nay."

Warburton's face snapped toward her at the

sound of her voice, and Tessa met the nobleman's gaze with a courage she did not feel. "I would prefer to remain here."

"Here? You would rather keep company with a Spaniard than serve in my bed?" A laugh ripped like a jagged blade from the lord's mouth. "I could force you, Tessa of Ravenscroft, drag you screaming to my chamber, bend you to my will. But I will not. Nay, 'twill be far more diverting to watch you break yourself, to watch that stiff-necked pride crumble away. For I promise you, you will be glad enough to escape these walls and fly into my arms when the rats begin gnawing on your pretty white flesh."

Tessa steeled herself against his scathing gaze, fighting the urge to shrink away. She could almost feel rodents' claws skittering over her skin, see the beady eyes glittering hungrily. Yet she could not, would not, show Warburton weakness.

Sucking in a deep breath to steady herself, she forced her feet forward, her lungs squeezing tight as she entered the cell. "I shall have need of clean water to tend the captain's wounds, aye, and fresh bandages. If your cook could bring a heartening broth made of—"

She started as Warburton's hand flashed out, seizing a flask from one of his men. With his other hand he ripped free a sash of saffron silk and then with an oath hurled both objects to the floor of the cell.

"These will have to serve," he snarled. "He's an enemy, not an honored guest! But since you have chosen to act as his healer, you would do well to heed my warning: If the Spaniard dies, I shall personally hurl you into hell along with him."

His cruel laughter raked Tessa's raw nerves.

"Good night, milady." His words were like the toll of a leper's bell as he slammed the massive door shut, abandoning her to terror.

Despite herself, Tessa rushed at the bolted portal. Her fingers curled against the iron-bound wood as she fought a detestable urge to break into tears. By sheer force of will she dammed up the cries of the child who lurked inside her, frightened, grieving, alone.

"Nay, damn you." She whispered the words, a fierce aching in her breast. "I'll not let you turn me into a sniveling babe."

Squaring her shoulders, Tessa stepped back from the barred cell door, and pulled deep bracing air into her lungs. But dread clamored within her, cutting her ever more sharply as she slowly turned to face the limp figure silhouetted against the filthy straw.

" 'Tis your fault we're in this cursed tangle!" Tessa took refuge in berating the senseless Santadar. "I warned you against building that blasted fire! But did you listen? Nay, your ears were too stopped up with notions of chivalry and honor to heed good counsel—"

"F-forgive me."

Tessa's mouth gaped open at the words, scarce a whisper in the silence of the cell. Catching up her skirts in her hand, she ran to Rafe.

"Captain Santadar?" She knelt beside the mound of straw, her flesh crawling as a small creature skittered deeper into the filthy mass of makeshift bedding. "Captain Santadar, are you awake?"

A wave of surprise jolted through her as she found herself drowning in wide-open indigo eyes.

"Awake enough to know I hurt like hell."

" 'Tis little wonder. Nay! Don't try to sit up, you bloody witling! If you damage the wound any further, you'll be making your last confession at St. Peter's gates."

"Serve . . . me right." Disregarding her warning, Rafe attempted to sit up, the corded muscles of his arms standing out in stark relief against his skin. Sweat gilded his brow and upper lip. She heard him groan and curse, and after a few agonizing seconds, he sagged back in defeat.

"I warned you, you ox-headed oaf! You couldn't lift a butterfly, let alone haul up that great carcass of yours!" Tessa laid her hand on his forehead to test for fever. "You'd best resign yourself to lying still and enduring what little nursing you get, because I'm all you have."

"Should . . . should have sent you . . . away." The soft words broke through Tessa's tirade, and she stopped, her hands stilling above the blood-matted fabric of Rafe's breeches.

"What did you say?"

Thick ebony lashes drifted down to high cheekbones, and that beautifully carved mouth twisted into a grimace. When he spoke again, there was a thread of weakness in his voice, as though the pain had robbed him of breath. "I should've sent you away the moment we escaped the mob. I knew I should . . . but you looked so fragile, so hurt."

Tessa squirmed inwardly, bedeviled by images of herself weeping in this man's arms the night before, sobbing out to him secrets she had shielded for so long. And she wanted to flee from the light in his eyes, flee from his gentleness.

"I've been fending off the wolves from my own

door since I was a child," she snapped, "and I promise you, there is naught fragile about—"

"About the dreams misting your eyes? Sorrows . . . an angel's smile, but so sad."

She stiffened, started to turn away, but the seafarer's fingers caught her wrist in a grasp that was stunningly strong, considering his condition.

"Don't," he breathed. "Tessa—"

Her gaze darted to his, her eyes blazing. She expected to discover subtle scorn in the Spaniard's handsome face, but she saw nothing except compassion and an unsettling understanding.

His fathomless blue eyes gleamed in the flickering torchlight, and she thought fleetingly of the tales of noble heroes her father had strung for her like pretty beads when she was a child.

Honor and courage were etched deep in the lines of Rafael Santadar's lean face, mingled with a bewitching aura of otherworldliness, as though he had never been tarnished by the ugliness all around him.

Tessa started at the fanciful thought, and reality came crashing down upon her with dizzying force. Witling! she cursed herself and tried to drag her shattered defenses about her and again conceal from the world the starry-eyed girl she had been, the child who had believed in love ballads and quests and gallant knights who gave their hearts.

"You shouldn't have come here with me." Santadar's deep voice drew her from her thoughts. "You should have left me to my fate."

Clenching her jaw, she pulled away from his touch. She had uncharacteristically exposed her vulnerability to this man but now it frosted over into her accustomed diamond-hard mask.

"Aye, I should have dashed into Warburton's arms like some lusty harlot and just let you bleed to death." An ironic laugh choked her. "Not that my actions will matter in the end—for the soldiers will kill you, and I—I'll be forced to play the whore."

"Nay! If that bastard touches you, I'll kill him!" Santadar's cheeks flushed dull red with fury, and he tried to stand up. His leg cracked hard into a half-rotted timber, and a black curse split his lips as he fell back onto the hay. Tessa stared in horror as fresh crimson spread over his tattered breeches, the new, bright blood stain mingling with the earlier, darker one.

"Lie still!" she commanded, rushing to retrieve the sash and flask from where the nobleman had thrown them. "God's teeth, if you don't stop having temper fits every time I turn around, that wound will never have a chance to heal!" she railed as she hastened back to his side.

He had pressed one hand over the wound, and scarlet blood was flowing between his fingers. Tessa saw a pinched, sickly expression steal across his face. "That has ever . . . been a fault of mine. Temper fits, I mean." She could see a muzziness in Rafe's eyes, and his breath came in short gasps as a weak laugh breached his lips. "I'll have to take . . . lessons in patience from . . . you."

Tessa's cheeks flamed as she dropped to her knees beside him. "If you had but tended the blasted thing earlier—"

"I had precious . . . little time. I was shipwrecked; I crawled up on shore. Then you—you fell off the cliff into my lap."

Against her will, Tessa felt a smile toy with the

corners of her mouth. "And Warburton had the ill manners to carry you halfway across the country-side."

A wobbly grin slashed across Rafe's face, making him appear achingly boyish. "*Sí*, wildwitch. 'Twas most uncivil of him."

"I should have looked at it last night." Guilt gnawed at Tessa as she tried to still the fluttering in her stomach. "I should have insisted."

"It would have done no good. I wanted to hold you. Just hold you." Rafe's grin faded, his gaze shifting to her lips with a wistful sadness. "But much as I'd like to do that now, I fear"—a muscle in his jaw knotted as his gaze fell to his wound— "we dare delay no longer. Whatever is in my leg, 'tis embedded deep, and 'tis tearing my flesh."

She felt a chill steal over her skin, dread thick in her breast.

"Tessa." His voice was whisper soft, bracing. "It will have to come out. I don't think I can do it."

Tessa choked back the bile rising in her throat. "I can." She desperately wished she felt half of the confidence conveyed in those two words.

"I know you can, *querida*. Any woman who defies the flames and mocks Neville Warburton would scarce be disconcerted by a tiny sliver in a man's leg." There was a gentle teasing in his voice. He lifted his bloodstained palm from his thigh, revealing the jagged gash beneath.

Tessa pressed her fingers to her lips as she fought the urge to retch. In the raw, gaping wound, she could just see something dark, buried a finger's depth beneath the skin. The agony Rafe had suffered must have been horrendous, she thought. How had he survived in the ocean, let alone come to her aid upon the rocky shores?

She raised her eyes to his, and she could not keep the fear from being reflected in her face. She had nursed Hagar diligently, but she had never had the inborn skill of a true healer. Yet her fingers were deft with the carving tools she used to fashion her marionettes. If she could draw on that ability, perhaps there was a chance. Her gaze skittered back to the wound.

Never had she—practical, cynical Tessa—expected to experience such raw sensation or this frightening feeling that seemed to slam into her stomach with the force of a blow. She wanted to blurt out that she couldn't possibly aid him, that she would only injure him the further. But his gaze was so steady and the planes of his face held such a rugged masculine beauty that it tugged at Tessa's soul.

A wounded Galahad. A captive king.

She turned away hastily, plucked the torch from its sconce, and wedged it between two stones so that the light shone on the wound.

" 'Tis only a scratch, wildwitch."

Rafe's voice seemed to come to her through a haze, but she shoved back the hateful weakness that threatened to overtake her. She glanced at her hands and saw that they were smudged with dirt. She dampened the sash with water from the flask and scrubbed her fingers as best she could. She heard fabric ripping, heard Rafe cursing, and when she turned back to him, she saw that he had torn the breeches free of his leg.

Muscle-hardened flesh the hue of burnt sugar surrounded the injury; a sprinkling of dark hair dusted the sun-browned skin. Tessa's fingers trembled. She stilled them.

" 'Twill take but a moment," she said briskly, but her whole body ached with tension. "Ready?"

"As much so as I'll ever be." He shot her another blinding smile, only the whiteness about his lips betraying his pain and his dread.

Tessa sucked in a deep breath as her eyes focused on the object lodged in Santadar's leg. Slowly, as gently as possible, she probed the wound, attempting to grasp the end of the splinter that was tormenting him. She heard a hiss of pain, glimpsed white-knuckled fists clenched in the straw as she battled the sickening sensation of that warm, wet wound closing about her fingers.

Tessa could feel the edge of the hard object, could feel the texture of wood slick with blood. She struggled to grasp it, draw it out, but it slipped from her fingertips. The splinter was very firmly lodged.

She glanced up at Rafe's face. His head was flung back against the hay, his eyes clenched shut. Agony was gouged deep in every line in his face; every tendon seemed ready to burst from its shield of skin. Yet he made no sound. No sound.

"I can't hold on to it," Tessa choked out.

"Do it! Are you afraid of hurting me?" Even in his pain, Rafe taunted her, baited her. His eyes were open now, glinting challenge. "Such weakness is forgivable in a mere woman."

Fury shot through Tessa, fire-hot. She thrust her chin out as her fingers dug faster, deeper into the torn flesh around the sliver of wood. She grasped it firmly and pulled with all her strength.

A ragged groan escaped Rafe's lips as the splinter slid free, and Tessa staggered back, her eyes fastening on the object she held in her hand. She swallowed, her stomach lurching, as she stared at the sliver of wood that had buried itself in Rafael Santadar's whipcord-taut muscle. It was as wide as two of her fingers and as long as her hand.

Tessa flung the wood away from her, then hastened to cleanse and bandage the wound, her fingers infuriatingly awkward.

"Wildwitch . . . "

She stilled at the soft word, her gaze shifting to his death-gray face. The tiniest of smiles tipped his lips. "I knew . . . knew you would brave the devil . . . if I dared you."

Tessa's mouth dropped open as she watched his lush, dark lashes flutter down onto high-chiseled cheekbones. Sweat born of agony had beaded on his brow and along the hard line of his jaw.

Indignation had welled up inside her, but as she glared at Rafael Santadar's perfectly carved features, the anger drained away. The lines of pain had softened in sleep; his lips were now curved into a half-smile, and his breathing was steady, peaceful.

Tessa watched him for a long moment, her hands absently winding the bandage around his leg. He was handsome, this Spaniard, and brave. Yet even if he had been cursed with the visage of one of the gargoyles on Warvaliant's parapets, Tessa knew she would have found him beautiful, for his inherent recklessness, courage, and raw masculinity were tempered with soul-deep compassion.

Her fingertips drifted to his face, brushing back one wayward strand of raven hair that had fallen across his temple. "They could not touch her . . ." Tessa could hear his voice in her memory, tender, achingly gentle, as he strove to comfort her. "God scoops innocents up in the palm of his hand before the flames can touch them."

"But before God swept her up, did she send a sea phantom to bewitch me as one final bit of mischief?" Tessa whispered, her fingers gliding down the curve of his beard-stubbled cheek. "Did she send you?" As she tested the firmness of his full lower lip, something she thought long dead stirred in her breast. "Oh, nay, Rafael Santadar," she said, shoving the emotion away. "You are but another man, one who will most likely lie dead soon, or be imprisoned in the Tower. And because of you, I may well rot there as well, after Warburton finishes with me."

Dread skittered up her spine, and she shuddered at the image that loomed in her mind—Neville Warburton, his thick red eyebrows, his eager, slack lips. She could almost feel the weight of the nobleman bearing down upon her.

"I'll kill him if he dares touch you," Rafe had snarled, death a blue flame in his eyes.

"Bloody fool." The words caught in Tessa's throat. "Do you not know 'tis hopeless to fight? Camelot crumbled to ashes centuries past. Merlin lies trapped in Melusine's cave, while Galahad . . . " She let the words trail off, tears stinging her eyes. "Nay, 'twould make no difference to you if the whole world crawled on its belly, would it, Rafael? As long as you stood true. But your pride cannot batter down this dungeon's walls, nor can your honor defeat Warburton's power. And after they have done with us, there will be no one in all of England to champion the cause of a peddler girl and a Spanish sea rover."

Unutterably weary, she curled up beside him, letting her head sag until it rested on the muscled plane of his chest.

"I wish to God I *were* a witch," she breathed against the thrum of his heart. "I'd conjure up a key to fling wide that cursed door. I'd cast open the gateway to hell and shove Warburton into its depths, and I'd sail off with you on a sky ship, with canvas woven of clouds and a rainbow hull." She stopped, suddenly aware her fingers had been stroking Rafe's chest, aware, too, of a metal circlet warm beneath her fingertips.

She raised her head, her hand closing over the object that hung around Rafe's neck on a gold chain.

A ring.

A shaft of something akin to jealousy shot through Tessa as she stared at the delicate bit of jewelry that could only adorn some woman's dainty hand.

Did the ring belong to the Spaniard's lady fair? A wife who awaited him in Spain, serene amid a bevy of indigo-eyed babes? Or a convent-bred beauty being readied for the return of her betrothed?

Tessa pushed herself to a sitting position, her fingers open to display the gold circlet in the palm of her hand. Torchlight gilded it in flame, picking out the intricately wrought device; a stag *courant* on a chevron. Tiny gold letters were just visible on the crest's enameled border. Though she could not read, Tessa knew in that heartbeat what the words proclaimed: "Honor's Sword."

She gasped, feeling as though an invisible fist has slammed into her stomach as the crushingly familiar crest tumbled her back to the great hall of Renfrew Castle, where the hawklike countenance of her father's benefactor, the noble Tarrant, Earl of Renfrew, flashed before her.

Where in God's name had Rafe come by such a ring? she wondered wildly. What in God's name did it mean? Had he stolen it? Was it booty from one of his sea clashes? Nay, 'twas not in Rafe to flaunt thievery, even if he had raided another ship.

Then what if . . . ?

Her fingers closed about the ring, pressing it into her palm. Mayhap there was no need for conjurings or magic. For if Rafael Santadar was somehow linked to the mighty house of Renfrew, the Spanish sailor might well have just performed a miracle more astonishing than any a mere witch could have wrought.

Chapter
Six

"RAFE?" Tessa squeezed his name through a throat thick with tenuous hope as she reached out and gently shook his shoulder in an effort to rouse him. "Rafe, wake up."

A rumble came from his chest, and his eyelids opened slowly, as though weighted down with lead. "Tired . . . wildwitch."

"Dammit, you blasted witling, wake up!" Tessa loathed herself for the anger in her voice. Her fingers tightened about the ring, and she rippled the chain up over his head.

Rafe cursed as the links raked his neck. "What the blazes—" His lips were pale with pain, and the ravages his wound had inflicted upon him were still carved upon his face. Befuddled by sleep and slowed by weakness, he groped at his throat where the chain had raked his skin. Confusion clouded his face; then his eyes narrowed in fury as he realized the ring was gone.

His gaze locked upon the gold links dripping from Tessa's fingers. "What the devil—"

She pressed her fist against her breast, her breath catching in her chest, as she saw the weal on Rafe's skin where she had torn the chain free.

"I—I'm sorry," she stammered, trying desperately to sort out the thoughts roiling in her mind. "Rafe," she managed at last, "I have to know how you came by this."

She extended her hand, then opened it. The enameled crest caught the light from the torch, reflecting it on Rafe's taut face.

" 'Tis mine." There was defiance in his voice, and fury. "It belonged to my mother."

"Your mother?" Tessa echoed, scarce hearing Rafe's angry words, her eyes filling with tears of relief as a laugh bubbled from her lips. She heard Rafe struggle upright, felt his eyes boring into her.

"*Sí*, wildwitch, I had a mother."

"Tell me. Tell me about her," Tessa implored. "Tell me everything, Rafe."

"She was beautiful. Gentle. Kind. And she died when I was but a lad. I scarce remember her."

"Her name? Rafe, what was her name?"

"My father called her Nanita."

Rafe's brow crinkled in confusion, his eyes reflecting some long hidden pain. " 'Tis the only name I ever knew for her." He seemed to gaze into the past, his voice softening. "But I can still see her in the garden of a beautiful castle among the orange trees and the vineyards, her hair all gold about her face as she caught a butterfly for me."

"But you must know something about her—something else!" Tessa urged.

" 'Twas a long time ago." It was as though the memory had raked open in Rafe some aged wound, and he stiffened, his face hardening again. "I've spent a lifetime trying to forget it. Why should it matter now?"

"It matters, Rafe. More than you know." Tessa clasped his fist in her hand, her voice low, earnest. "There is an Englishman, an earl who owned the ships on which my father sailed. His daughter, son-in-law, and grandson were killed by cutthroats years ago in Spain."

"But what has that to do with me? I know naught of your earl, nor of your father, Tessa, and as for the man's grandson, I—"

"I believe you may be that grandson."

Tessa started as Rafe ripped his hand from her grasp, and she was stunned at the rage and dread that crossed his features.

"No, 'tis impossible! My mother . . . could not have been English."

"You said but a moment ago that you have few memories of her, that you know naught of her name except that your father called her Nanita. The earl's daughter's name was Anne. *Anne*, Rafe. She wed a Spanish grandee and sailed off with him."

"That means nothing, Tessa! There is no proof that—"

"That you are Lord Tarrant's grandson? Then tell me, Rafael Santadar, tell me where your mother got this ring." Tessa thrust it at him. " 'Tis the stag *courant*, the Renfrew crest!"

Rafael uttered a black oath, and his hand flashed out and snatched the ring from her grasp, as though to shield the treasured memento of his mother from some heinous scourge. "There are a hundred ways she could have come by it!" Rafe snapped. "Whatever scheming you're about, you can cast it to the winds, for I'll have no part in it."

"No part in it!" Tessa exclaimed incredulously. "Don't be an idiot! Don't you see? This ring is your salvation! If we can somehow smuggle it out to Lord Renfrew—or escape Warvaliant and reach the earl's castle, mayhap 'twill buy your life."

"No!" Rafe's roar stunned Tessa, seeming to reverberate off the damp stone, echoing back his anguish. She froze, staring into his face, his inner pain wrenching at her heart. 'Twas as if, in that moment, she could see into his very soul.

They were his enemies, the English. They had destroyed his ship and nearly taken his life as well. How many of his crew had Rafael Santadar watched drown in his hours adrift in the sea? How much had his helplessness to aid them cost his fierce pride? And now she was telling him that the blood of his hated foes ran in his own veins . . .

Tessa swallowed hard, sympathy rising inside her. Yet she could not—dared not—allow Rafe to cut himself off from this, his single hope. She would not allow him to indulge his pride, because . . . because she could not bear to watch him die.

That realization shook Tessa to her very core, terrifying her. She knew not what she felt for Rafael Santadar, this man she had met only one night ago. She wondered if some sprite had woven their spirits together when they were naught but their parents' dreams. It was as though the tales of the sea phantom were made real the first time she looked into Rafe's blue eyes.

Nay! she chastised herself sharply. The only reason she cared about Rafael Santadar was that he was a truly good man and, as such, was rarer than the most precious of jewels.

"Rafe," she said softly, searching for the words that would wound him the least, "I understand what you are feeling—the anger, the confusion. But—"

"You understand nothing." His gaze pierced her. "I loved my parents, Tessa. My mother was an angel, always smiling and laughing, and my father was like a magnificent knight riding out of a legend. I remember him tossing me astride his horse and racing out across the fields. I remember him weaving flower crowns to place upon my mother's hair as I wandered about in our favorite grove." His mouth hardened, and his eyes narrowed. "But most clearly of all I remember how they died—cut down by a band of murdering brigands as we traveled the road from Seville."

Tessa winced at the picture his words painted, the grief in her own heart still so fresh she could sense Rafe's agony.

"I saw them," he went on relentlessly. "I saw the sabers bite into their flesh, heard my father's death cry as he struggled to gain time for my mother and me to escape. I was four years old, tall even then, with a wooden sword my father had bought for me at a market. I wanted to help him fight but my mother caught me up in her arms and tried to run. They caught her, stabbed her, and left her for dead, and they slashed me with a knife—here." His fingers knotted around the high neckline of his shirt and wrenched it open.

Tessa flinched as her eyes locked upon the scar

arcing across the muscled column of his throat. "Sweet God!" she cried out, her hand rising of its own volition, fingertips touching the faded white line that marred the bronzed perfection of his skin. "How did you survive?"

Rafe shrugged, bitterness filling his eyes. "Mayhap the murdering bastard who sought to slay me was distracted by my mother's jewels or by the riches to be found upon my father's body. Mayhap one of the saints held back his blade. I know not. One of the thieves bent over me, his features masked by harlequin paints, and cut me. I must have lost consciousness, for I remember nothing after that, until some movement jarred me awake."

Rafe ground his fingertips against his eyes. "It was my mother. I'll never forget her face, Tessa. Her eyes were like wounds, brimming with agony; her skin was like ice. She was delicate, small and badly wounded, but she half dragged me to a hermitage tucked up in the hills. She laid me in the arms of Brother Ambrose and begged . . . begged him to care for me. And then"—the slightest tremor shook his voice—"she died."

"Rafe . . . " Tessa's own voice broke, and she reached up, cupping his face in her hands. "The ring—"

" 'Twas Ambrose who gave it to me. Somehow it had escaped the murderers' eyes. Ambrose worked a chain in gold for me, and hung it around my neck. And he honored his promise to my mother, loved me as though I were his own son."

"But you never knew who your parents were? Never knew where you had lived? Did no one search for you?"

" 'Twas most remote, Ambrose's hermitage. He liked to stay far from the temptations of the world. If anyone ever came looking, they never found me. Two years passed before Ambrose could even get me to speak. And by then any memories I might once have had as to where I belonged had faded."

"Then 'tis possible your mother was the Renfrew heiress," Tessa ventured.

Rafe cursed, slamming his fist against the unyielding stone of the dungeon wall, raking the skin from his knuckles. "I am Rafael Santadar, once captain of the *Lady of Hidden Sorrows*. I am a Spaniard, milady. A Spaniard, with no taint of English blood."

Tessa glowered at him, the sympathy she had felt changing into anger. "Aye, you're a Spaniard—stiff-necked, arrogant, with the world beneath your heel! Even as she was dying, your mother sought to save you, God knows what she suffered. But you—"

"Tessa." 'Twas but her name, yet more menacing than the darkest of oaths.

"Nay, you'll hear this, and your pride be damned!" she said. "You are so high and mighty that you'll throw your life away rather than use the one key that might save you from the queen's wrath. Why? Because you might have to admit that your mother was English? Does that tip her halo? Are you ashamed of her now, Rafael? Ashamed of the mother who sacrificed so much for you?"

"Enough!" he bellowed, his face white, his fists clenched.

For an instant, Tessa half expected him to strike her, but he only turned around, his glare burning into the wall. He was trembling with fury. Tessa could see, feel, taste his rage. And she could sense as well that she had dealt the proud Spaniard the most masterful of sword strokes, cleaving his defenses.

Pain? Aye, she knew well the suffering her words had inflicted, but that was small price to pay for Rafe's life. Years of learning to be careful and canny had taught Tessa when to leash her tongue. She forced herself to remain silent and let her words gnaw at Rafe's conscience.

Shaking back her hair, she curled up on the straw and pillowed her face upon her folded hands.

"What the devil are you doing?" Rafe snapped.

"I'm going to sleep." Her eyelids fluttered shut. "I am weary of your arrogance and idiocy."

She lay there a long time, feigning slumber as she listened to Rafe muttering harshly in Spanish, and she was glad she could not understand a word he said.

Rafe stared at the guttering torch, the wound in his leg paining him not half as much as Tessa of Ravenscroft's harsh accusations. Curse the witch— she had clawed open wounds Rafe had tried all his life to heal. She had laid bare the foul pride that had driven him even so far as to deny the woman who had endured such pain for him—his mother.

The image of her face made Rafe's heart ache, a hundred tender caresses and kisses sweet as honey rising in his mind. Tessa had jeered at him, goaded him, scorned him for having betrayed his mother's love. And damn her to blazes, the woman had been right.

Was he so blinded by arrogance that he would disown the woman who had borne him rather than discover she was of his enemy's blood? Was his love for her such a fragile thing?

Rafe's fists knotted, his fingernails digging deep into his palms.

Was he one with the pirate sea dogs who roved on Elizabeth Tudor's leash? Was he the spawn of some thrice-damned English earl?

" 'Twould be better to think myself bastard born," he murmured.

Never to have known your mother's touch? Never to have run among the lemon trees and grapevines? Even his thoughts mocked him in Tessa's voice.

His gaze moved to where she lay, infuriatingly serene, totally oblivious to the blaze she had started within him.

Oblivious? His lips curled in a scornful smile. He much doubted it. The little witch had known exactly what she was doing when she scalded him with her words. And then she had closed her eyes, leaving him alone with thoughts that would give him no peace.

He had wanted to wake her many times during the hours that followed, but instead, he had only fumed inwardly, hating the fact that she had spoken the truth, hating even more the way her hair fell, like curtains of night, over her face.

He shifted, gritting his teeth as he maneuvered his leg into a more comfortable position. What was it about her that drove him to madness? Intrigued him, entranced him, infuriated him? Was it her beauty? Her spirit? The temper that could wax white-hot even beneath the blaze of his own formidable rage? Despite her seeming fragility, there was a strength in her. She was like the finest rapier wrought by the masters of Toledo. And she had cut to the heart of him, burying herself deep.

"Wildwitch." He whispered the name he had given her, remembering the cherubic innocence upon her face as she had feigned sleep. Not even the *Lady*'s cook could have been oblivious to his tirade, and the old Castilian had been stone deaf, Rafe thought wryly. Yet Tessa had lain there, so peaceful he had felt an urge to dash her with what little water remained in the flask, startle her to wakefulness so that he could rail at her.

Sí, and be masterfully outmaneuvered again? he thought wryly. He had already suffered humiliating defeat at Drake's hands. He would scarce lock into battle again with this wisp of a girl who would most likely best him.

His gaze traced the pure line of her throat, the stubborn curve of her chin. Thick lashes the hue of sable lay in rich crescents on her rose-blushed cheeks, while her lips . . . berry red they were, and thrice as sweet.

They parted, the tiniest of sighs drifting from her, and Rafe's mouth went dry. What would it be like to brush those lips with his own, to gather up the dewy moisture that clung to the delicate curves? How would it feel to see those eyes, bright as onyx, blaze not with the fire of anger but with heady passion?

With an oath, Rafe wrenched his mind away from images of Tessa's lips eager upon his, of his hands delving deep into the silken waterfall of her hair. 'Twas blasphemy, somehow, to think of her thus while she lay there trusting as a child.

"Are you through, yet?"

The low voice made Rafe jump, his gaze flashing to where tip-tilted eyes glinted up at him, touched with amusement.

The lips he had been contemplating moments before softened into a smile.

"Have you ceased your rumbling?" Tessa stretched, her lithe body outlined to perfection against the cloth of her gown, her breasts pressing tantalizingly against the thin fabric. "At first I thought the castle was toppling down upon us, but then I realized 'twas naught but a foul-tempered wretch in the midst of a tantrum."

"A tantrum which you, milady, took the greatest of delight in bestirring."

The wood sprite's smile vanished, and the light in Tessa's eyes dimmed. "Nay, Rafe, I can assure you I took no pleasure in it at all." She sat up, curling her arms about her bent legs and resting her chin on her knees.

He regarded her in silence, uncertain how to deal with this Tessa, devoid of fire, anger, and sparkling wit. A sad-eyed waif, she seemed, lost in shadow.

"Rafe, I am sorry for hurting you. But what I said was true. And I don't want you to die."

Something in that tremulous admission made a lump rise in Rafe's throat, and her liquid, limpid eyes filled him with some unnameable emotion, driving him to want to shield her. He had known this instinct with countless women. This need to protect was an impulse born of the honor on which he prided himself.

Yet with this wood witch, with her devil-dark curls and her angel's face, 'twas different. For while he wanted to guard her from the rest of the world, he also needed to plunge past her defenses, delve into her soul until there was nothing left hidden.

"Tessa." Her name rasped from lips parched for the taste of her. He scarce felt the throbbing in his leg as he shifted to her side, his fingers threading into the lush waves of her hair, his palms framing her face. "Who are you, wildwitch? What sorcery have you worked upon me?"

She caught at the fullness of her lower lip with her teeth, and Rafe smoothed his callused thumbs across the moist swell until she released its tantalizing curve. He saw her lashes dip over eyes glossed with confusion and longing.

" 'Tis no witchery." Her breath was soft upon his skin.

The need that throbbed in her voice twisted in Rafe's loins, unleashing a tempest within him. With a groan, he sought her mouth, his lips tender, yet aching for the sweetness she promised. And she gave it to him, gave him far more than he had ever dreamed possible.

Velvety warm as the petals of a new-blown rose, her mouth opened beneath his, searching with both an innocence and a wantonness that drove him past endurance. She tasted of courage, she tasted of hope. He eased his hands down from her hair, curving them around her shoulders as he drew her deeper into his kiss.

And it was as though the earth tilted upon its axis, swirling away from brutality, ugliness, despair. She whimpered, and for an instant he thought she wanted to pull away from him. But when he started to release her, her hands caught at his shoulders, and the two of them sank back into the straw.

Had it been the most luxurious of feather beds, it could have seemed no softer, and Rafe could feel in the woman beneath him eagerness, passion. "Tessa . . . " He whispered her name, kissing her cheeks, her chin, his loins pounding with a need so fierce he could scarce hold it in check.

And then her fingertips skated over the wedge of flesh bared by his open shirt, and the trails of sensation she left in their wake burned like flames.

"Cristo!" He ground out the oath, his mouth slanting over hers, hungry, his tongue plunging past the barrier of her lips into the hot sweetness beyond. He wanted to devour her, take her into himself, make himself whole again. "You taste like summer," he moaned against her lips.

He wanted to slide his palms over her skin to see if it was indeed the spun satin it seemed. As though they possessed a will of their own, his hands charted a path down to her slender waist, then up again, his thumbs grazing the ripe swell of her breasts. He felt her shudder, heard her gasp against his lips. His eyes opened at the tiny sound, fixing upon her face, flushed with pleasure, eager, willing, so willing, and yet . . .

He stiffened as his gaze swept the babe-soft wisps of hair that clung to her delicate cheeks and the eyelashes fanning sweetly against her skin. Innocence wreathed itself about her like the first blossoms of spring, whispering of treasures far too precious to defile. His fingers tightened about her ribs, and he desperately wanted to shove such thoughts away, immerse himself in the sensations she was evoking. But he let his lips soften against hers, then slowly, reluctantly, drew away.

The chill of the dungeon seemed to raise an invisible wall between them, driving back the wonder he had known in Tessa's kiss, leaving instead the certainty that he should never have touched her at all.

She had endured the death of her mother, the terror of Warburton, and imprisonment, and she might well be forced to stand trial at the queen's hands for having aided him. And now, as if she had not suffered enough, he had taken her with his mouth, his hands, and had brought that look of turmoil to her eyes.

Her fingers had closed about the fabric of his shirt, as if to hold on to something elusive, and her small knuckles were pillowed against his skin, sending unwanted heat to his already throbbing sex.

"Stop," Rafe said through gritted teeth, his fingers encircling her wrists, gently pushing her away.

He saw her flinch, hurt welling in those incredible dark eyes, and he damned himself to the hottest fires of hell. "I should never have allowed that to happen. 'Twas unforgivable."

"Unforgivable?" The dazed expression faded from her face, the graceful line of her upswept eyebrows lowering with puzzlement.

"To kiss you, to touch you, to make you want me." He fell silent, his own desire harsh in his throat.

She lowered her head for a moment, her cheeks staining red. He glimpsed the soft curves beneath the ebony of her satin hair. He saw her draw in a deep breath before she lifted her chin, her eyes meeting his. " 'Tis wrong, then, to want to touch lips that have given me such comfort?"

He felt her wrist slip from his grasp, his hand suddenly lifeless as her fingertips traced the curve of his lips. "You're so gentle, Rafael Santadar, so good. You almost make me believe . . . in magic." The tiny catch in her voice wrenched at Rafe's soul. Her eyes shimmered with tears. "If this is sin, milord phantom, then hell can have me and welcome."

Rafe arched his head back, his face contorting with the anguish and the ecstasy her whispered words spawned in him. He wanted to tumble her back into the straw and make love to her with a fury that would consume them both.

'Twas insanity, this wild, deep stirring within him, this lifting of the weight of despair that had crushed him for so long. For the love of God, they were lying in Neville Warburton's dungeon, facing nigh certain death. Why, then, did he suddenly feel so free?

He reached out to touch her, tell her how she affected him, but a sudden sound sent raw dread through every muscle in his body.

Iron grated against iron on the other side of the cell door, and muffled voices penetrated even that daunting panel of iron-bound wood. Rafe scrambled awkwardly to his feet, his wound grinding with pain. He felt the fear in Tessa as she stood close beside him, saw her eyes, wide as a child's, and knew he would do anything, honorable or no, to protect her from harm.

"Warburton." Had she whispered the name "Satan" she could have infused it with no more loathing.

Rafe grasped her chill fingers and pulled her behind him so that she was shielded by the breadth of his shoulders. At that moment he would willingly have bartered his soul for a saber or a dagger with which to defend her. His eyes narrowed upon the door, watching it swing wide upon protesting hinges.

Shadows dripped over the rich velvets, glowing gems, and white ermine robing Neville Warburton's bearlike form. He stood flanked by two stone-faced guards, his lips curving back from jagged white teeth. Power and cruelty oozed from every line in his face, and his small eyes glinted with a foul anticipation that made Rafe's blood turn cold.

"Captain Santadar, I trust you slept well?" the nobleman purred, his thick fingers fondling a ruby that clung to his breast like a gobbet of blood. "I desire that my guests enjoy the finest hospitality Warvaliant has to offer."

"Your *hospitality* moves me beyond words," Rafe said. "I only hope I can return it in kind one day."

The twisted enjoyment in the lord's face deepened. "Unfortunately, I much doubt you'll ever have the opportunity to repay me for this night," Warburton chortled. "But at least, Phantom, you will be gracious enough to share with me the one comfort I did afford you."

Hooded eyes roved slowly to Tessa, and Rafe felt her fingers clench in his.

"Of course," the nobleman observed, examining his fingernails with diabolic interest, " 'twas with much reluctance that I sacrificed our little puppet mistress's company last evening. It put me in a most surly humor; my servants will attest to that. My only comfort was in plotting what pleasures I would indulge in when she and I met again."

"Damn you, Warburton, if there is a wisp of

decency left in your black soul, let the girl go." Rafe struggled to reason with the man. "She is innocent of any wrongdoing."

"Innocent?" Warburton guffawed. "After a night with a rutting dog the likes of you?"

His eyes were fixed suggestively upon Tessa's breast, and an oily smile snaked over his thick lips. "I have seen you, puppet mistress, your hands moving over your puppets with much genius. Do your fingers dance as daintily over a man's body?"

"Bastard!" The thin leash Rafe had held on his temper snapped, freeing him to spring into rage, to lunge at the leering nobleman, heedless of the consequences.

But at that moment one of the guards drew his blade. The gleaming point flashed out, digging into the flesh at the base of Rafe's throat. He froze, his razor-honed reflexes saving him from impaling himself on the sword.

"Nay!" he heard Tessa cry. "Don't hurt him! I'll go with you, my lord."

"Tessa—" She leapt past him into Warburton's reach, and Rafe's gut clenched with frustration and rage as the nobleman's fist tangled in her hair.

"So help me, God," Rafe said, "if you touch her—"

"Nay, Rafe." Her words burned him with hopelessness, helplessness. "There is naught you can do."

"Most sage advice, my pet, most wise, though 'twould be diverting to watch the Spanish dog being torn apart by my English wolves." He gestured to his guards. "Methinks our prisoner could do with a leash of iron, my friends. Though I fear, Captain Santadar, the manacle's embrace will be less entrancing than that of the fair Tessa."

"Don't do this, Warburton." Rafe heard the plea in his voice, but he cared not. He was willing to humble himself before the brutal Englishman if it would spare his wildwitch the horrors that the lust-bloated nobleman had planned.

Warburton cocked his head to one side, his upper lip curling, and Rafe could see in his eyes nightmare visions of Tessa trapped in the brutish man's arms, Warburton's massive fingers gouging into her soft flesh, his knees forcing her thighs apart.

"I intend to dare much this night, Phantom," Warburton sneered. "More than you can imagine."

As though he had sensed Rafe's deepest fears, the nobleman reached out a beefy hand and closed it over the swell of Tessa's breast. A choked sob rose from her throat, and Rafe saw her face flood with shame and terror.

"Dammit, I'll kill you, Warburton!" Rafe strained toward Tessa, felt blood trickle warm upon his skin as the sword point dug deeper into his neck.

He saw the English lord's fingers move up and grasp Tessa's chin. "Look at him, puppet mistress, this Spaniard who claims you were naught to him, who says you had no part in aiding him when he crawled up on our English shore. Look at him. He is ready to cast himself to the devil on your behalf. Do you think any judge in the land will believe you innocent of treason once he sees your cursed Spaniard's face?"

"I care not what you or others think," she snapped, lifting her chin courageously. "Rafe . . . "

'Twas but his name, yet it was infused with comfort and deep longing.

Anguish wound itself like a band of iron about Rafe's chest. His eyes stung at the bravery he saw in her Madonnalike face.

A laugh rumbled from Warburton's chest, evil as the jeering of Satan. The nobleman wrenched Tessa around and dragged her toward the door.

In the open doorway he paused, knotting his fingers in Tessa's hair, yanking her around again so that her torment would be branded upon Rafe's soul forever.

"She is beautiful, Santadar, is she not?" the nobleman snarled. "But I wonder what the night's entertainment will do to this face, this body. 'Tis fragile, for all its delights. And 'twill suffer—"

"Warburton!" Rafe roared the name, hate blazing hell-hot within him as the Englishman stalked into the shadowy corridor, dragging Tessa with him.

Her eyes, velvet black and desperate, caught Rafe's, held them for a heartbeat, and he could feel her fear inside him like a living thing.

"Tessa!" Agony tore through him, ruthless and devastating. Never had he thought anything could wound him more deeply than watching his ship sink. Never had he thought grief and terror could torture him more savagely than they had as he watched Bastion and Rique and the rest of his brave crew drown in the sea.

But as the cruel Warvaliant disappeared with Tessa of Ravenscroft, 'twas as though Rafe had plummeted into the depths of hell.

Chapter
Seven

THE chamber bled crimson velvet, and the dark wood panels reflected the light from scores of burning tapers. Tessa fought the urge to retch, as the walls closed in about her, trapping her in Neville Warburton's hellish lair.

Jewels and ermine garments lay everywhere, cast about by a careless hand, and the mullioned panes of the narrow window glinted like rats' eyes in the night. Yet though the massive bed loomed before her, its black velvet draperies whispering of the horrors to come, all she could see was Rafe's face as she was dragged from the dungeon. All she could hear was his voice as he pleaded with Warburton to show her mercy.

Tessa's stomach churned when her eyes flicked back to where Lord Warvaliant stood, ripping his doublet from his massive chest, as thickly furred as an ape's. There was no mercy in Neville Warburton, no trace of the innate honor that glowed in Rafael Santadar's face. The English lord would use them both, take the greatest of glee in breaking them, and then forget they had ever existed.

Warburton was greedy for their pain, thirsting to

grind Rafael beneath his heel, hungering to crush Tessa with his body and then use her destruction to torture the Spaniard below.

Her gaze narrowed as she looked at Warburton's slack lips, dull-red with lust, and despite the fear roiling within her, Tessa steeled herself to show the cruel beast no sign of her terror. She would rob his lordship of that bloody pleasure, at least, God curse him.

Her neck arched, her lip curled with that same fiery arrogance she had seen in Rafe as he faced impossible odds, and she vowed that no matter what happened in the hours to come, she would not let Warburton break her.

A sudden hot strength seemed to pour into Tessa as Rafe's indigo eyes, dark with nobility, rose in her mind, and her chin jutted upward in stubborn resolve. She was no cowering court belle, afraid of her own shadow, no delicate Spanish blossom tended by duennas and scowling uncles.

Would she endure Warburton's brutality? Allow herself to become the nobleman's victim? Abandon Rafe to the English earl's cruel whims? When England sinks into the sea! Tessa swore silently. Nay, she would contrive to best the dull-witted beast, escape him. And then . . . then she would find a way to gain the release of the Spaniard who had touched her heart.

Her resolve faltered when she remembered the massive door sealing off the dungeon, secured not only by bands of iron but by two stout men-at-arms as well.

She drove the doubts from her mind, clenching her fists in determination. Leap one fence at a time, Tessa, she warned herself, gazing around the opulent chamber. First find a weapon and dispatch Warburton. Then—she glanced at the door and was unable to suppress an inward shudder as she remembered the nobleman bellowing to his servants. What was it that he had threatened? That he would break the arm of any who dared disturb him this night? Even if she was unable to escape rape at Warburton's hands, mayhap she could slip out later while he lay sleeping.

She jumped as a coarse laugh shattered her feverish plotting, her gaze snapping to where the nobleman stood.

"This is the finest chamber you have ever been bedded in, eh, wench?" he jeered, hugging his doublet off and throwing the elegant garment on the floor. "And *this*—" His fingers moved to the fastenings of his hose, one hand lewdly cupping the bulge of his codpiece. "I vow to you this will be the stoutest sword you have ever been impaled upon."

Bile rose in Tessa's throat, raw panic surging through her, but she forced it back, her nose crinkling as if scenting something rank. She needed to find some way to goad the nobleman, enrage him so that she could quell the awful sense of powerlessness eating away at her courage.

She tossed her head and let a scornful laugh trill upon the air. "I fear your sword will seem a frail reed indeed, my lord, next to the Spaniard's bold blade."

Fury exploded across Warburton's features, and it took all of Tessa's will not to turn and flee before the nobleman's rage.

Warburton's barrel chest heaved beneath its fuzz

of red hair, his belly quivering where it spilled out over the band of his hose. But despite the ravages of excess evident in his body, his meaty clenched fists and his savage snarl left no doubt as to the ferocity of which the earl was capable. As he turned on Tessa, she saw the folly in baiting a hungry bear.

"So, puppet mistress"—Warburton's rage hissed in his voice—"you were fool enough to sample the Spanish swordsman's thrusts?" Lord Neville stalked toward her, his hands flexing. "Our queen will find that most disturbing. But 'twill banish any question she might have had as to where your loyalties lie."

Tessa swallowed hard, then wheeled and walked away from the earl in an effort to conceal the effect his words had had upon her. She paused and looked out the window, but from the corner of her eye she glimpsed a heavy bronze candelabrum.

"A night in Captain Santadar's arms was well worth incurring the queen's displeasure," she said.

"*Displeasure*? You will face a damn sight more than Her Majesty's displeasure, puppet mistress! Tell me, was your night with that Spanish dog worth the traitor's death you now face, milady? Will you clutch the memory to you as the hangman's noose half strangles you? When they cut you down while you still breathe? When the knife bites into that soft, sweet belly of yours, will you be thinking of Santadar?"

The mullioned panes of the window swam before Tessa's eyes, her imagination painting vivid pictures of the hideous fate she had heard described in such detail. To be hanged, then drawn and quartered— 'twas the most agonizing death that diabolical minds had been able to devise—hours of torture inflicted before a jeering crowd.

She flinched as the earl's hand crushed the soft flesh of her cheeks, and was stunned to find him inches from where she stood. Her gaze snapped up to his glowing devil's-eyes. His fetid breath soiled her face; his lips were wet and eager.

"Nay, Tessa," he sneered, his thumb grinding against the fragile pulse in her throat. "Don't try to hide your fear from me. I can smell it on you, taste it. It makes me hungry, puppet mistress, for what you gave Santadar."

Confusion pierced Tessa's terror for an instant as she sorted through her muddled thoughts. What she gave Santadar? She clenched her eyes shut, a sob lodging in her throat as she pictured the perfectly honed planes of the Spaniard's face, remembered the fierce tenderness of his lips upon hers. If only she *had* given Rafe what Warburton would so brutally wrench from her, mayhap she could have lost herself in the wondrous memories while the English nobleman fell upon her. But to cast her maidenhead before a swine like Warburton—

Pain drove itself through her breast as Warburton's greedy fingers squeezed the tender flesh. Tessa could not keep a cry of pain from breaching her lips.

"Are you thinking of him, whore?" Warburton sneered. "Your Spanish lover? Well, this I vow to you: When I have done with you, the only man you will remember betwixt your legs will be Lord Warvaliant, and the memory will be like a nightmare."

Tessa stifled a scream, panic bolting through

her as the nobleman slammed her down on the bed, pinning her against the sheets. Bruising fingers groped beneath her gown, the flesh of Tessa's inner thigh burned as though doused with acid, and Warburton's thick lips raped her mouth.

And in that instant Tessa understood the full scope of the horror that was about to befall her. "Nay!" She cried out the denial, desperation raging through her as she sank her teeth deep into the earl's lip. Blood spilled into her mouth. Her stomach turned, and she was nigh deafened by Warburton's roar of pain and fury as the hulking Englishman reared away from her. She caught a glimpse of his face, and her heart froze.

Crimson gushed from the gash in his mouth. His eyes glowed with a crazed, murderous light. "Bitch!" he shrieked, one hand swiping at his chin. "I'll kill you!"

Tessa, fingers clawing at his face, legs thrashing, struggled to escape from beneath his weight. Warburton's fist flashed back, then swung, cracking into her jaw. A hundred shards of pain shot through Tessa's skull, but she fought against them, then saw her chance as the nobleman drew back to deal her another blow.

With a strength she hadn't known she possessed, Tessa slammed her knee into the hard bulge at the apex of Warburton's thighs. Warburton bellowed, raging like a wounded beast, agony lashing his massive arms to his torso as he rolled to one side. With a mighty shove, Tessa scrambled from underneath him, searching desperately for something, anything, to use as a weapon.

Her gaze again locked upon the candelabrum, and she lunged for it.

"You'll die for that," she heard Warburton vow. "You'll die!"

A sob rose in Tessa's throat as her hand closed around the heavy chunk of bronze. With a cry, she whirled and swung the candlestick with all her might, driving it into Warburton's skull with sickening force. His head reeled to one side. Tessa couldn't breathe. Horror choked her as she saw him crumple back onto the bed, crimson blood flowing from a jagged cut arcing across the left side of his face.

The eyes that had regarded her so cruelly rolled back in their sockets, and his mouth gaped wide, as though frozen in a scream.

Tessa wanted to shriek herself. Sweet God, had she killed him? she thought wildly, her hands shaking as she clutched the chunk of bronze. She flung the candelabrum away and staggered back from the massive bed, her eyes fixed upon the inert Warburton. Scum though the man was, renowned for his brutality, and regarded with distaste in Elizabeth's court, he was nevertheless of noble blood while Tessa was naught but chaff to be trampled beneath the feet of the nobility.

If she was discovered . . .

Panic surged in her breast, her gaze darting to the massive carved chamber door. It was still closed, and no sound emanated from the hallway beyond. As she held her breath, she half expected to hear a shrill alarm and the sound of heavy footfalls running toward the chamber.

No one knew what she had done, she told herself, desperately trying to wade through the waves

of panic into calm. Even Warvaliant's minions could
not see through thick stone walls, and his lordship
had threatened bodily harm to anyone who dared
disturb him.

She forced her gaze back to where Lord Neville
lay sprawled on the bed, then wiped the back of her
hand against lips that felt soiled by his mouth. She
knew she had to get out of there before her crime
was discovered—if she could remember the way.

She closed her eyes a moment, struggling to recall
the maze of corridors that was Warvaliant Castle.
Thrice before she had been here to peddle her wares;
thrice she had wandered about the forbidding stone
fortress, discovering ways to slip from its grasp. It
had been a game then, like trying to unravel the secret
of a mythical labyrinth, but now she would play in
deadly earnest. For somewhere, lost among those
corridors, lay Rafael Santadar.

If she could free him and get him out to the gardens, they could escape together.

The absurdity of her plan struck her like a bolt of
lightning. It would be a feat worthy of legend if she
could slip from Warvaliant's grasp alone. To even
attempt to find Rafe was insanity. She could not
even remember the way to the dungeon, let alone
to the cell where Rafe was imprisoned. And how
could she gain possession of the key to the cursed
door?

Tessa pressed quivering fingers to her throat. Her
memory filled with the glowing hues of the ring that
had hung about Rafe's neck, and the Renfrew device
engraved thereon seemed to whisper of hope. If she
could escape Warvaliant herself and go to Renfrew
Castle, Tarrant, that mighty nobleman, could then

hasten to Warvaliant and rip Rafael from the fortress's stone fist.

Unless Rafe by then lies dead, a silent voice jeered, and Tessa's fingers clenched as she faced another horror: When Warburton's men discovered that their lord had been killed, would they not be mad for vengeance against the peddler girl who had cost Warburton his life? And when they realized she had slipped out of their net, would they not turn upon whatever victim lay vulnerable to their wrath?

Rafe's wound was hideous enough already. Tessa tried to blot out the memory of his jaggedly torn flesh, swollen and raw. Even if Lord Neville's men did not murder Rafe, fever could seize him in the time it would take her to reach Renfrew Castle afoot. The injury could putrefy, and there would be no one to care for him.

But to try to free Rafe from the dungeon herself was madness.

Tessa sucked in a shivery breath.

"Let the girl go . . . "

Rafe's words echoed through her, spiraling her back into the dank cell alight only with the Spaniard's honor. His features haunted her, the sharp planes and harsh angles softened by tenderness, his eyes warm upon her face.

"Rafael Santadar," she murmured to herself, "I'll not leave you to rot in that hellhole."

Yet if she hoped to rescue him she would need to arm herself. Her gaze flashed about the room, searching for a deadlier weapon than the candlestick. With shaking hands she flung open a carved chest and plundered its contents.

She found a sable mantle trimmed with ermine and

threw it about her shoulders, along with another of sapphire satin that she intended to use to shield Rafe from the chill night winds, should the two of them escape to the moon-dark wilds. Next she affixed a dagger with amethysts bunched like grapes upon its sheath about her waist with a cloth-of-gold sash. Though the knife provided her some small comfort, she knew it would be of little use against the broadswords of Warburton's retainers.

She bent over the chest one more time, digging deep, and caught her breath as her fingers brushed something long and metallic. Her hand closed about it, and she pulled it out from among the satin doublets and wool shirts. Triumph surged through her as she straightened, clutching a lavishly engraved pistol.

She hefted it, the weapon incredibly heavy in her hands. Never before had she held one of these new weapons, and she had no notion of how to fire the thing even when it was primed and ready. She hoped no one she confronted would sense her ignorance.

Tightening her grip on the pistol, she hastened toward the door and eased it open a crack. There was no one without. The halls of Warvaliant yawned before her like an empty tomb. With the greatest of care, she slipped into the hallway.

The very shadows that pooled upon the floor seemed to be specters of earls long dead, whispering and watching. Tessa ignored them as she hastened through the dim tapestry-draped passageway, her heart thundering in her breast, her fingers icy. She wound her way deeper into the castle's bowels until her gaze caught the glow of light from a stairway that plunged downward. She ran toward the steps, fear thrumming through her.

She was about to slip into that torchlit stairway and plunge down to the dungeon when suddenly the clomp of footfalls drifted toward her from the bottom of the steps. The sound struck terror in Tessa's heart.

God's wounds, someone was coming!

The pistol almost slipped from her sweat-soaked hands as she threw herself behind a leather trunk, banging her hip painfully on an iron-bound corner as she concealed herself.

Yet there was small hope of that. Even if whoever was climbing the stairs could not see her, the hiss of her breath seemed deafening and the thundering of her heart was certain to betray her. She knew her fear must be radiating off the stone walls in waves that seasoned warriors could scent as easily as wolves scented their prey. Tessa struggled to calm herself, her fingers clenching about the pistol as the footsteps drew nearer and nearer.

It was more than one person, she deduced by the sound, and there was little doubt but that they were men. Some of the retainers she had seen swarming about the castle when she and Rafe were dragged through the gates?

She swallowed hard at the memory of the guards, their armor glinting, their eyes savage, and she peeked out from behind the trunk, half expecting a horde of them to descend upon her. But the curving passageway still hid them from her view.

She heard them jeering at someone as they approached. She could sense contempt in their voices, even though their words were muffled by the thick stone walls. As she strained to understand them, gleaming silver and rich scarlet suddenly flashed against the ashlar.

Her hands shook as the embodiment of her worst fears stalked out of the shadows—four of Warburton's men, their lips curled in hate-filled snarls as they turned their scorn upon the man who walked in their midst. Tessa tried to peer through the maze of armor-clad legs to see the poor wretch they held at their mercy, but she could see no one—until, as though moved by her very will, one of the guards shifted out of the way.

Tessa's gaze swept over the solitary captive among the guards as light from the sconce bled over his flowing shirt and gray-blue breeches.

Rafe.

She gaped at him from behind the trunk, almost betraying herself with a stunned gasp. Sweet Christ, what had they done to him? His face was ravaged by anguish, and his bound hands were raw and bleeding as though his knuckles had been ground against the cell's stone walls. A wicked bruise encircled one eye, yet even that ugly swelling did not conceal the desperation in those indigo depths.

Had they beaten him? Tortured him? Nay. Tessa knew instinctively that mere brutality could never have carved such agony across Rafael's features. 'Twas Tessa herself, his helplessness to save her, that had nigh broken that fierce will.

Her eyes burned, but she drove back the sob knotting in her breast. 'Twould do Rafe precious little good to cower here, weeping over him. She needed to aid him. Yet if she leapt from her hiding place and tried to wrest Rafe from the guards' grasp, 'twould be to no avail. The four of them would lunge for her despite the pistol, trusting the others to overpower her if she managed to fire.

But where were they taking Rafe? The question roiled in her mind.

Had Warburton given orders regarding the Spaniard before he dragged Tessa to the chamber above? Had he decided to dare Elizabeth Tudor's wrath by disposing of the hated Santadar himself? Or was Lord Neville merely sending his caged lion to London to await the queen's punishment? If so, this would be Tessa's only chance to help him.

She steeled herself, ready to burst forth, regardless of the consequences, when suddenly her gaze locked with eyes of pure indigo, eyes wide with stunned elation.

Pale lips formed her name, soundlessly with aching sweetness, and the crushing anguish that had ravaged Rafe's face was replaced for an instant by triumph.

As quickly as the emotions had streaked across his face they were gone, but a fierce pride now stiffened Rafe's shoulders, as though the sight of her, free, had given him strength.

Tessa sank back into the shadows and watched him stride away, surrounded by the guards. She would cling to Rafe's strength, be patient and careful, and hope that Dame Fortune would cast her dice in their favor.

Drawing in a deep breath, she slipped from behind the chest and followed Rafe and his captors.

Chapter
Eight

TESSA was free!

Free! Rafe battled to keep his reactions hidden
from the guards clustered about him as he forced
himself to move forward at a steady pace.

He strained to hear any sound of alarm rising in
the castle, strained to hear bellowing or the heavy
fall of booted feet as Warburton's men pursued her.
Yet there was nothing but the grumbling of Rafe's
own guards. Warvaliant, that great brooding behe-
moth, had failed to stir.

Rafe gritted his teeth, his mind roiling with questions. Sweet God, how had Tessa escaped Warburton and made her way down here into the depths
of hell? He wanted to catch her in his arms, whirl her
around in joy, shake her for her idiocy, but most of
all he wanted to shield her, protect her, drive the
fear from those incredible dark eyes.

His fists clenched, his hands straining instinctively
against the coarse hemp ropes that held him, as the
guards urged him onward, away from the vulnerable wraith with her riot of dark hair. Along the
winding corridor they prodded him, toward some
unknown fate, and 'twas all he could do not to fling

himself at one of them, heedless of the cost, in an effort to reach Tessa.

But if he did reach her, would he not bring these eager-eyed men-at-arms with their swords and their hatred down upon her? No, he could best serve Tessa by playing out this charade with Warburton's men, by facing whatever they had planned for him. That would buy Tessa time to escape the fortress and lose herself in the windswept crags she knew so well.

But would she flee? Would she realize his own plight was hopeless? Would she know that to attempt to aid him would be suicide?

The fire in those ebony eyes haunted him, icing his stomach with fear. Don't be a fool, wildwitch, he silently pleaded.

"Santadar." Rafe started at the sound of his name, unable to stop himself from knocking into the guard ahead of him, who had come to a halt in front of a closed door. His gaze snapped up to the man's face.

The men-at-arms had been savage when they dragged Rafe from the cell. They had clearly enjoyed slamming their fists into a hated Spaniard's ribs and eyes. But their viciousness had melted away during the trek through Warvaliant's corridors and had been replaced by something that set Rafe's instincts humming with foreboding.

His gaze raked the ring of faces about him, and he scented on the massive soldiers the subtle tang of fear. What, by God's blood, could bring that darting nervousness to the eyes of men who had faced death on the battlefield a score of times? Men hardened to butchery? The hair at the nape of Rafe's neck prickled.

One of the guards cleared his throat as his eyes flicked from Rafe to the door. "Ye're—ye're to be presented within," the man said gruffly.

"Presented?" Rafe echoed, eyes narrowing, wary. "And who the devil am I to be presented to?"

"You'll know right soon enough." The guard's pronounced Adam's apple bobbed once, twice, in his bullish throat, his rugged face paling as though something Rafe had said had fed his gnawing unease.

Death-chill fingers seemed to trail down Rafe's spine, and he hated the stirrings of his own unease. He steeled himself, clinging to the memory of Tessa, so small in the shadow-shrouded passageway. If he wanted to aid her, he would have to meet whatever fate lurked beyond this cursed door, and he would meet it with the arrogance and courage befitting the Phantom of the Midnight Sea.

He squared his shoulders, forcing a sneer to his lips, as his gaze shifted to the doorway. "Well, sir guard, if I am to be 'presented,' should we not open the door? Or do you expect it to swing wide of its own accord?"

"Hold your cursed tongue, Spanish dog, or I'll hack it out," the guard said roughly, his voice unsteady. Like a nightmare-stricken child confronting ghosts in the shadows, the man reached out a gauntleted hand and swung open the heavy door.

Rafe tensed, his eyes struggling to focus on the dim chamber. But he had no time to glimpse what lay within before a hard hand shoved him forward. His foot caught on one of the thick rush mats lying on the floor, and he stumbled, his thigh cracking into some unseen object. Pain shot through his wound, and he cursed.

Yet even the red-hot throbbing in his leg held no power to drive back the shudder that swept over him as his eyes focused and he scanned the shadowed chamber.

A sense of danger drifted over his skin like breeze-borne cobwebs. The haze of a specter seemed to hover over what looked like a macabre shrine. Black velvet draped the walls, and a huge bed loomed like some night-spawned ghoul. Bunches of dried herbs dangled from pegs above the narrow windows, the wilted leaves rustling like bat's wings. On a stand in the far corner of the room a single slender taper glowed like a demon's finger, throwing light on the ceiling above.

Rafe's eyes followed that slender column of light, as though he half expected to find the chamber's inhabitant hovering there, hellish mouth gaping wide, soulless eyes aflame.

With an inward oath, Rafe shook himself, banishing the absurd imaginings. From the time he was a lad, he had dismissed superstitious stories, preferring tales of mortal men performing acts of valor to those of the netherworld and spirits who stalked the earth. In a Spain weaned upon tales fostered by the Inquisition, he had been a rarity, and, by Christ, he would not succumb to those cursed whispers now.

"Captain Santadar." Breath-soft and malignant, the voice seemed to drift from the shadows themselves. The scent of dying roses hung cloyingly on the air.

Rafe stiffened, his gaze moving to the huge tester

bed. "I am Santadar." His own voice echoed back to him, laced with unease. "You wished to see me?"

Laughter trilled across the chamber, seeming to stir even the dried herbs, which rustled as though the claws of some small unseen creature had skittered over them, and had Rafe's hands been free, he would have felt the urge to cross himself.

"Aye, my good Captain. I wished to see you."

Whoever possessed that haunting voice was toying with him, and that toughened Rafe's resolve to show none of his unease.

The bed curtains fluttered as if swept by a draft. Yellow eyes gleamed like twin devils in the darkness. Rafe's stomach lurched as his gaze locked with those glowing orbs, and he felt a thin film of sweat bead his brow. As he turned and ambled toward the candle with forced nonchalance, his gaze fell upon a tattered volume that lay on the marred surface of a heavy table. The book was open to a drawing that made the fear cinch itself tighter about Rafe's chest. It was an image he recognized all too well— Ojancanu, the cyclops described in legends from the far reaches of northern Spain. Fiery red hair burst from the creature's head, and its one sinister eye possessed a nigh palpable menace.

" 'Tis the symbol of the black side of the soul." The spectral voice chilled Rafe's skin. "That side we all possess, but deny."

Rafe looked at the crude drawing and saw that the words inked below the picture were in Spanish.

"I am aware of Ojancanu's power." Rafe kept his tone level.

"Mayhap you have confronted the beast recently, Captain Santadar. Perhaps you saw his face as the

Spanish ships were being shattered. Mayhap you tasted his bitterness as you lay in chains. Did you, my fierce seafarer? Did you touch the devil in your own soul?" The voice was so much closer now that Rafe could almost feel it on his skin.

Feigning indifference he turned away from the ragged volume to face whatever ghost the chamber possessed. His heart slammed to a halt and his breath froze in his lungs as his gaze fell upon the figure now gliding out of the shadows.

The meager candlelight snaked in glistening whorls along thread-of-gold crewelwork on blood-red velvet. The rich fabric flowed about a body so small and thin, it looked like that of a child. But the face framed by the pearl-encrusted escoffion was not that of an innocent. Webbed with tiny lines it was, the cheeks startlingly pale, the lips tinted like frosted roses, the silver hair rippling down over narrow shoulders.

Long bony fingers stroked the fur of a cat; the creature regarded Rafe with its devil-gold eyes. But it was the woman's eyes that arrested him, forcing him to stifle the urge to take a step backward. For those eyes beneath thin black brows were nigh color-less; the irises were the palest green Rafe had ever seen.

For a moment he wondered if the woman was blind, but then her gaze shifted to him, and he knew in that instant that she could see him. Indeed, she seemed to look into the very core of his soul.

"Who . . . are you?" he asked.

The woman regarded him with unblinking eyes. "Chatelaine of Warvaliant, Morgause Bledford War-burton."

"The lady of the castle?" Rafe stared incredulously at the woman who was apparently Lord Neville's mother. "I am—"

"I know who you are and all there is to know about you. Your ship was sunk, and you managed to swim to shore. And then you were captured and hurled into chains."

"I was locked in the castle's dungeon." Bitterness edged Rafe's voice, and he felt again the fierce tug of Tessa's vulnerability, and his own cursed helplessness.

Lady Morgause's lips curved into an enigmatic smile, revealing tiny white teeth. "You must forgive my son's appalling manners," she said. "He is far too conscious of his duty to these wretched English lands, and with the fear of invasion running rampant over the countryside, I fear he became a bit overzealous. 'Twas unconscionable, the way he treated you."

"He could have cast me to the devil, and welcome! But Tes—" Rafe bit off the name, fear racing through him as he caught himself.

Those strange eyes searched his face, and Rafe had the sensation that Morgause Warburton was looking for some crack in his soul, but her voice held all the sickly sweetness of honey. "You have been through a most trying ordeal, Captain Santadar, but your fortunes are about to change if only you have the courage to . . . " The woman's voice trailed off, her gaze flicking to where the guards still stood in the doorway. Their faces were impassive, but every muscle in their bodies appeared to be tensed.

"You will close the door, Smythe," Morgause directed in silky tones.

"But, milady, the Spaniard is dangerous despite his bonds. Lord Neville would not like it if we left you alone with him."

"I am aware of exactly how dangerous Captain Santadar is—especially considering where his thoughts are now."

Rafe's gaze slashed up to Lady Warburton's enigmatic eyes, but she betrayed not a glimmer of the meaning behind her words.

"Smythe, get out and bar the door now."

"Milady, please—" Sweat trickled down the guard's face as he begged her.

"Do it at once!" Morgause's voice was cutting and and the guard started as the cat leapt from her arms. A feline yowl split the air, and Rafe saw the hulking man cower as though the animal were a tiger.

"Aye, my lady. Aye." Smythe's hand whipped out and closed the door with such a force that the sound reverberated through the room. The candle flickered and nearly went out, and another ripple of apprehension seized Rafe. He forced himself to focus upon the fact that the absence of the guards might afford him some chance of escape.

For the man called Smythe was right: Rafe was dangerous. More dangerous now than at any other time in his life. For somewhere in the labyrinth of passageways below was the woman who had burrowed into his heart with her courage, with her wit, with those eyes that seemed to warm the very core of him.

"She is very beautiful—the woman."

Morgause's words startled him, and Rafe stiffened. He dismissed the notion that the ice-pale chatelaine could read his mind, and yet Morgause

Warburton seemed to peer into him and see there the delicate curves of Tessa's face, the cascade of her black hair, the budding emotions she had stirred in him. 'Tis absurd, Rafe railed inwardly, furious with himself for thinking such crazed thoughts. Most likely some servant had carried tales of Tessa up to Lady Morgause, and the woman was merely toying with him.

Yet what if she *was* able to see into his mind? What if she discerned that Tessa was free?

As though hoping that distance could somehow diminish the noblewoman's power, Rafe turned and walked away in silence, the inky shadows suddenly seeming less sinister than the penetrating light of that pale green gaze.

"You should be grateful, Captain Santadar. Grateful to Neville for ridding us of your little peasant doxy. For if she were still clinging to your breeches, we would not be enjoying this chat."

Rafe stifled the surge of relief that shot through him at this evidence that Morgause had no knowledge of Tessa's escape.

"I was never beautiful." The woman's words drew Rafe from his thoughts. The black velvet drapes stirred as she glided past them like a scarlet slash against the flowing cloth. Rafe watched her warily as she went to the mullioned window, her fingers caressing the strange emerald ring on her finger.

He scanned the room again for some means of escape, his hands working surreptitiously against the coarse hemp that bound them. His wrists burned and stung.

"What, Captain Santadar? No gallant denial? No protestations that I must have been comely as a girl?" The woman's gaze flicked down the half-bared expanse of Rafe's chest to where his breeches clung to powerful thighs, and Rafe's stomach lurched as her pink tongue peeked out, moistening her lips.

He felt his cheeks burn. "Lady Morgause, what do you want of me?"

White fingers fondled the gem's glowing facets, the emerald ring seeming to gleam with a light of its own. "I want nothing *of* you, Captain Santadar. I wish to give something *to* you."

Rafe's hands stilled in their struggle against his bonds as the woman's words rasped against his already strained nerves.

"You see, I spent a good deal of time in your country as a girl, Captain Santadar. I loved Spain. I cannot express the pain I felt when Elizabeth Tudor's bumbling forced your honorable king to make war on England. And now to have the proud España broken by a ragtag muddle of howling pirates . . . "

The unexpected words slashed through Rafe, splitting wide raw wounds, releasing the burning shame. "Spain is not broken!" he blazed. "The defeat of the armada was mere luck on the part of the English. Spain will rise and crush—"

He stopped when he saw the cold glitter in Morgause Warburton's eyes, his mind conjuring the image of a golden-scaled serpent hiding beneath a stone, waiting, watching.

"There are other ways to defeat one's enemies than in battle, Rafael." She floated toward him, her gown trailing across the floor like death's shadow. "Let me show you."

A shudder ran through Rafe, and he felt as though

a fine layer of silt had drifted down upon his skin. Yet he stood still, some instinct warning him not to show his revulsion to the woman before him for fear of revealing a vulnerability that would prove a formidable tool in Morgause Warburton's hands.

His jaw knotted as her corpse-chill fingertips skimmed his cheekbone and the dark hair at his temple. "Tell me, Rafael, are you hungry?" Her throaty whisper turned his stomach. "Hungry for vengeance against those who crushed you? Your pride—that raging Spanish pride—is broken now. What would you barter to gain it back?"

Rafe's jaw clenched as he remembered tales of Satan's angels tempting men. He felt the urge to draw away, yet those pale green eyes held him.

"Would you sacrifice your soul, Captain Santadar, if I told you I could put into your hands the tools to bring this infernal land to its knees?"

Lady Warburton's words spun about him, seeming to catch him in some intricate web, the threads poisoned with his own hate, his own pain.

"You're speaking in riddles," he said, the feel of her fingers trailing down his throat repulsing him.

"Am I? Then I shall provide you with the riddle's solution." She extended her fingers toward him, the emerald winking. "Do you know how much power this hand holds, Captain? With a wave of my fingers I can bring death—swift and certain death."

Rafe tensed as he heard the soft metallic click of a tiny latch snapping free and saw the shimmering green emerald rise out of its clasp of gold. What lay beneath the stone was obscured by shadows, but Rafe had heard of such deadly ornaments before, had seen them in exotic ports he had voyaged to.

The compartment hidden beneath the jewel was just large enough to secrete away deadly powders, sleeping potions, any number of sinister substances to strike at one's enemy in the most loathsome way possible.

"Poison! You want me to—" Rafe heard a hiss of breath and felt the chain cut into his flesh as Morgause's icy fingers closed about the ring that dangled around his neck.

The outrage that had surged within him vanished, leaving him chilled to the core of his soul as he peered down into the woman's face. Her gaze was riveted to Rafe's ring; her glazed eyes stared at the crest as though it were some demon made real. Those eyes that had been so chill were burning now with an unholy menace, and if his hands had been free, he would have ripped his mother's ring from Morgause Warburton's grasp.

"Where did you get this ring?" she demanded.

"Hold." The command from a shadow-shrouded corner of the room made Morgause spring away from him and wheel about as though summoned by some ghost. Rafe's stomach plunged to his toes as his eyes fixed upon a pale angel's face and a pistol barrel aimed squarely at Lady Morgause's breast.

"Tessa!" Rafe was as stunned as if the girl had appeared out of thin air. Yet she was real; he knew it the instant that impudent voice cut through the clutching silence.

"If you make a sound, milady, I'll kill you." Tessa strode forward, drafts wafting the velvet curtains behind her, baring what looked to be a hidden door carved in the stone. She looked ready to fire the weapon, her dark eyes steady and unyielding.

Yet Rafe was certain if the pistol had suddenly been transformed into a dove, Morgause Warburton would not have moved, for she stood, wild-eyed, as though stricken by her own sorcery.

One of Tessa's slender hands flashed to her waist and slid a silver dagger free of its scabbard. In a heartbeat, she severed Rafe's bonds. His hands seemed afire as the blood rushed into his numb fingers, and she thrust the pistol into his grasp, then swept up a silken cord from the bed and bound Morgause's birdlike wrists.

"Nay, you're not Anne." The woman's voice was as shaky as a frightened child's. "She had golden curls and—"

"Hasten!" Tessa's voice cut through Rafe's thoughts as she lashed the other end of the cord to the huge bedpost. "We have to be quit of here before the guards return." She headed to the concealed doorway. "There is a way out through the garden, and I saw some horses."

Rafe thrust the pistol into the waistband of his breeches, then cast a backward glance at the sinister chamber as he followed Tessa out the door. "Where the devil will we go?" he demanded, catching Tessa's hand.

"Renfrew Castle."

"No. I'll not go there."

" 'Tis our only chance."

He cursed, but then surrendered to her will as they bolted down the precipitous stone stairway and out into the night. Yet even as they stole two horses, mounted them, and thundered toward Tessa's wild lands, Rafe fumed at the knowledge that he would soon be forced to confront the earl who might well prove to be his own grandfather. He could not shake the sense of doom crushing down upon him as he remembered the crazed light in Morgause Warburton's eyes as she stared at the enameled crest on his mother's ring.

Chapter
Nine

TESSA clasped her torn, dust-smeared skirts with smudged hands, an odd thickness in her throat as her gaze swept the room. Renfrew Castle had not changed. She felt as though a gentle hand had reached out and forced time to pause in its flight.

The great hall, spacious and grand, spanned the length of the huge stone edifice, a monument to generations of noblemen who had brought honor to the English kings. Walls that had been raised in the reign of the fourth Henry were draped in tapestries depicting the battles at Agincourt, Crécy, and Bosworth Field; walnut screens carved by masters' hands provided a backdrop for massive chairs of bog oak and chests inlaid with subtly shaded woods.

A huge trestle table stretched majestically in a seemingly endless sweep of cherrywood inlaid with Tudor roses. Though deserted now, the great table echoed with the memory of countless revelries past. At the head of that table the mighty Tarrant, Earl of Renfrew, had stood, an eternity ago, addressing the somber gathering of sailors' families.

"Lost . . . " Tessa could still hear the earl's voice,

harsh with his own grief. "All hands were lost . . . "

She could see Hagar's face, stricken, as though the nobleman had cleaved her heart with his sword; she could hear her foster-mother shrieking in disbelief, dying inside. And Tessa could feel again the terror that had seized the child she had been as the world that had seemed a magical, wondrous adventure shattered around her.

Her life had never been the same after she learned William Ravenscroft was dead. And after the death of his son-in-law, his treasured daughter, and the grandson who would have been his heir, the bold, blustery Tarrant Renfrew had become as savage as a wounded wolf. All joy had been driven from the castle that had once rung with his hearty laughter.

Tessa wrapped her arms tight about her body and attempted to chafe warmth back into her limbs as she walked slowly into a pool of light spilling from a high-arched window, but the sunshine did nothing to warm her; the golden rays offered no comfort.

'Twas the starkest of ironies that here, in the chamber where she had learned of her father's death, she would now give to Tarrant Renfrew the grandson he had lost. What would the earl say when she raised the ghost of his grandson before him? And what would happen in the soul of the man standing so stiff and hostile before the flames writhing upon the massive hearth?

Tessa's gaze shifted to Rafe, her heart aching at the dread she sensed in the powerful Spaniard. His feet were planted apart as if he stood on the deck of his beloved ship, ready to weather a storm. This would be the most devastating tempest he had faced in his life.

She wanted to go to him, smooth away the lines of
pain carved about that sensual mouth. She wanted
to thread her fingers through the silken midnight
of his hair and assure him that all would be well.
But she could not, dared not, for to do so would
be to chip away yet another bit of the fierce pride
that was so vital to Rafael Santadar, the man who
had fought to save her on the hellish beach where
Hagar had burned, the man who had kissed her with
a fearsome passion that had melted her very soul.

She wished she could assure him that things
would not go awry, that Renfrew would accept him
with open arms, draw him into a protective embrace
that would shield Rafe from the queen's wrath, but
Tessa could offer no assurances.

Rafe was enraged by the mere thought that he
might be tainted with the blood of his enemies. And
with the precious lives Spain's offensive had stolen
from England, 'twas possible that Tarrant Renfrew
would be less than pleased that a Spaniard, a captain
of the great armada, was seeking haven within his
walls.

Mayhap that was the reason it was taking the earl
so cursed long to enter the great hall, Tessa thought,
her lips compressing with impatience. It seemed as
though hours had passed since the wide-eyed page
had skittered from the room in search of his master.

Mayhap the earl was even now ordering his soldiers to hurl the enemy captain into chains, or
mayhap the addle-brained page had muddled the
message Tessa had sent, and Renfrew had no idea
that they waited below.

Her gaze flicked again to Rafe. His strong fingers
were tracing the circlet of gold about his neck, and

his eyes were dark with confusion and skepticism. If Renfrew didn't hasten, she had little doubt the Spaniard's patience would snap and Rafe would stalk from the castle, for he was afraid.

Tessa caught her lip between her teeth. She could feel Rafe's fear, though 'twas not betrayed by any shadow on his face. He knew a fear that Warburton's dank cells and threats of agonizing death could never have spawned in him. A lump formed in her throat; the need to break the horrible silence clamored within her.

She drew in a shaky breath and paced closer to the blazing fire before which Rafe stood. She extended her hands toward the bright orange ribbons of flame as if to warm them.

"Once, when I was a little girl, I worked my marionettes in this room," she said, her voice soft with memory. "My father was passing proud of my puppetry, and he had promised the earl's spit boys that he would bring me here to play for them. They were roaring with laughter, the lot of them, nigh bringing the buttery down about their ears, most likely because I was mixing up the odd voices I had given to each of my figures."

She stole a glance up at Rafe, saw him staring at her, his face impassive. "I was fair bursting with my own importance," she continued, "when suddenly the room went still. 'Twas the earl come to see what the disturbance was. He had been strolling through the castle yard when he heard the laughter. He sent the servants back to their tasks and demanded to see my father and me here in this hall.

"I was only six years old, too young to understand the trouble my father might have been in. I skipped into the room at his side and then ran up to the earl and demanded to know why he had spoiled my fun."

She saw Rafe's head turn toward her, the steely hardness in his gaze softening a little. Then his eyes narrowed as if in anger at her effort to distract him.

"My father nearly collapsed into apoplexy at my brashness. But the earl merely looked at me—all blustery and brimming with childish indignation—and burst into laughter. He roared until tears poured down his face. I can still remember standing a hand's breadth from his chair, glaring at him, my hands on my hips. He caught me up and held me on his lap, and told me I was a bold puss, like his own daughter when she was a girl. He bade me fetch my marionettes, and then he sat and watched me with the most determined interest until the strings on my figures were so tangled even Papa couldn't unwind them."

"Oh, no doubt your earl is a blasted saint," Rafe snapped. "If he'd but grace us with his presence, we could cease this foolery and away."

As though conjured by Rafe's very words, the militant tramp of footfalls reverberated from the corridor beyond, and both Tessa and Rafe turned as the Earl of Renfrew stalked through the archway.

A full head of tousled iron-gray hair gave Tarrant Renfrew the appearance of having just been dragged from his bed, yet there was nothing sleepy or serene about the old warrior. Despite the gout that ofttimes confined him to his chamber, and that had barred him from his beloved soldiering, he reminded Tessa of nothing so much as a petard about to explode.

Piercing falcon eyes glared out at the world from

beneath enormous coal-black eyebrows, and his features were ornamented by an aged scar earned in battle in the Low Countries. Tessa fancifully thought the earl wore his disfigurement like a badge of courage across his craggy jaw.

Tessa felt Rafe go rigid, and she drew herself up to her full height, knowing Tarrant Renfrew accepted timidity in no one. Yet the look in the old earl's eyes almost made her falter.

"What the bloody hell is this about?" Tarrant boomed, a gleam of such stark violence burning in his gaze that Tessa's breath caught in her throat. "That witling boy said there was a man here, some fortune-hungry vulture greedy for Renfrew lands."

Tessa started to speak, to cut off the harsh words she knew would be fire to the smoldering fuse of Rafe's temper. But she was too late. The Spaniard, his indigo eyes afire with fury, took a step in front of her, as if to shield her from Tarrant's angry words.

"I want naught of you, old man! Were it not for Tessa's insistence, I would not have sullied your cursed door. You can cast your lands to the devil, and be damned." He spun and caught Tessa's hand in a hard grip. "We'll away from here at once, take our chances upon the highroads."

"The devil you will! You claimed to possess a ring. *My daughter's ring*—"

"Nay." Tessa strained against Rafe's grasp. "Lord Renfrew, 'twas I who made that claim."

Her interference only infuriated Rafe further. His eyes, now laced with loathing, flashed to the earl's face. " 'Tis not your daughter's ring!" Rage burst free in Rafe. " 'Tis naught to do with you!" He seized the golden circlet and held it close to the warrior's scarred countenance. " 'Twas my mother's!"

"Your *mother's*!" The earl's voice threatened to split the timbers girding the ceiling. His face was ice-white as his gaze locked upon the object in Rafe's hand. Rafe stared at the aged Englishman's features, knowing instinctively that no blow from a mace, no thrust of a broadsword or pike had ever given the old warrior a more agonizing wound than the sight of the ring that glistened in the firelight.

Disbelief, horror, and sick certainty ripped through Rafe, and he closed his fist around the ring as if to shield it from what he now sensed was the truth.

" 'Tis not your mother's ring." Tarrant Renfrew's voice was broken, anguished. "This is not the trinket of some scurvy Spanish wench. 'Tis Anne's . . . Anne's!" The earl's hand flashed out and crushed Rafe's wrist in a bruising grip. Rafe burned to drive the Englishman's hand from his, but his limbs seemed deadened, immovable.

"My lord, please!" Tessa cried, her hand closing upon the earl's arm.

"Where did your mother steal it, you accursed Spanish scum? Tell me, by God!"

"My mother was no thief!" White-hot claws seemed to tear at Rafe's vitals, and he wanted to stop his ears so that he would not hear the agony in Tarrant Renfrew's voice, close his eyes so he would not see the earl's face tormented with grief, pain, and loss.

"Mayhap she was a murderess, then," Renfrew bellowed. "Mayhap the bitch aided her men while they cut down my Anne and her husband and their babe. We never even found their bodies."

The old warrior flung Rafe's wrist away from him and wheeled away, but not before Rafe had seen his lips contort and heard him utter a harsh sound akin to a sob. " 'Twas twenty-eight years ago. Sweet Christ, the pain should not wrench at me so deeply still."

"But, your lordship"—Tessa's voice was earnest and soft, like a cool mist on his fiery pain—"Captain Santadar was a *child* twenty-eight years past!"

Tarrant Renfrew's face blanched, and Rafe was stricken by the storm in the nobleman's eyes as his gaze slashed from Tessa's face to Rafe's own. "Santadar—is your name Santadar?"

"Santadar." Tessa repeated the name softly, and Rafe felt as though his very soul had been ripped from his body.

"Then you . . . " The earl's voice caught. His eyes were fixed upon Rafe's face, and Rafe had the strange sensation that the Englishman was seeing him, truly seeing him, for the first time. "My God, you might really be . . . Anne's son."

The ring had fallen from Rafe's numb fingers, and Tarrant reached out and grasped it as though it contained magical powers. Aye, and mayhap it did, Tessa thought. It had raised someone from the dead.

"No. I mean, I know not." Rafe hated the fear in his voice. "My mother died when I was four years old. I don't even know her name. But she was Spanish. Dammit, she must have been. I don't believe my own mother was English."

"Would you remember her face, if you saw it, lad?" The sudden gentling of Tarrant's gravelly voice unsettled Rafe as nothing else had, feeding his own unease.

"Of course I would! She was my mother!"

"Look you here."

Rafe started as the earl drew from beneath the collar of his slashed-silver doublet a small object, a delicate oval that looked out of place in the palm of his battered hand.

"This is a likeness of my daughter, Anne."

For long seconds, Rafe only stared into the old warrior's eyes, unable to look down at the picture he held, unwilling to confront the truth he knew would shatter all that he was.

Lost in his own secret pain, the earl let his voice drop low as he began to spin skeins of memory, tales of a past Rafe had never known. "Anne was the most beautiful maiden at court, and Ruy Santadar was handsome and gallant, the nephew of a diplomat come from King Philip. Anne loved him, but if I'd known I was sending her to her death, I would never have consented to their marriage."

Rafe closed his eyes against the spell Tarrant's words were weaving about him, but the darkness only haunted him more deeply still, tormenting him with images of lemon trees and laughter and a wooden sword his magnificent father had bought for him at market. Rafe's jaw knotted as those glittering remembrances melted into a hideous memory of death, screams, terror, and flashing blades.

He could hear his own childish shrieks, feel the burning pain as the brigand's knife bit into his flesh. And he could see his mother, her golden hair a tangle about her savaged angel face, as she fell beneath the beasts who had attacked them. He tried to block out the pain of the memory, but it only drove itself deeper into his heart.

Renfrew's voice intruded into Rafe's consciousness. "Their son was the joy of Anne's heart. My only comfort lies in the knowledge that few people know such happiness as Ruy and Anne did in the few years they were given. And if you—if you are their son . . . " The earl's voice cracked, and Rafe opened his eyes to see his own face reflected back at him in the old man's eyes.

"Look you, boy," Tarrant urged, his brawny hand trembling as he held the delicately wrought miniature. "For the love of God, look at her likeness."

Rafe felt gentle fingers drift down the muscled plane of his back, and he knew them to be Tessa's. He drew strength from the warmth of that hand. And yet a sense of foreboding stole through him, as though he would witness his own death if he looked upon the painted face.

With agonizing slowness he forced his gaze down the broad expanse of the earl's doublet to where the aged nobleman's hand lay open before him. Rafe sucked in a deep breath, his whole body feeling like a whipcord ready to snap.

And then his eyes fixed on the fragile oval of porcelain that lay on that scarred palm, and it was as though Renfrew Castle and indeed the world itself had crumbled away beneath his feet, hurling him into a void of anguish and disbelief.

Curls that shone like spun gold wreathed a face as delicate as a Madonna's; sweet lips curved as if they possessed some wondrous secret. Eyes, dark blue like Rafe's own, sparkled with mischief, and a challenge that Rafe well knew would drive a man to sell his soul for but a single smile.

And he had known that smile, seen that smile a

thousand times in his dreams; he had watched the
quicksilver flashes of love and merriment brighten
those angelic features. And he had seen them savaged by grief and agony.

"Nanita, run! Leave me!"

The deep, desperate voice of Rafe's father cut
into his memory, and Rafe could feel his mother's
anguish, a living thing within her breast, as she
seized her son in her arms and fled across the night-
dark land.

A fist of iron seemed to clench itself about Rafe's
throat. His eyes burned with tears that he refused
to shed.

No! a voice inside him screamed. *'Tis impossible!
Impossible!*

Yet of their own volition, his fingers reached out,
and took the likeness from Tarrant Renfrew's hand.
Confusion, hatred, and a crushing sense of helplessness ground deep within Rafe's soul, and he
felt again the terror of the child he had been, lost
and alone.

He skimmed a trembling thumb over the intricate
brush strokes that had captured his mother forever.
Then he raised his eyes to those of his grandfather
and stared into the face of his own uncertain future.

Chapter Ten

TWILIGHT wreathed Renfrew Castle in wisps of mauve; clouds of royal purple trailed about its majestic turrets like the robes of an ancient king. Tessa peered across the courtyard from the window of her chamber, her arms and legs aching less than her heart.

'Twas time for her to leave. Aye, in truth, if she were wise she would leave now that she had paid her debt to Rafael Santadar. She should slip out into the night and let the Spaniard tilt with his own demons henceforth.

She had delivered him to a grandfather who was prepared to protect him with his life if need be. And although she was sure that Lord Neville and the eerie Lady Morgause would like to hurl Rafe back into the sea, Tessa knew that neither Warburton possessed the courage to defy the mighty Tarrant. She suppressed a shudder at the memory of the aged noblewoman's pale visage, the hidden menace that skulked beneath, and her mind filled with the sinister and vengeful fate that could await Rafe at the woman's hands.

Tessa banished her fears and clung instead to the

strength in Rafe's broad shoulders and the power
of the Renfrew name.

He was safe. Safe. Yet as she leaned against
the wall of the bedchamber that had once been
Anne Renfrew's, Tessa drew little comfort from
that knowledge, feeling suddenly desperate and
alone.

Her gaze swept over the beautiful gold-framed
portrait that hung on the tapestry-draped wall. It
was the image of a girl poised on the brink of wom-
anhood. The eyes, so like Rafe's, glowed beneath
the painter's masterful strokes, shining with the
confidence of a woman who is much loved.

Anne Renfrew. The artist had painted the girl's
name in flowing letters, formed as daintily as the
features he had portrayed on his canvas. The girl
was Rafe's mother and Tessa recognized in Anne's
face the same sensitivity that now marked her son's
features.

Most likely Rafe thought that trait was well hidden. But the moment she had met him, Tessa had
seen in Rafe an innate gentleness that was rare
indeed. Did it embarrass him? she wondered. A
tiny smile curved Tessa's lips. For some reason she
was certain 'twas one trait Rafe Santadar tried un-
successfully to hide.

He had also tried to conceal from her the pain he
felt as he rode away from Warvaliant Castle, and
the misery that had beset him when Warburton
taunted him about the armada's defeat. He was
no longer the proud captain of a vessel. He was
not even a full-blood Spaniard. That, too, had been
taken from him. She had seen the stricken look on
his face when he learned he was half English. He

had not wanted to believe it. How long had he stood there, staring at his mother's miniature, the eyes that had once burned with honor, courage, and fierce passion filled with the anguish of a devastated child?

She remembered the tales she had heard of Anne Renfrew's hideous death, remembered Rafe's torment as he described to her the grisly scene when he had been ripped from his mother. Tessa had wanted to take him in her arms and drive back the demons that gave him no peace. ·

And what would he have done if he had not learned that Renfrew blood flowed in his veins? Tessa wondered. Would he have abandoned himself to the queen's fury? Dashed off to Spain where there were no bold ships for him to captain? Could he have faced the bitterness of his defeat?

She laid her hand on the door betwixt her own chamber and the one where Rafe now paced like a caged lion, chafing in bonds far more confining than those Warburton had locked about him. There was no escape from the shackles that had been clamped about Rafe when he confronted the truth of his heritage. They would be there always, grinding against his pride.

Tessa looked down at the crack beneath the door. Rafe's shadow darkened the slit of light again and again, his pain seeming to reach out invisible fingers to clutch her heart.

What, she wondered, had passed between Lord Tarrant and his grandson in the hours after the earl had banished Tessa to the luxury of a hot, scented bath and a fresh gown? What plans had the earl devised for Rafe? What demands had he made of him?

And how must Rafe feel now that he had learned he
was heir to an earldom in a land he despised?

Tessa felt her eyes sting with tears for him. She
wished there were something here for him, something that would soothe his pain, but there was
nothing in this vast castle, no one. Except herself. The Spaniard's fierce pride and independence
gnawed at Tessa. Were she to intrude upon his
musings, he would most likely bid her leave him
in peace. He would not want her to see his pain.
But she could bear the elegance of Anne Renfrew's
chamber no longer; she wanted only to go to the
restless man who paced beyond that heavy door.

She unlatched the door and eased it open, and
the light from a dozen tapers suddenly warmed her
face. Rafe stopped pacing, but no sound came from
his lips.

She looked at him across that magnificent chamber, but instead of going to him, as she had longed
to do, she froze, as if seeing a stranger.

The battered, rakehell seafarer who had swept her
away on the craggy beach was gone. In his place was
a somber man whose face was lined with turmoil.
Tessa had the urge to flee back to her own chamber
and slam the door between them.

And yet he was beautiful, more beautiful than
she had ever dreamed. Waves of dark hair fell in
glorious disarray about his chiseled features. His
broad shoulders were encased in a magnificent doublet of emerald velvet slashed through with silver
satin. His long legs, well muscled from scaling the
rigging, were encased in hose of apple green, only
the slight bulge of a bandage betraying the fact that
he had been wounded.

But it was his eyes that struck her most deeply, eyes so haunted they wrenched Tessa's soul.

"Wildwitch." There was a world of longing and despair in his rough-edged voice. She thought for a moment he would reach for her, knew that he wanted to, but he only turned back to the mullioned window, his eyes roving out across the horizon to the distant purple sea. "A storm is brewing out there on the waves. I can feel it, taste it."

"But you need not dread it," Tessa said quietly, trying to judge what it was that he needed of her.

"I do not dread it." His sensual lips curled back in a half-smile tinged with pain, his teeth flashing white in his sun-bronzed face. "I love it when the sea pits herself against me, sweeping my ship up in her skirts, and swirling it in her temper. 'Tis wondrous. Exhilarating in a way nothing else could be. No pretenses, no pretty lies. Just a man dancing with the sea, facing death, mayhap, but more alive than ever before."

He raised his hand to the leaded window panes, his strong bronzed fingers trailing against the glass as though he wished to touch the cresting waves. And Tessa was stunned at the jealousy that stung her, and the nagging sense of loss.

"You'll be chasing after the sea's skirts again before you know it," she said. "With a new ship, aye, and a crew."

Rafe's bitter voice rumbled in his chest. "I think not, wildwitch. My grandfather has other plans for his sweet Anne's son. I shall be forced to face tempests on this infernal island before I'll again be free."

"Tempests? Here? What does his lordship want of you?"

"Only that I rig myself out in full regalia and hie myself off to the heretic queen's court like a monkey on a chain."

Tessa blanched, fighting the fear she felt for Rafe. "Has the earl gone mad? What if you are arrested and tried? The queen could imprison you!"

"They could lock me in your blasted Tower of London and welcome. But I'll not be so fortunate. My grandfather will call in a score of favors, hurling the might of the Renfrew name behind me. I'm to grovel before the cursed Tudor witch, disavow my Spanish heritage, and crawl—but I'll not do so, damn him. I told him I'd hang before I'd kiss Gloriana's feet."

Tessa watched him, feeling his pain, understanding his resolve, but she could not keep herself from asking softly, "But the earl, too, faces the headsman, the loss of his lands, Rafe. England is brimful of ambitious courtiers who would like nothing more than to use you against Tarrant Renfrew. They are eager to steal this castle and to assume the power of the Renfrew name."

"The old man scarce knows me! If I leave the castle this night, none will even know I was here."

"The earl is your grandsire, whether you will it or no. And by now every servant who stalks these halls knows who you are, Rafael Santadar. The news that you have been found has no doubt spread like wildfire across half of England. Most dangerous of all is the fact that Morgause Warburton suspects you are Anne's son." Tessa paused, seeing a shudder run through Rafe at the mention of Lady Warburton. "And Neville Warburton would like nothing better than to break your grandfather."

"Curse it, Tessa, I thought that you at least would understand."

"God help me, I do understand how this hurts you, and it tears me apart! But I can't forget Lord Tarrant, Rafe. He is an aged man who has spent a lifetime serving the queen and carving out a place for himself in the annals of bravery and honor. He has only this pile of stone and the windswept crags to call his own. And now you, the grandson for whom he grieved for eight and twenty years."

Rafe wheeled away from the window, brows slashed low over his eyes, fists clenching and unclenching as if itching for something to hurl against the wall. "If he grieved for me, why did he not search for me, send some of his soldiers, at least, to inquire how it was that his grandson had vanished into the air? If *my* daughter and *my* grandson were set upon by murdering thieves, I would have ripped Spain apart in an effort to find him!"

"And to what purpose, if the child was hidden in a hermitage in the wilds of an isolated mountain?" Tessa flung back. "If the earl had searched for an eternity, he'd never have found you. He thought you were dead, Rafe." Her harsh words faded beneath the anguish streaking across his face.

"Do you know what it feels like to be a terrified child, Tessa? To have the people you love torn away from you? Murdered before your eyes?" Rafe ground the heel of his hand against his brow, and she could feel the hurt and grief throbbing within him.

"Nay, Rafe, I know naught of such loss." Her voice was threaded through with her own pain— the death of her wondrous father somewhere upon the relentless sea, the nightmare vision of the eager mob's flames consuming the frail body of the mother she had cherished.

She wrapped her arms around the thin silvery gown. The delicate fabric felt like a sea breeze against her skin, but nothing could drive the hollow ache from her soul. Rafe lifted his gaze to hers, and there was hopelessness in his indigo eyes, and something more.

"Wildwitch." He choked out the name he had given her, his voice raw. "Forgive me. What befell me . . . 'twas all a long time ago." He drove his fingers back through the rich waves of his hair. " 'Tis just that. I don't even know who I am anymore. When the *Lady* went down, all that I was perished with her. For the first time since my mother laid me in Brother Ambrose's arms, I— I don't know where the devil to go or what to do."

Tessa felt her own throat thicken with tears. She swept across the space that separated them and gently touched his pain-ravaged face. "You've lost nothing, Rafe, nothing of the honorable, brave, and wondrously gentle man you are." She let the tears rimming her lashes fall free. "I used to spin stories when I was a girl, tales of a bold sea ghost who would steal me away. 'Twas my father who began telling the stories. They delighted me by the hour, filled my imagination. But none of those dreams could touch the sweet reality of you, Rafael Santadar."

"Wildwitch—" Rafe's voice caught, his eyes overbright. " 'Tis madness, the feelings you loose in me. I'm crazed. Scarce three days have I known you, and yet if I had known you my whole life through, I could not be more certain than I am at this moment that . . . I love you, Tessa of Ravenscroft."

He saw her eyes widen with astonishment, disbelief, and wonder, saw her lips part.

He reached for her then, his fingers tangling in the curling tresses at the nape of her neck. "Tessa, God help me, I—" Fire flared in Rafe's eyes as his face arched downward toward Tessa's.

Her lips parted in a cry of joy as Rafe's mouth closed over hers with desperation and need and piercing, piercing sweetness. She dug her fingers into the hard muscles of his shoulders, pressing herself against him as though the warmth of her body could somehow drive back the chill despair webbed about him. Yet he gave to her far more than she had given him, pouring into his kiss such roiling emotions that Tessa felt swept away by them.

Drowning. She felt as if she were drowning in the love he offered, and she was glad to sink deeper into the honeyed warmth Rafe was pouring about her.

Instinctively her hands swept up, her palms bracketing that stubborn, beard-roughened jaw, her fingertips skimming the silky midnight richness of his hair. At that instant she realized he was trembling, this bold seafarer who had faced the might of Sir Francis Drake without quavering, who had hurled defiance at Neville Warburton, England's cruelest nobleman.

Rafe's whole body was shaking with need. And she wanted to give him all he asked, wanted to take the very essence of his soul inside herself and make it hers.

Tessa skimmed her fingers beneath the velvet doublet, hungry for the sensation of his skin against her palm.

"*Querida*," Rafe ground out. "*Madre de Dios, querida*, I want you. I need you."

A tiny gasp tore from Tessa as she parted his heavy slashed-velvet doublet and felt his hot flesh under the thin shirt beneath. She could feel the roughness of the mat of hair spanning his chest, could feel his nipple, pebble-hard, against her fingertips.

"Rafe," she whimpered, her nails nigh tearing at the fabric that separated them.

A groan breached Rafe's lips, and she could sense that he was fighting his passions, trying to be chivalrous, gallant.

"I love you." She sobbed out the words, her lips hungry upon the corded flesh of his throat, her hands knotting into fists against his chest.

"Damn!" He ground out the oath between clenched teeth and she could feel the leash he had been holding upon his passion snap. He dragged her closer still to his emerald doublet, crushing her breasts against the hard plane of his chest, his mouth slashing over hers, as though he were starving for the taste of her. Tessa reeled beneath the hot, heady flavor of his need, slipping her tongue into his mouth, tasting him with a hunger she had never felt before.

A hard arm curved under her knees as Rafe swept her up against him and carried her to the huge bed. The fragrance of cedar and heather whirled about Tessa, mingling with the heady scent of male passion.

And then he was beside her on the soft mattress, his hard palms skimming over her body, his mouth seeking hers.

"Tessa . . . " He rasped out her name against the fragile skin of her throat, his lips hot and moist against her pulse point. "We shouldn't do this." But his fingers were already tearing loose the fastenings of the silver gown, baring the milky curve of her shoulder, freeing her breasts to his burning gaze.

Candlelight spilled over his features, limning them with wonder as he drew the fabric back from her skin. His fingers paused in their quest, his face suddenly wire-taut and still, so still. For a moment Tessa feared he would stop the magic he was working upon her, draw away. But then she looked into his eyes, and what she saw there made a sob knot in her own breast.

Love. Aye, love, and an awe that drove the breath from her lungs.

His hand, rope-toughened, sun-browned, swept across the coral tip of her nipple with infinite tenderness.

His face blurred before her; her eyes burned as tears flowed unchecked down her cheeks. Love . . . How could it have happened so swiftly, so thoroughly? It had swept down like a sea storm and whirled away her very soul. Her father had told her a thousand stories so beautiful they had made her weep—tales of love, courage, honor. Yet none of the feelings they had evoked had been as wondrous as the one rushing now about her heart, carrying her away.

"Rafe." She whispered his name, reaching up to take his face in her hands and draw him down.

His lips moistened the swollen crest of her nipple as they skimmed across it. "You're so beautiful, wildwitch . . . " His voice trailed off as he drew her nipple into his mouth, suckling her with agonizing sweetness. Tessa cried out, feeling desire shoot deep into her womb as a hollow ache began at the apex of her thighs.

She wanted, needed, the fierce gentleness only her phantom could bring.

"Please," she choked out, "let me touch you. I need to touch you."

A sound akin to a cry of pain was ripped from Rafe's chest, and he tore away from her, freeing them both of the garments that lay between them, tossing his emerald velvet doublet on the floor, sending her gown to pool upon it like a beautiful silver lake on a verdant shore. And then he loomed over her, magnificent, naked, the hard lines of his body burnished by the sun and sea winds. Rafe's shoulders, honed by fighting the heavy canvas sails, tapered into a narrow waist; whorls of dark hair misted the muscles carved into his broad chest. A pale scar slashed across his ribs, a reminder of some battle past, that slight imperfection only serving to add to the virile power inherent in Rafe's tall body. Around his thigh, a snowy white bandage swathed the wound he had suffered in his battle with Drake—the wound that could well have cost him his life in the chill and merciless sea.

He would have another scar when his leg wound healed, further testimony to the dangers faced by the Phantom of the Midnight Sea. Tessa suppressed the thought, not wanting to think how close he had come to losing his leg—and his life.

She shuddered at the thought of him lost or

drowned, then banished that shadow upon her joy. For he was here. He was safe. And for this single moment he was hers.

She drank in the sight of him, wanting to brand it on her memory forever, to capture it, keep it. " 'Tis you who are beautiful," she whispered, reaching out and tracing that pale scar. "So beautiful." A blush fired her cheeks, and for the first time she felt fear—fear that she would somehow disappoint this man who had captured her heart.

She heard his breath, harsh in his chest, and resolve flooded through her. Aye, he was beautiful, and she would not play the simpering miss, not cheat him of knowing what the sight of him did to her.

Slowly, so slowly, her fingertips traced the line of one of his ribs to where a ribbon of black satin hair bisected his flat stomach. She caught her lower lip between her teeth as her hand glided downward, her eyes following the course her fingers were charting. The ribbon widened, coarsened, and her palm brushed the velvety-hard heat of that which made him a man.

"Tessa!" Every muscle in Rafe's body snapped taut.

" 'Tis just as I imagined it to be," she whispered, her breath wisping over her fingers onto the throbbing length of Rafe's sex. "Hard, so hard. I want to feel it inside me."

With an oath he flung himself down beside her, kissing her with a dizzying intensity that stole her very soul. The hands that had driven her close to madness skimmed over the gentle curve of her hip, his lips leaving burning trails across her skin as he threaded his fingers through the downy softness between her legs.

Tessa quivered, her head arching back against the pillows as Rafe parted the dewy petals cradled in the dark silk down, the rough-callused pads of his fingers finding the hardened nub that pulsed with desire.

"Rafe," Tessa gasped. "I need you." She tugged on his shoulders, struggling to draw him atop her, but he only made a soothing sound deep in his throat.

"Soon, wildwitch, soon."

A cry of protest welled within her, then shattered into a gasp of agonized pleasure as his fingers moved upon that delicate knoll. Her hands knotted in the softness of the bedclothes, her nails clawing at the silky fabric as he eased his finger into the tight opening, softening the seal of her virginity.

"I don't want to hurt you. Tessa, you're so sweet." He shifted over her, his weight pressing her into the downy softness of the feather tick, his body hot, so hot and trembling. He braced his arms on either side of her, then slipped one muscled thigh between her legs, parting them gently.

She felt him probe the liquid center of her, the beautifully carved planes of his face rigid with the effort it cost him to hold himself back.

And then his eyes found hers, held hers for long moments that seemed to spin into eternity. "I love you, Tessa." His mouth closed over hers, a ragged groan reverberating through his chest as he plunged deep, burying himself inside her.

A stinging pain bit Tessa, but she heeded it not,

reveling in the feel of Rafe within her. And just as she thought there could be no greater joy than their joining, he thrust his hips forward, stroking deep, the spiraling madness he had awakened within her moments before building again, expanding.

"Sail with me, wildwitch." His voice whirled to her through a rainbow haze of passion.

She dug her nails into the flesh of his back, searching for something, anything to cling to in the tempest he had unleashed. Again and again he thrust, as though trying to reach some wondrous secret within her.

Then suddenly the passion-hazed veils fell away, revealing beauty such as she had never known. The world burst, shattering into a thousand jewel-hued droplets of joy. She tossed her head as she clutched Rafe to her, opening her eyes as she felt his body shudder, then stiffen. She watched him, her heart filled with love, as his face contorted with the power of his own release.

Long moments he held himself above her. Then he buried his face in the tumbled waves of her hair, his body racked with the tremors that still jolted through him.

"Tessa." Her name was the most tender of caresses. His fingers stroked her cheeks, gathering up her tears as though they were the rarest of treasures. "Did I hurt you, wildwitch?"

Tessa traced the line of his jaw, the fullness of his lower lip, unable to keep the quaver from her voice. "Nay. 'Twas the most miraculous thing that has ever befallen me. 'Twas beautiful, Rafe. 'Twas . . . " Her fingers fluttered as though trying to grasp the right words to describe what had happened between them, but there were none wondrous enough, none magical enough.

"God forgive me, wildwitch," he whispered, his voice breaking. "For at this moment I'm glad I lost my *Lady*, glad I was cast upon these shores to taste of you just once."

Tessa stroked the silky softness of his hair, her throat too tight to speak.

Then he raised his head, his eyes warm and tender as he gazed on her face. "Come with me, wildwitch," he said, trailing kisses across her eyelids, her nose. "I need you. Want you."

"Come with you? Where?" She tried to clear her mind, remember his earlier words.

"Come with me and stay with me forever. I've naught to offer you, Tessa—no ship, little money. By Saint Michael, I might well lose my head if Elizabeth Tudor cages me in her Tower. 'Tis madness to ask this. 'Tis insanity . . . and yet I've been searching for you my whole life. I can't let you go, no matter what the cost."

"I'll not leave you, Rafe."

"Marry me."

She gaped at him, stunned, his words showering her with hope and joy and a soaring sense of wonder.

"Marry you? You are heir to the Earl of Renfrew, son of a Spanish grandee. I was but an orphan when my mother and father found me. I know not where I came from or who my real parents were."

"It matters not. I want you, Tessa. Only you. I'll go to your blasted court if it will make you happy, and I shall try to keep a civil tongue in my head to protect this earl you respect so much. But at least give me some small hope that once this madness has ebbed, you might be my wife."

My wife . . . Had Tessa ever heard words fraught with more longing?

"I've been lonely, Tessa. Christ, I've been alone so long. I was beginning to believe I would never find you."

His hands curved about her cheeks, his lips drifting closer, his breath softly mingling with hers. A chuckle rumbled low in Rafe's throat, and Tessa was struck by how seldom she had heard that rich, wonderful sound.

"I thought I would never find you, *querida*, and then—then you tumbled off of a cliff and into my arms. I looked into your face, and you . . . you bewitched me. When I was a lad I scoffed at the sailors of Odysseus, risking death for the Sirens who lured them onto the reefs, but I would join them now, and gladly, Tessa. I would face any peril to ensure that this sweet enchantment will not end."

Tessa kissed his cheek, his jaw, the curve of his lips, and she felt a whispering of dread deep in her stomach. If only the peril confronting them could be as simple as the sea reefs Rafe had often faced, rather than the sinister shadows of Morgause Warburton and the looming danger of the queen.

She closed her eyes, scenes whirling before her like some dreadful nightmare—the majesty of Elizabeth Tudor's court, magnificence she had never thought to see, the lurking danger in the cruel, power-hungry courtiers, and the savagery of Neville Warburton.

What weapon could a man like Rafael Santadar wield against the intrigues he would be hurled into?

To what lengths would the Warburtons—aye, and Tarrant Renfrew's other enemies—go to destroy this grandson whom the earl so obviously treasured? And what of her? Would she not be the perfect tool with which to crush the bold Santadar?

Nay, she resolved inwardly, her arms tightening about Rafe. I shall aid him, shield him. Guard him against the daggers they will try to slip betwixt his ribs with their honeyed words, their evil minds.

She started from her musings, finding Rafe regarding her with solemn eyes. "Wildwitch?"

" 'Tis naught, Rafe, naught," she struggled to assure him, burying her face against his shoulder for an instant. She pulled away, her gaze meeting his steadily, dark with strength. " 'Tis just that I'll not ask you to cast yourself upon any reefs where I am not willing to follow, my bold sea phantom. After we've confronted whatever demons await you, we'll see whether you truly want a Siren at your side."

Chapter Eleven

RAFE had expected the glittering court that surrounded Elizabeth Tudor to be decadent, but even in his wildest imagination, during the week he had healed at Renfrew Castle, he had not dreamed of the excessive lavishness of the English court.

Precious gems were scattered upon garments and hair as carelessly as flower petals tossed from a child's hand. The throne room was filled with treasures that dauntless adventurers had carried back from countless voyages to shower upon the queen who held not only their loyalty but, 'twas rumored, their hearts as well.

The Virgin Queen, they had named her, and yet 'twas well known that her majesty possessed a highly cultivated taste for a well-turned masculine body, although she rarely showed it, except in bawdy jests or in the patterns of the dance—the only time she was seen touching her male courtiers, even her renowned favorite, Leicester. But her passion was there, all the same, in her eyes and in the aging lead-painted face that men had once called beautiful.

Rafe's gaze flicked across the crowded room to where the queen was ensconced upon a magnificent throne, her gem-starred hair like flame surrounding her pale cheeks, her mouth a tad selfish, her eyes keen.

She was the enemy ruler, and yet even as he watched her from a distance Rafe could feel her magnetism. It was a kind of silken thread that drew the greatest men in her kingdom to her and made them trip over themselves like puppies in search of her smile.

"What think you?" Tarrant Renfrew's voice broke through Rafe's thoughts. Though Rafe wanted to tell the earl that his queen paraded about like a strumpet, that the lavish trappings of the Elizabethan court were vulgar, he found himself unable to do so.

Instead he heard his own harsh whisper. "She is magnificent."

The earl's lips curved in an indulgent smile. "Every man in this room is half in love with her, be he ten or a hundred. Once I believed 'twas the power she wielded, and that men flocked about her only in the hope of gaining a crown. But now I know 'tis something within Elizabeth herself. An aura that kept her safe even as a princess whilst her enemies plotted against her."

"Mayhap 'tis the fact that she changes her loyalty the way a chameleon shifts his hues," Rafe said. "Or that even though she be a monarch, she is not averse to using feminine wiles, seeming helpless whilst she waits to pierce a man's heart."

Tarrant scowled. "You think you know so much of our queen, and our ways, eh, stripling? You know Elizabeth not at all. She can be the most loyal of friends. The kingdom she inherited from her sister was as somber as one of your Spanish courts, the fires of Smithfield still poisoning the air. Now look at it. For a generation—aye, since even before Henry died—factions warred within England, tearing apart her very soul. Men cared not what damage they did to this island, cared only that their own special puppets sat upon the throne. Elizabeth changed that, though even I never suspected that she could."

Rafe gave a snort of disbelief, clinging to the scorn he had always felt for the Tudor queen. Instead of the outraged response he expected from his grandfather, the old earl's lips curved in a grin.

"And now she has even defeated your Philip," Renfrew observed, "king of the high seas, master of an empire. Not a bad tally for a child who was called a bastard and raised more like a captive thief than a princess, eh, boy?"

Rafe winced as the earl's elbow dug into his ribs. The nobleman's eyes were twinkling, as though Elizabeth had provided him with some grand jest.

"You called her magnificent," Renfrew said, "and you were right. But she is more than that, this Elizabeth. She will be immortal."

A harsh laugh broke from Rafe's lips. "I never thought to hear the English speak such idiocy, unless, of course, 'tis true what is whispered of your queen—that she is in league with the Dark One."

Instead of growling with anger, Tarrant laughed. "Well, my son, if in truth she is in league with the devil she will be in good company. It seems to me half the great men in society have been thus accused in whispers. 'Tis the only way those envious of them can explain away their own failures."

Renfrew's eyes narrowed, and Rafe felt an urge to squirm beneath his intense regard. "I have heard of a Spaniard who was wooed by the devil's mistress," said the earl. "A seafarer, he was, who bargained away his soul."

Rafe felt his cheeks burn.

"So tell me," Tarrant said. "How did you find his highness, Prince Lucifer, when last you spoke?"

Rafe felt chilled to the very marrow, visions of his homeland skittering through his mind. Consorting with the devil was no jesting matter in sultry Spain. He blinked, his imagination filling with the horror that was the Inquisition. During the auto-da-fé, the death ceremony for those condemned by the inquisitors, pristine white robes, hand-stitched by dainty Spanish maidens, draped the unfortunates who filed into the town square. Stakes surrounded by piles of faggots awaited. The repentant were allowed the mercy of strangulation before being put into the searing flames.

"That tale about me," Rafe snapped, "is absurd."

"Aye, but it could also be very dangerous, could it not?" The old earl's eyes flicked to Rafe's, the merriment within them tempered now with understanding. "Trysts with the devil are a serious matter in England as well, especially when the subject of the whispers is a queen who has numerous times sensed the cold kiss of an ax blade up her neck. No matter what you think of our Elizabeth—either her faith or her form—she is still a monarch. She is bold Henry Tudor's daughter, and no son could have served him better. She has not survived by being weak. And she holds your fate in her hands, Rafael."

Rafe felt his grandfather's hands close tightly, about his upper arms. "Listen to me, boy. I know you are not used to buckling before the will of any man—let alone a woman. But do not bait the queen. Nor should you make the mistake of thinking that Elizabeth can be won with pretty words.

"You have a future here, a chance at more than you could ever hope for in Spain. What were you there? Captain of some leaky ship, existing on weevily biscuits and stagnant water, searching for treasure that Englishmen would snatch from your hands? You were no one there."

With an oath Rafe tore from his grandfather's grasp. "I was Captain Rafael Santadar, a man known for countless battles on the high seas. But I would rather be a peon working in a grandee's vineyard than an earl in the land of my enemies. You say that you love me, that your blood runs in my veins. If this is true, you will forget you ever saw me once this farce is finished. You will let me go away with Tessa."

Rafe saw the earl's craggy features harden, and hated him for the contempt he saw in those falcon eyes. "Away to what, Rafe? Life upon the seas with the daughter of a common sailor?"

Anger flared in Rafe, and his eyes flashed blue fire. "I care not if she is the daughter of the devil himself. I love her, blast you. And had it not been for her intercession on your behalf, I would have left Renfrew Castle the first night I had the misfortune to darken your door."

"Oh, aye, I am the most heinous of villains, am

I not? Sheltering you in a castle legendary for its strength, offering you a fortune to rival that of the queen and a name—"

"A name I will give Tessa of Ravenscroft when she is my bride, whether you will it or no. It sickens me—*sickens me*—that she has shown you such loyalty these past days while you have shown her nothing but scorn."

"Scorn? I have treated her in a manner befitting one of her station. By Mary's crown, boy, I've not flogged her or abused her. And did I not dispatch my own men to retrieve her trinkets from the hovel she and the old woman lived in?"

"Those *trinkets* are all she possesses. They are her memories."

"Then the wench has precious little worth remembering, lad. Trunks full of half-finished ruffs, a score of puppets—God's wounds, I've not even objected to the trysts in your chamber these nights past. The girl discovered your identity, brought you to me, and for that, I'll always be grateful to her. If she eases this period of transition for you, I'll see that she's provided for for the rest of her life."

"Something you neglected to do when her father lost his life on one of your vessels?"

Tarrant's eyes narrowed beneath his craggy brows, and his voice became a dangerous growl. "Do you know what I was doing when that ship went down? I was still tearing myself apart with grief, aye, crazed with it. Still thinking that you and your mother . . . ah." The earl drew out the final syllable. Then suddenly his stormy gaze paused on something visible over Rafe's shoulder. His rough-carved features softened a little, but Rafe mistrusted the canny light in those eyes that were so like his own.

He turned, his gaze following his grandfather's to a group of courtiers who were entering the vast chamber. It took Rafe but a heartbeat to identify the object of Tarrant Renfrew's attention. For there, among the powdered and perfumed dandies with their oiled beards and the glittering jewels dangling from their pierced earlobes, stood Tessa, a pristine lily in a field of garish flowers.

Rafe's heart lurched at the sight of her. The dark mass of her untamed hair was caught back from her face. A French hood of bronze velvet edged with pearls added luster to her rose-blushed cheeks and rippled down past her shoulders like a veil of amber.

Bronze velvet also encased a waist so tiny it seemed but a wisp above the generous skirts that swept out from her hips. A ruff rose behind the slender column of her neck. His eyes shifted to where a jeweled stomacher pushed up her high, firm breasts, and he saw a glorious necklace of amber and topaz nestled in the valley between those two ripe mounds.

He and his grandfather had been speaking of devils but a moment before. Perhaps that was why Tessa now seemed like an angel.

But as Rafe's astonishment at her beauty faded, his wariness deepened yet again. He had left her in their chamber earlier to rest. When he had bent to kiss her before meeting his grandfather, she had been plying her knife over a bit of wood she had been working on the past few days, guarding it from his eyes with a jealousy that both surprised and amused him.

There had been no sign of the magnificent trappings garbing her now. His eyes flashed to his grandfather who leaned complacently against a pillar. "What by Mary's crown is she doing here?" Rafe snapped. "I want her spared whatever ugliness transpires."

"Tessa will be my insurance that as little as possible transpires." The earl flicked a speck of lint from his saffron doublet. "I fear you have a most formidable Renfrew temper, and it will be lashed by the sharp tongues in this room. I advise you to remember that Tessa's future, as well as your own, depends upon your behavior this night. I could think of no better way to remind you than this."

With one scarred hand he gestured to Tessa, who now hovered, like a shy roe deer, in the carved wood archway. Her eyes were wide, and despite their melting dark beauty, Rafe could see in them the slightest shadow of fear.

How many times had he watched her, in the past days, gazing at the richness of the Renfrew stronghold? It had been as if she were staring into some chasm plunging between the two of them—noble heir and humble mistress of marionettes.

And now she was confronted by the scintillating grandeur of this room, these men and women of daunting power, and Rafe could feel her slipping away from him like grains of sand cupped in a child's tiny hand.

His jaw knotting, he turned his back on the earl and hastened toward Tessa. Her perfect white teeth caught the fullness of her lower lip in the nervous gesture that had become so achingly familiar to him. The hands that had swept over his body with such wonder were now clenched in a death grip about a delicate feather fan. As her eyes caught his, Rafe could see the relief shudder through her.

"Rafe!" Her lips formed his name as she rushed forward, and he fought the urge to draw her into the shield of his embrace. "Your grandfather asked that I present myself, but . . . " Her eyes swept the assemblage, and Rafe hated the look of uncertainty that defiled those usually intrepid eyes. Her fingers, one marked by a tiny cut, no doubt suffered while she was carving, fluttered to where her breasts plumped above the stomacher, and her cheeks flushed deeper still.

He wanted to rage at his grandfather for putting Tessa through this, but knew he dared not reveal his anger to Tessa, for 'twould only serve to make her more uncomfortable still. Instead he murmured, "I am glad you are here to show these posturing courtiers what true beauty is."

Tessa gave a shaky laugh. "I feel as if I've been cast adrift in the middle of your cursed ocean with not so much as a keg to keep me afloat. 'Tis all so grand, I might well drown in it. Unless, of course, the queen discovers who and what I am and hurls me from this chamber herself."

Despite the milling courtiers all around them, Rafe could not stop himself from reaching up to Tessa's face, its curves as pure and smooth as an apple blossom. His voice, when he spoke, was gravelly with the emotion she stirred in him.

"If Elizabeth Tudor banishes you from this assembly, 'twill be because she is but a guttering candle in the face of such beauty."

He was rewarded with a smile, poignant and

sweet. "What? And have these peacocks already filled the mouth of my bold Spanish rogue with pretty compliments that mean naught?"

"They mean everything, Tessa. *You* mean everything to me. I—"

"Open your eyes, you dolt!" Tarrant Renfrew's gruff whisper shattered Rafe's words, driving back the veil of loving that had seemed to surround the two of them. "Her Majesty awaits you, and—curse it all to hell—look you who stands by her side!"

Rafe's gaze flashed up to the dais where Elizabeth Tudor was ensconced, a gaudy butterfly amid a hive of bumbling bees. Beside her, among the most handsome beaux in the land, lurked a man whose countenance drove a fist into Rafe's gut.

"Warburton." Tarrant spit out the hated name. "And if the son be snapping about Her Majesty's heels, that she-wolf mother of his is no doubt prowling about as well."

Rafe's whole body snapped taut as his gaze locked onto the face of his enemy, the man who had hurled him into the foul dungeon of Warvaliant, the man who had tried to brutalize Tessa.

The malevolent eyes glinted hatred, and Rafe saw that one heavy jowl was marred by a wicked-looking gash while the man's huge fists clenched as though eager to crush someone's throat. Rafe sensed in the nobleman a thirst for blood and a pulse of raw fury throbbing beneath Warburton's anger-flushed skin. Those eyes, filled with hatred and violence, bored into Tessa's pale features, and as Rafe saw that seething gaze fixed upon the face of his woman, his blood ran cold.

"Wildwitch?" 'Twas the softest of questions, but

he felt her fingers close about the sleeve of his doublet as if she were trying to steady herself.

"I fear Lord Warburton won that ornament on his cheek at my hands," Tessa said. "I was in a bit of a hurry to seek the company of a gallant Spaniard."

Rafe's jaw clenched as he recalled all too clearly what had almost happened to Tessa at Warburton's hands.

"Dammit, boy," the earl said roughly, his keen mind obviously having deduced the reason for Rafe's fury. "The girl escaped but a little worse for the encounter. Now fix a smile to that blasted face of yours. The way your eyes are spitting flame, they'll think you plan to drive a dagger 'twixt the queen's ribs!"

Another voice resounded nearby: "And you would like that, would you not, Santadar?"

Rafe jerked his gaze away from his grandfather's features and turned to the loathsome Warburton, who was stalking toward them. The nobleman's lips were twisted in a sneer, and his voice, when he spoke again, was edged with such menace that Rafe turned his broad shoulders to shield Tessa from the man's gaze. "Or would you let your doxy strike out at the queen in your stead?" Thick fingers touched the gash marring his face.

"You bastard. She should have slit your cursed throat!" Rafe took a step toward Warburton, fists clenched, battle-ready. The magnificent chamber and all within it melted away, leaving only Rafe and the man who had tried to harm Tessa. But before Rafe could strike, Tarrant's brawny hand flashed out and grasped his arm.

Rafe yanked away, the legendary fury of the Phantom of the Midnight Sea roiling in his eyes as he glared at the aged earl. "Go to the devil, old man!" Rafe's words echoed in the sudden silence, and he became crushingly aware that every eye in the room was regarding him with curiosity, suspicion, hate—and ghoulish anticipation.

He heard Tessa breathe his name, that single, pleading sound, steadying him as nothing else could have. "Rafe," she whispered, "the queen is watching you!"

He raised his eyes to the dais that lay in a wash of golden candle-shine. At that instant Warburton and all his evil whirled away, time seeming to crash to a halt as Rafe's gaze locked with that of Elizabeth, queen of England.

Nothing had prepared Rafe for the force of those dark eyes—eyes that had known betrayal and pain, eyes as lusty as a new-blown maid's, yet as shrewd as those of the most ruthless statesman. *Queen.* Elizabeth Tudor was the embodiment of that single word.

"Lord Renfrew." A voice well seasoned with command cut through the stifling silence, and the queen's lips curved in an enigmatic smile. "I am told you have brought us a most intriguing guest."

The earl swept the monarch a bow, then surreptitiously dug one elbow into Rafe's side, bidding him to follow suit. Gritting his teeth, Rafe stiffly acknowledged the woman on the throne.

"My grandson, Rafael Santadar, if it please Your Majesty." The earl strode forward, Rafe following in his wake with a reluctance he was certain must radiate from every line of his iron-taut face.

Elizabeth Tudor's thin lips curled and Rafe sensed

the needle-thin point of danger in the woman's smile.

"If it pleases us?"

Her gaze moved slowly over Rafe's body, and he felt like a prize stallion being readied for a mating.

"Your grandson pleases us mightily, my lord, in his face and form. But 'tis miraculous, is it not, that the sea should have spit him up after . . . how long has it been? Fifteen years?"

"Past twenty, Majesty."

"Truly?" The queen's face took on a pensive expression and she picked up a tiny mirror affixed to a golden chain about her waist. Her eyes swept her reflection for a moment, then darted away. "It seems like yesterday that sweet Anne was frolicking in the gardens, bewitching every man who saw her. She was a babe of six years when first I looked upon her, her cheeks apple-rosy." There was a tenderness in her voice that had not been there before.

"I was a frightened captive princess then, being transferred to yet another gilded prison." Elizabeth's fingers fluttered up to the ruff encircling her neck, as though she still felt the threat of an executioner's blade on her skin. "We had stopped to rest a moment, for I was sickened by the swaying of the coach. Then Anne darted out into the road, an imp in a torn dress, her ribbons all askew. She had eluded her nurse in the meadows and had woven a circlet of gillyflowers."

The queen's words stroked Rafe's imagination, and he conjured a most tender portrait of the mother he had loved.

"For the pwitty pwincess, the child lisped, settling the flowers atop my head. That was the first crown I had worn in a long time, Captain Santadar—and it gave me hope."

Rafe felt an uneasy sense of kinship with the flame-tressed woman, and he had to battle to remember that she was an enemy—a heretic who might well cast him into a prison far worse than the gilded chambers in which she had languished. Yet he wanted to ask her more about the mother who darted about in the shadows of his memory, his need to know about Anne Renfrew Santadar gnawing within him. He did not trust himself to speak, so he remained silent.

"Aye, we recall Lady Anne's loyalty with much fondness, good Captain. Yours, however, we find disturbing."

"Do the English find it *disturbing* that a man should love his own country?" Rafe met her gaze levelly. "Patriotism is a trait much valued in Spain."

He saw in the queen's eyes a subtle sparkle, and he knew he had risen in her estimation.

"We value loyalty in England as well, as you will soon discover, Captain Santadar. In fact, before we graced this assemblage with our presence, we were conferring with our advisers on how to reward the brave seafarers who recently defended our shores against unwarranted Spanish aggression."

Rafe flinched inwardly, the taste of defeat brassy in his mouth. He could not stop himself from allowing the slightest of sneers to cross his face. "I would scarce call it unwarranted for a country to retaliate against the thieves who have plundered its treasure ships, Your Majesty."

Two lines carved between the queen's brows, displeasure obviously banishing whatever tenderness the royal Tudor had felt toward Rafe's mother. "Come now, Captain. One can scarce blame an entire country for the actions of a few . . . er, over-zealous men."

"Men who have the silent approval of the one they value most?" Rafe raised one eyebrow, making his meaning crystal clear. He heard his grandfather's muttered curse, felt the tension binding the room pull tighter still.

"You will not deal Her Majesty any more of your insults, Spanish dog." Warburton's voice, eager and resonant with hate, cut through the room as the nobleman stepped forward, one hand clamped about the hilt of his sword. "Nay, neither you nor your peasant doxy."

"We do not need your interference, Lord Warburton." The queen's voice was an ice-edged dagger, her eyes snapping with anger as they fell upon Rafe. "But we can assure Captain Santadar that we are quite capable of deflecting his veiled barbs ourselves—and with astonishing permanence."

Never had Rafe heard a warning delivered so eloquently or with such killing effect.

"With Your Majesty's permission," Tarrant Renfrew plunged into the sudden silence, "I beg your indulgence. Rafael is still disconcerted by the events that have transpired upon these shores and in the Channel. He was wounded, and he lost his ship."

"Aye, praise God!" An ugly laugh rang out from Warburton. "I hope it plunged to the ocean floor with five score bloody Spaniards aboard." Murmurs of agreement rippled through the room, threaded through with bursts of hearty laughter.

Hot fury pulsed through Rafe's veins, his fists

knotting. "Aye," he bit out, "and every one of them a better man than you, Lord Neville."

He heard the hiss of steel as Warburton ripped his sword from its scabbard. One of Elizabeth's favorites lunged to stay the nobleman's hand, but had scarce seized Lord Neville's thick wrist before the Earl of Renfrew sprang between Rafe and Warburton, his craggy features filled with anger and fear.

"Enough! Sweet Christ, Rafe, I—" As though he had just remembered where he was, the earl cut off the curse and turned to his queen. "Your Majesty, please forgive my grandson. I fear he and Lord Neville ran afoul of each other a few days past."

"I have heard of their altercation, but I have no patience with such bickering," the queen said smoothly. "Lord Neville, you will cease blustering in our presence. And as for you, Lord Renfrew, you have already pleaded our indulgence once in your grandson's behalf. But we have found that children who are indulged too frequently become uncontrollable."

"I am inclined to agree with you, Your Majesty, but I have also discovered that when children are prone to fits of temper it is best to deal with them another way—by ignoring them."

Rafe wanted to wring the old man's neck, but at that moment he caught a glimpse of bronze velvet and wide ebony eyes. Tessa had hastened forward, despite her awe of the queen, and he sensed that she had done so because she feared for him. And 'twas for Tessa that he managed to leash his clamoring fury.

The earl's eyes seemed fixed upon the girl as well,

and Rafe was unsettled by the fleeting expression of relief that crossed his grandfather's face.

Renfrew again addressed the queen: "I would propose, Your Highness, that we indulge ourselves for a while. I have taken the liberty of arranging an amusement."

Elizabeth Tudor regarded the earl with a frigid glare. "That is good, my lord, for I find your grandson far from amusing."

"May I present, for Your Majesty's enjoyment, Tessa of Ravenscroft, a skilled mistress of marionettes and an accomplished player."

"Blast you!" Rafe swore and started to cross to Tessa's side, but the earl's hand closed in a bruising grip about his wrist.

"Curse you, boy," the aged warrior hissed. "If you give a damn about her neck, and your own, you'll hold your blasted tongue!"

Rafe pulled away from the earl's grasp, but remained silent, hating the impotence he felt as Tessa, ashen-faced and wide-eyed, took a halting step toward the great throne.

The sea of courtiers parted, all eyes now fixed upon the slender beauty in their midst.

"So you call yourself a master player, girl?" The queen's voice held a thread of subdued anger and a hint of belligerence that made Rafe doubt whether a troupe of angels could bring a smile to those pale royal lips.

Tessa raised her chin and held her shoulders stiff with pride. "Others so label me. But I fear Lord Renfrew is mistaken. You see, Your Majesty, my marionettes are—"

"In the trunk near the door." The earl's eyes met

Tessa's, and the girl blanched as two servants hastened forward with a decrepit chest. When they set it before the queen, the monarch regarded it as though she half expected a creature with soiled fur and sharp teeth to scuttle from beneath its lid.

Outrage and determination surged through Tessa when she saw the expression on that royal face, and she hurried toward the chest.

What lay beneath the wooden lid was more precious to Tessa than any gem, for the creation of the marionettes had been a labor of love carried out over a lifetime, a legacy from the father she had lost. As she opened the lid, the candlelight limned dozens of carved figures, their joints carefully hinged, their faces painted with the loving strokes of an artist, their velvet gowns and slashed doublets as elegant as those garbing the guests in the hall.

The queen leaned forward on her throne, her eyes scanning the marionettes with a boredom that fired Tessa's blood. Then suddenly that canny gaze lurched back to a somber, black-garbed puppet that lay staring up at the ceiling.

A hearty laugh rose from the queen, startling all within the room, but when Tessa looked at the proud Spaniard, chafing under the crushing burden of failure and scorn, she could not bring herself to scoop up the puppet that had so fascinated the queen. Instead, Tessa hastily seized a harlequin, displaying it before the queen.

But the monarch would not be distracted. One heavily beringed finger pointed to the black-garbed puppet.

"That one. Take out that one, girl," the queen commanded.

Tessa's gaze flicked to Rafe. The pain in his arrogant features made her hands unsteady as they hovered over the marionette Elizabeth had indicated.

"Your Majesty, I . . . I would rather—"

"You would do well not to try our patience any further than Captain Santadar already has. Show us that figure, girl, at once."

Tessa felt a veil of despair drift over her. She and Rafael were trapped among their enemies, sharks scenting blood and closing in for the kill. She saw it, sensed it, and knew she had no choice but to curry the queen's favor any way she could.

Slowly she delved into the chest and pulled out the puppet that had so intrigued the queen. It was a most unflattering likeness of King Philip of Spain, modeled after a caricature Tessa had seen of Spain's mincing monarch. The puppet's deftly carved nose was pinched with self-righteousness, and the small eyes betrayed a dull-wittedness that made Elizabeth shake with laughter.

As the crowd strained forward to see what held Elizabeth's attention, Tessa sensed the stiffening of Rafe's shoulders, heard his muttered expletive. Tessa had expected anger but she had not been prepared for the depth of the hurt in Rafe's indigo eyes. Her fingers tightened upon the marionette's protuberant belly, but there was naught she could do to spare him, for the queen was already leaning eagerly toward her.

"By God's wounds, Hatton, look you!" Elizabeth dug her finger into the arm of a man standing beside her. " 'Tis King Philip himself, I'll stake my very soul!"

Tessa forced herself to untangle the strings, trying

to block Rafe's expression from her mind. She took a deep breath to steady herself, then drew upon the expertise gained during years of practice with the marionettes.

At that instant, the caricature seemed to spring to life in her hands. "Your soul?" Tessa spoke for the puppet in a whining voice. "I want not your soul, fair lady. 'Tis your heart I crave." She stole a glance at Rafe, and her fingers slipped on the strings, but she covered her mistake, tearing her gaze away from the rage-flushed Spaniard. "Have I not courted you these countless years past?" she said in King Philip's mock voice. "Have I not pleaded for your hand? Of course, your treasury . . . would not come amiss."

A wave of laughter rolled over the chamber that had been so tense a moment before, and Tessa felt a surge of relief.

Then the queen turned her gaze toward Rafe. "Sit you down, Santadar," she bade him. "Mayhap we can cure your sulks with this clever child's entertainment."

"With your permission, I would prefer to retire," Rafe said. "As my grandfather has said, I am still afflicted with this wound." His fingers touched the thick bandage beneath his hose.

"And we are afflicted by your boorishness."

Tessa saw Rafe's cheeks stain dark, and the tendons in his jaw stood out as he met the queen's gaze.

"Now you will cease this unseemly sulking, milord Captain," Elizabeth said, "or we will cart you off to the Tower, where the grim surroundings will better match your mood."

Tessa saw Rafe's face go still, sensed that the storm brewing within him was savage and fierce and that if it broke, Rafe would destroy his only chance of making peace with Elizabeth Tudor and proving himself a worthy heir to the old earl.

And Tessa also knew that she was the only one in that vast chamber who could lighten the queen's mood. She stole a glance at Warburton, who was still fuming under the queen's displeasure, and she prayed that he would remain too fearful of Elizabeth's anger to wreak any more havoc upon Rafe's barely leashed temper. She sensed that it would take little to send the two men lunging for each other's throats. And as for the queen—there was a new grimness about Elizabeth Tudor's mouth as she commanded, "Now, Tessa of Ravenscroft, you will proceed."

Tessa sucked in a deep breath, trying to block Rafe from her mind as she fished in the wooden chest. She displayed some of her favorite figures, including one of Sir Francis Drake looking like a posturing peacock in a primrose satin doublet, his chest so puffed out with pride that one was tempted to reach out and prick it with a pin. A tiny silver saber was clasped in the knight's carved hand, and his legs were a bit bowed to give him a delightful swagger.

Tessa had carved several new puppets in recent months to calm the fears of the village children as the threat of invasion loomed nearer. From her trunk she removed Spanish grandees with long pointed beards and weasely smiles as well as an inquisitor with intricately detailed Spanish money sticking out of his rope-bound cassock.

"You have enough Spaniards to man another armada," the queen observed. "Have you no more proud Englishmen?"

"Methinks the wench prefers Spanish curs," Warburton's voice cut in.

"*Enough*, Lord Warburton!" the queen warned. "One more word and we'll banish you from this chamber and from our court. We are taking great pleasure in this diversion, and we'll not have it ruined by your tantrums!"

"Your Majesty—" Warburton began to protest, then fell silent, cowardice evident in his broad face.

A silence fell over the room for long seconds. Then suddenly it was broken by a man's resonant voice. A stunningly handsome stripling of about twenty, resplendent in rose-colored velvet, swaggered closer to Elizabeth. "I know not whether Lord Neville's charges are true, but I do know that Mistress Tessa has more English figures in her trunk. I saw one of her delightful puppet shows a while past, and I can tell you that somewhere in that trunk she has a likeness of you, Your Majesty."

"A likeness of me?"

Tessa winced inwardly, dread gnawing at her stomach. The queen's sensitivity regarding her once dazzling appearance was renowned throughout England. And Tessa's carving of her was far from the complimentary image a fading beauty would enjoy.

She cleared her throat, fighting to find some excuse not to humor the monarch, but then her gaze locked upon the face of the queen, and she saw in that animated countenance how incredibly similar her carving was to the woman she had attempted to depict.

She took out the wood-jointed queen, resplendent in ermine and gold chains. The figure's gown of crimson slashed with gold flowed about a miniature farthingale, and red hair formed a nimbus about the proud Tudor visage.

A tinge of greed pursed the carved lips, and the shrewd dark-painted eyes glinted in the candle-light, but there was also a soft reminder of the princess Elizabeth had once been. A certain vulnerability was buried deep beneath the robes of power.

She held her breath as the royal hands reached out to take the figure from her, and Tessa's fingers shook as she dipped the monarch a deep curtsy and released the bright-hued marionette.

For what seemed an eternity the queen stared at the figure, her eyes unreadable. The entire chamber was swathed again in suffocating silence. Tessa well knew that the courtiers dared not express any opinion of the carving until they had gauged the queen's reaction.

Tessa's palms sweated, and she hazarded a glance at Rafe, praying that he, too, had looked at the puppet and seen that she was as ruthlessly honest in her portrayal of her own countrymen as she had been in her images of the Spanish. But those tempest-filled indigo eyes only stared at the tapestry-draped wall, rebellion, arrogance, and a deep, savage pain evident in the planes of his face.

"And so"—there was an ominous purr in the queen's voice—"you think us a bit greedy, eh, Tessa of Ravenscroft?"

A shiver coursed down Tessa's spine, her breath catching in her chest.

"You see us as a spider, spinning her webs about England?"

As the queen's words penetrated Tessa's dread, a

strange strength seeped through her, a strong confidence in the work for which she had been given such a special gift.

"Aye, Your Majesty." She met the queen's gaze squarely, hearing about her the sharp intake of breath, the murmuring of disbelief and shock at her boldness. She went on just as boldly, "And without your shrewdness and your ability to leash the royal purse, England would have been swept away by France or Spain by now." Tessa couldn't stop the smallest hint of impudence from curving her lips. " 'Tis a feat no mere king could have accomplished." Tessa felt Elizabeth's dark eyes boring into hers, but she stood unflinching.

"You make jest of the monarchy, girl?"

"Nay." Tessa's respect for the woman who had shielded England from countless perils shone in her eyes. "I seek only to praise the greatest ruler England has ever known."

The royal eyes took on a warmth, a light of kinship that drained the crushing tension from Tessa's limbs. "Play for us, Tessa of Ravenscroft," Elizabeth commanded. "Give us something to make us laugh. With Philip's vultures lurking upon the horizon these past months, we have had precious little to laugh about."

"With Your Majesty's pardon," the young man who had spoken before piped up, "the wench does a most diverting farce in which grandees trip all over themselves in their arrogance and witless Spanish captains are outwitted by bold Sir Francis. I vow, when I saw it, I nigh fell from my horse with laughter."

"That does not surprise us, Percy, for you are the worst horseman in our kingdom. However, we would like to see this farce ourselves."

"Nay!" Tessa could not stifle the plea. Her gaze slashed to Rafe, and she saw in him an awful stillness, an anticipation that made her want to scream. "If it please Your Majesty, I—"

"It would please us for you to obey our command. At once." Sharp-edged steel was in Elizabeth's voice again, and the threat of Rafe's banishment to the Tower bent Tessa to the monarch's will. She sensed this was no idle threat. 'Twas a warning to the proud Spaniard, to his grandfather, and to Tessa herself that Elizabeth was still undecided concerning the fate of the man who had been washed up on her shores.

Tessa stole a surreptitious glance at Warburton and felt the hideous nobleman's loathing and lust eating at her skin like poisoned nettles. Then her gaze swept the room's other occupants, bursting with intrigues, jealousies, ambition. And she knew that she had no choice but to give the performance of her life, in the hope that it might in some small way influence the queen's ultimate decision.

She took out the marionettes and set up the tiny props she had fashioned. Soon bellows of delighted laughter filled the huge chamber as Tessa worked her magic with the wooden figures, bringing them to life with her hands. But with each movement of her fingers, with each shrill voice and bawdy jest that she put into the mouth of Sir Francis or the cowering King Philip, she felt as though she were slicing away what remained of Rafael Santadar's battered pride.

Please, Rafe, understand! she silently pleaded with that impassive figure. I love you. I have to aid you the only way I can.

As she plunged onward, the light of Elizabeth Tudor's favor shining upon her, Tessa could feel as well the burning fury, disgust, and incredible pain in the proud countenance of the man she loved.

Her gaze swept to his for an instant, and her fingers nearly fumbled at what she saw. Fury? Pain? Nay, they were not uppermost after all. In those wondrous indigo depths only one emotion now blazed, stark and crushing.

Betrayal.

Her marionettes and her words had dulled the fierce light in Rafael Santadar's eyes as naught else had held the power to do—not defeat at the hands of Drake, not Warburton's cruelty, not even the certainty that the blood of Rafe's enemies flowed in his veins.

She had betrayed him.

And Tessa knew with a sickening certainty that the ransom for her sea phantom's safety would be the loss of a love that was more precious to her than her own life.

Rafael would never forgive her.

Chapter
Twelve

RAFE stalked from the noisy chamber, the guttering candles and threads of dawn peeking through the glistening windows doing naught to dampen the merriment that still rippled from the room.

It seemed an eternity that he had been imprisoned there by the cursed queen's will, manacled by invisible chains to watch the destruction of the one tiny glimmer of joy the fates had allowed him in the days since he had sailed his *Lady* from distant Spain.

She had betrayed him. Tessa, his wildwitch. The thought twisted in Rafe's gut like a knife. She had scorned him, scorned the men who had died so bravely on his ship. She had jeered at timid Rique, at brash Manolo, at the ever-smiling Bastion who had sacrificed himself that the *Lady*'s end should not have been in vain.

Rafe's face contorted with the pain of it, and a choked animal sound issued from his throat as the shadows pooling within the silent corridor shifted into scenes that had been played out in the past few hours.

Images of adoring courtiers and of the queen herself swam before Rafe's gritty eyes. The throng had encircled Tessa, slavering praise over her as though she and her puppets had single-handedly saved England from Spain's mighty sword. Even the old earl—the grandsire who supposedly loved Rafe—had hovered near her, grinning like a sated crocodile. Only Neville Warburton, his face purple with anger and frustration, had seemed as offended as Rafe was. Seething over what was transpiring, the nobleman had stormed from the chamber even before Rafe's own exit.

Sweet Savior, how could she have done this? Rafe cried out silently. How could she have torn away what little pride I still clung to?

To save your life, cried another voice.

'Twas simple, so simple. He had seen the plea for understanding in those onyx-bright eyes, had seen the tremor in those lips that had healed the many gaping wounds in his soul. She had played the wily queen's game that he might be spared. Spared from the grinding misery of London's Tower. Spared, mayhap, even from death. But did she know him so little? Did she not know that he would rather face the horrors of Elizabeth Tudor's torture chambers than see his love, his lady, defile the honor that was so precious to him?

Rafe clenched his fists, his eyes burning with fury and desolation. Mayhap 'twas true, what his grandfather had said—that he and Tessa did not know each other at all.

The tapestried corridors, set about with looming statuary, blurred before Rafe's gaze, and he wiped at his eyes with the back of one hand. Even the force of will that had seen him through countless battles—the mighty will that had enabled him to make the treacherous journey from the wreckage of his ship to the distant English shore—now failed him. He was unable to banish the anguish that seemed to shatter his very soul.

Love. He had waited a lifetime to drink of its splendor. Had tasted it, drowned in it . . . and then watched it turn to poison.

"Wildwitch, come away with me," he had said. "Be my wife." The words he had spoken spiraled back to haunt him, haunt him along with the memory of the small, callused fingertips that had worshiped every inch of his body, brought him the most excruciating pleasure. He was haunted, too, by the morning-soft voice that had whispered to him about the most fragile of dreams.

Dreams broken now forever.

Forever.

A Saracen's blade seemed to cleave Rafe's heart, all joy and hope ebbing away as though they were his lifeblood. And he cursed himself, cursed her, cursed the fates that had been so cruel as to capriciously hurl them together when there could be no hope for the tomorrows he and Tessa had so desperately wanted.

When he was a lad curled up near Brother Ambrose's companionable fire, listening as the holy man spun legends of love, Rafe had been touched by the stories of Orpheus and Eurydice, Troilus and Cressida, England's own Lancelot and Guinevere. He could still remember the thrill he felt as each tale unfolded, could remember, too, how hard he fought to hide the shameful tears that had stung his eyes at the lovers' unhappy end. It had seemed so wondrously painful, and yet the honor and chivalry had captured Rafe's imagination.

But now he saw no beauty in love shattered, sensed no wonder at the magnificent tragedy of it, felt only an agony such as he had never known.

He drove his fingers back through the unruly waves of his hair, fighting to banish Tessa's voice, which still whispered to him from the clustering shadows.

"No, wildwitch," Rafe said aloud. "No more bewitching."

A sudden chill skated down Rafe's spine, the drafts within the corridor fingering the tapestries covering the thick stone walls. They rustled and rippled, as though moved by the breath of some unseen specter that lurked within the palace. Mayhap it was Anne Boleyn, searching for her severed head, or poor Catherine Howard, shrieking for Henry's mercy as she was dragged away to die. Centuries of spirits no doubt lurked within these royal halls. Rafe could hear them whispering.

With an oath, he reined in his imagination, berating himself for the whimsy of a child. Yet as his gaze pierced the rippling shadows at the corridor's end, he saw within them a figure that made his breath catch in his throat. For but an instant his eyes widened as they fixed upon the flowing white robe worn by a small, willow-thin form. Pinched features, gray as death, rose above the neckline of that wispy gown; eyes glittered with a light of their own.

Unbidden, Rafe's hand flashed to his waist, but there was no dagger affixed there.

"Come, Captain Santadar, we are old friends, are we not?"

The shrill feminine voice made Rafe tense. "You have no need of a weapon."

The figure stepped from the shadows, but Rafe had identified that thin, strangely unsettling voice even before the meager light glimmering in the passageway fell across the pinched features of Morgause Warburton.

More than ever, the lady of Warvaliant seemed to hold in the palm of her hand minions of the other world. Rafe's hand rose in the beginning of the sign of the cross, then froze as he was assailed by the absurdity of the action. Odd Lady Morgause might well be, but Rafe had little patience with superstition and unfounded fears.

"My lady." The words were bland, and he met her gaze levelly, remembering the last time he had seen the lady of Warvaliant, her hands bound, her face suffused with a kind of confused terror as she babbled about the ring. Rafe raised his hand to touch the gleaming gold circlet that had been his mother's, as though it were some talisman to ward off a lurking evil.

Morgause's pale gaze flicked to Rafe's fingers, and a sly smile split her lips, as though she could see through to the niggling unease that beset him.

One of those ice-white hands fluttered out and traced a line down the rich cloth of his doublet, and Rafe fought the revulsion that washed through him.

"Mayhap I was hasty, when I spoke a moment ago," the lady trilled. "After all, when last we met you were most . . . unchivalrous. Perhaps I should draw a weapon with which to defend myself against you. Yet I must confess, I would have little will to do so."

Rafe tensed, as those cold fingers inched up to his

throat, but he did not pull away, knowing instinctively that to do so would be a subtle triumph for the woman before him. Her fingers rested on the pulse in his neck, and Rafe was beset by an image of a black spider, hungry for a mate and hungrier still to cause death.

"I seem to recall that my reception within Warvaliant's walls was somewhat lacking in civility," Rafe replied. "However, 'tis not my way to be ungentle with ladies, no matter what deviltry they have on their minds. Restraining you was a regrettable necessity, but a necessity, nonetheless."

Morgause's tongue flicked out to moisten her lips, and Rafe misliked the heat that shone in those eyes. "I would much like to ascertain your way with ladies for myself, Captain Santadar," she purred.

Rafe's brow furrowed in confusion as he sensed that more lay beneath the woman's words than he was able to discern. Yet he understood full well the lascivious light in those eyes, had seen it before among the lush whores in their bright-painted houses in far-off Spain, had seen it as well in the wide, innocently sensual eyes of the native wenches who had often rushed to meet his ship. Those he had managed to meet with good-natured rebuffs, gently but firmly indicating that he had no appetite for the wares they offered. He had felt for them a kind of sympathy, the indulgence of a father with a spoiled but beloved child.

But for this woman, two decades his senior—this woman with her specterlike hands and her cunning, chill eyes—he felt only disgust and a sick stirring in the pit of his belly, as though merely with her gaze she had somehow soiled him.

Rafe encircled her wrist with his hand, the bones covered by the thin layer of the lady's flesh seeming to grate against his skin. And as he put the woman's hand away from him, he found that he had wearied of her game.

His gaze flicked up to the door of the bedchamber he was to share with several of Elizabeth's other men, then back to the face of Morgause. " 'Tis evident you were awaiting someone here, so far from the ladies' quarters. If you will excuse me, I am wearied by the day's events. I will leave you to your business here."

The laugh that rippled from the woman's throat made chills skittle up Rafe's spine. Morgause arched her long white neck, shaking back the silvery waves of her hair. As the shadows cast dark hollows in her cheekbones and the sockets of her eyes, her smile suddenly looked like that of a death's-head.

" 'Tis you whom I awaited, my gallant captain," she said, her eyes locking with his. "I would wager that you are already tired of that plotting snake, Lord Tarrant, and his maneuverings, casting you about like a pawn upon his infernal chessboard. And that peasant witch you befriended—'twas beyond horrible of her to humiliate you in front of Elizabeth's strutting peacocks. After all you had sacrificed for her."

Rafe's skin prickled with wariness. "But you were not in the queen's chamber this night. I saw you not."

"I have ways, milord Spaniard, of seeing things. Not with my eyes but in other ways." There was a sinister delight in her voice. "And I had more important affairs to attend to than a girl with her play-things."

Rafe berated himself for falling into the trap of superstition the woman was weaving about him. He suddenly recalled that Morgause's son had left the throne chamber some time ago. No doubt he had run to his mother and spilled out to her the happenings beyond that royal door.

"And do these . . . affairs have something to do with me?" Rafe said.

Morgause's gaze swept the corridor, and Rafe was certain that if the devil himself had been hiding behind some stone, she would have been able to detect him with those pale, unholy eyes.

A smile of satisfaction crossed her face, her fingers twisting the huge emerald that glinted upon one small hand. "Aye, they have much to do with you. I would grant you the greatest of boons, Captain Santadar—freedom."

"Freedom?" Rafe's heart thudded.

"Safe passage to Spain. Escape from Tarrant Renfrew's clutches, aye, and from the faithlessness of that common wench upon whom you lavished your heart."

Despite his own anger at Tessa, outrage welled, quick and fierce, within Rafe at Morgause's words. "You'll speak no ill of Tessa, my lady!"

"Fine. I see that you still dance for the girl, like one of the figures upon her strings. You obviously have no wish to do aught but grovel at her feet and lap up the leavings your grandfather tosses to you. I will leave you to do so."

Morgause turned and started to glide away from Rafe. For a heartbeat, he almost let her go, but then his savaged pride and the fiery words the lady had flung upon it made his hand flash out to stop her.

"Wait." She swung to face him, and he regretted he had spoken.

Those glittering eyes watched his face expectantly, those frosted-rose lips infuriatingly smug.

Rafe spoke through clenched teeth. "I would hear more of what you have to say."

"Would you, milord?"

Rafe felt as though the words were being ripped from his very chest. "*Sí*. I would hear more of Spain and of safe passage. I want to be quit of this madness." He turned away. He wanted desperately to hasten away from England, away from Renfrew and the woman who had bewitched him. But he recognized the truth—that for the first time in his life he was running away. And he knew that Lady Morgause was aware of that shame as well.

"Your passage to freedom is all arranged, Captain Santadar. A ship waits upon the Thames to carry you to France. You will find a pouch on board filled with enough coin to pay for the rest of your journey home."

A sinking sensation beset Rafe's stomach, and he felt a stirring of loss deep within him. But he steeled himself against them. Escape was what he desired, was it not? He wished to return to Spain, never to have to confront the triumph in the eyes of Englishmen when they realized he was one of the enemy captains Drake had so handily defeated. Never to have to feel the tugging of his mother's heritage within him. Never to have to reveal to Tessa how vulnerable she had made him, how devastating it had been for him to watch her crush his pride in those hands that had brought him such wonder.

But why should he trust Morgause Warburton? Why would she endanger herself and her son to aid a man who, mere days before, had lain in Warvaliant's dungeon?

"What price must I pay for your aid?" he asked, meeting her gaze.

That eager, hungry light again played upon Morgause's pale features, and she strained forward, her bosom heaving with some emotion Rafe could not name. " 'Tis a small price, Captain Santadar. One that will serve your cause as well as my own. You have but to remove one small obstacle from my path this night."

"Obstacle?"

"Aye, I have been much troubled by someone seated high within this castle. I would like to be . . . relieved of this person's presence in the most permanent way possible."

Rafe stared into those pale witch's eyes. "What do you want me to do, my lady? Kidnap some enemy for you?"

"I wish you to . . . dispose of this enemy."

Rafe nearly choked, disbelief roiling within him. "You wish me to murder someone?"

"'Murder' is such an ugly word, Captain Santadar. I much prefer gentler terms. However, since you press me, aye. That is what I wish you to do."

"I know of no gentle term for cold-blooded killing, milady," Rafe said, his skin crawling. "And I know no gentle way to give you my answer. I have killed men aplenty, in battle, and have been nigh death myself a score of times. But never have I taken a life on a whim, nor will I ever do so. No, even if your ship had the power to carry me away to heaven itself."

Rafe swung away from her and stalked toward the door, but before he reached it, he felt Morgause's fingers catch at his sleeve.

"A moment, please, Captain Santadar."

He whirled on her, fury etched deep in his face.

There was a quaver in her voice, something that made him pause.

" 'Twas wrong of me, I know, to ask such a favor of you. 'Tis just that I am but a poor woman, widowed, alone, with enemies snapping at me."

"You have your son," Rafe said in steely tones. "Surely Lord Neville would take great pleasure in dispatching this enemy in whatever way you wish. In my brief acquaintance with his lordship, I found his taste for the pain of others to be most indiscriminate."

Morgause's lips quivered, and Rafe felt a brief stab of remorse that he had struck out at her through her son. Then he brought himself up short, dashing away the regret. Sweet God, this woman was no frail, gentle flower. She had just asked him to do murder!

"My son has such an . . . er . . . ill-begotten fondness for this person that I fear even his regard for me would not sway him." Her lashes fluttered, and tears glistened in her eyes. "But that is my cross to bear, Captain Santadar. I see that now." A sigh shuddered through her thin shoulders, the gauzy white fabric swathing them fluttering about her.

Rafe regarded her uneasily and watchfully, unsettled by the lightning-swift shifts of mood evident in

those strange eyes. Yet he could not stop himself
from drawing out his handkerchief and pressing it
into her hand as she continued a most *valiant* battle
against weeping.

"I kill for no one, milady." Rafe's words were not
ungentle, but they were firm.

She nodded, dabbing at her eyes with the square
of fabric he had given her. "You are most kind,
Captain Santadar. Most noble. 'Twas foolish of me
to . . . to put you in such a difficult position. I thank
you for your patience in listening to me . . . aye, and
showing me the error in my wishes. If you would
allow me, I would like to do what is within my paltry
power to make things right between us."

"Milady?"

"The ship." Morgause's lips curled in a watery
smile. "It still waits beyond these walls. Let me
redeem myself in your eyes by helping you escape."

Rafe stared into her eyes for long minutes, a battle
springing to life within him. He knew it would be
crazed of him to trust a woman who had asked him
to commit murder. 'Twas insanity to place his life in
the hands of one who disturbed him so deeply, who
stirred in him feelings of such stark foreboding.

And yet, what choice had he? Would Tarrant
Renfrew help him return to Spain? Would Elizabeth
release the Spanish captive who had afforded her
courtiers such amusement this night? And Tessa—
could he face the pleading look in her eyes? Could
he confess the truth to her—that his pride, savaged
at her hands, was more important to him than their
love for each other?

Pain cut, jagged-edged, within him, and he knew
at that moment he would risk anything not to look

again upon the sorrow in Tessa's angelic face. Besides, it mattered not that Morgause was tangled in some plot. Once he was free of this castle, Rafe could effect his own escape. He could stow away on some foreign vessel at anchor here in London.

"Please, good Captain," Morgause whispered. "Let me aid you the only way I know how."

Rafe straightened, his decision made. "I would be most grateful to be quit of this castle, these shores, as soon as possible."

"Before dawn fully breaks we can be away." Morgause wrapped her thin arms about herself, delight evident in her face. "Hasten to gather what things you wish to take; then meet me at the door below." Her fingers fluttered toward a curving staircase that vanished into inky shadows. "I will wait for you."

The sudden sound of footsteps at the far end of the corridor made the noblewoman draw back, her gaze flicking to a figure in amber velvet hastening toward them. Like a snake, Morgause Warburton slithered into the darkness. "Hasten, Captain Santadar. There is little time."

But Rafe scarce heard the woman's warning. His eyes locked upon Tessa as she came toward him. Had she seen Morgause? No. Rafe had scarce seen the noblewoman himself until he had all but tripped over her. And Tessa's quarters were far distant from Rafe's own.

By Saint Stephen, didn't Tessa know he would not want to see her? Not after she'd humiliated him with her puppet show.

Rafe stepped out into the meager light of the corridor and fixed an implacable glare upon Tessa's wounded Madonna face. The misery and the love that shone upon her features drove the pain deep into the core of him, but he clenched his jaw, wheeling away from her in a gesture of dismissal and stalked into his chamber.

Every other woman he had ever known would have retreated beneath the scathing fury in Rafael Santadar's gaze. Most would have fled, weeping, to be consoled by some buxom matron. But before he had time to slam the door of the chamber in which he sought refuge, she stormed up behind him, one delicate hand stopping the portal midway.

"Damn you, Rafael Santadar," she blazed, her eyes spitting black flame, "at least have the courage and honesty to tell me to go to hell instead of stomping off to sulk like a spoiled babe."

Rafe gazed at her face, at those features, which were branded on his heart, and the pain of her betrayal slammed into him again like a fierce blow.

"*Honesty*?" he roared, hating himself for the break in his voice. "You want honesty, madam? I'll give it to you! You betrayed me, blast you. Jeered at the men I commanded, the men who died under my command. You scorned them that you might play the jester before your strumpet queen and her perfumed fops."

"I performed to save your cursed stiff neck, plague take you! Because I loved you and wanted to spare you."

"You wanted to spare me?" Rafe gave a savage, anguished laugh. "I would have faced every horror Elizabeth had to offer to be spared the pain of watching you in that chamber this night, watching you, the woman I loved and trusted, hold up my men—

my honorable, loyal, dead men—to the ridicule of
the thieving pirates who killed them."

"Rafe." His name was a plea, and her eyes filled
with tears that rent his spirit. "Your men are dead.
You live. I had to do all I could to see that you
remained alive. I love you, *love you*, curse it. I grieve
for your men, because I see the pain you suffer for
their loss. But don't you see? Your *life* matters more
than your pride."

She reached up and curved her fingers about his
cheeks, and he could feel them shaking, see the
tears flowing down her pale cheeks. He felt a tearing agony in his heart, a wrenching pain so deep
it nigh drove him to catch her in his arms and
bury his face in that cascade of glorious dark hair,
regardless of the cost. But instead his jaw knotted
beneath her touch, and his eyes were cold as they
met her tear-glistened gaze.

"Nay, milady, I do not see." Gritting his teeth
against her anguish, he put her away from him and
turned his back on her pleas, her love.

Silence ground down upon him like a millstone,
torturing him with his idiocy, his cruelty, and the
certainty that he lacked the strength to forgive her.
Trying to spare himself the sight of her pain, he left
her outside the door and stepped inside the bedchamber, but he found that the walls of the empty
room hurled her image back at him a hundredfold,
jeering at his cowardice.

Behind him, in the doorway, her muffled sobs had
stopped, but he knew she still stood in the vaulted
corridor, watching him.

Then he heard her footsteps as she entered the
room and circled to stand once more before him.

He had thought he possessed pride in abundance, but his was but a light gilding in comparison to the strength that now shone within Tessa's eyes. She was all that was bright and good and beautiful in the world—all things that he valued. And he knew in that instant he had no right to touch her with his own tarnished arrogance.

For long minutes she stood there, her eyes delving into his with such sweet sorrow. Then she reached out and traced the stiff line of his lips. "When you fell beneath Warburton's sword, I was proud of you, Rafe. Aye, and when you had to face the certainty that your mother was English, I ached for the misery it caused you. But now . . . now I am only sorry for you."

"I want none of your sympathy."

"You have it. You have it in abundance, you stupid, stiff-necked Spaniard. I thought you loved me, that we loved each other. I dared hope so." Her eyes flicked away for a heartbeat, then found his again, giving him no quarter. "Love, real love, could never be crushed by such a selfish, worthless trait as pride, Rafael."

He pulled away, unable to bear her touch another instant, unable to bear the scent of her, the sadness in her.

" 'Twill not warm your bed at night, this pride," she went on relentlessly. " 'Twill not bear your children."

There was a catch in her voice, and a hateful longing throbbed in Rafe's loins.

"Your babes," she said. "How I wanted to lay them in your arms."

'Twas a knife thrust as she turned away and

strode from the chamber, leaving him with naught but empty, aching hands and a future so barren it crushed his very soul.

He waited until he was certain she was gone. Then he scanned the chamber. The rich garments his grandfather had had made for him lay packed in an inlaid chest, along with jewels befitting his station as Tarrant Renfrew's heir. Yet he took naught from the chest save a black mantle and the sword that had once been Tarrant's own.

He could hear the muffled laughter of the courtiers still waiting upon the queen in the distant chamber, and knew there was but little time to make his escape.

Tessa—her name wrenched his heart. Then he turned and descended the shadowy staircase. He sensed the presence of someone at the foot of the steps, felt a sudden wariness even through his pain.

Roses. The scent of withered roses that was Lady Morgause's own hung heavy in the darkness, but 'twas mingled with another scent as well, one more disturbing . . . familiar. Sandalwood and wine. The finest Madeira.

Rafe sensed danger, his fingers flashing instinctively to the hilt of his grandfather's sword, but 'twas too late.

Something heavy crashed into the base of his skull, plunging him into a world of hopelessness as dark and chill as his future without Tessa.

Morgause knelt beside Rafe's inert form and pressed her fingers to his heart. Her lips curved in a satisfied smile. "He lives."

"I can assure you, when I have done with him, he will wish he had died," a harsh, masculine voice cut in. "Died before he ever set foot upon English shores."

Morgause ignored the figure looming beside her as her fingertips trailed over the warm, muscled plane of Rafe's chest. " 'Tis a waste, you know. A most regrettable waste. He is . . . much like his father, Ruy Santadar. He was foolish as well, but so . . . hard, so wondrously virile. I still remember—"

"Do you remember that he would have cast us both into prison for spying twenty-eight years past?" the voice lashed out. "Had us executed as traitors if he had revealed—"

"He did not," Morgause interrupted dismissively. "You saw to that, and to the death of his puling wife. Yet it seems you were unable to finish the task, for the babe we thought dead has now appeared as a man."

"I knew not that he lived!"

Morgause waved away the angry protestations, plunging on as though the other had not spoken. "He returns as a man with far too much honor to rid us of our enemy or even to save his own skin." She laughed, a rippling, sinister sound. "Aye, 'tis a pity our good captain proved reluctant to thrust our blade through the queen's black heart, is it not, my dearest Lucero? Death to the Protestant usurper of what will again be a Catholic throne," Morgause purred, raising her eyes to the sharp features of the inquisitor. " 'Twould have been perfect for Anne Renfrew's son to have driven the knife home. But we will find another way . . . later."

Encina rubbed his hands together, fixing his eyes upon Santadar. "*Sí*, after I see to a most fitting demise for our captain. I shall be a hero, renowned for presenting to the Spanish king the reason for our defeat at English hands: witchery . . . witchery!"

"Do not fondle your hero's laurels too soon. 'Twill not be easy to mount a witchcraft case against a man so well respected, especially if he lets it be known that he is Ruy Santadar's son."

"Bah! Captain Santadar's little puppet mistress has taken care of that difficulty for me. The flames of the auto-da-fé will prove most eager for Captain Santadar's flesh, I promise you. And all of Spain will rejoice at his screams."

"The puppet mistress?" Morgause interrupted, chafing at wrists that still carried the marks of the ropes with which the girl had bound her. "Is she in captivity?"

"Nay, but she soon will be."

Morgause's lips split over small pearly teeth. "I care not how you use her once she is in your possession, but 'twould give me the greatest of pleasure to aid you in . . . securing her. There lies a debt between us."

"I have no time for women's games!"

"You have been gaming with me since that day in Seville when I enlisted you in my father's quest to restore Catholicism to England. Do as I bid you, Señor Encina." She let the full force of her pale gaze fall upon him and saw the Spaniard shrink back. Her gaze had bent the strongest of wills to her own. It was a frightening gaze whose power she used with relish.

Aye, 'twas far better, betimes, to have the strange features fate had given her than all the beauty Anne Renfrew had possessed.

"Have one of your men follow in my wake and wait, hidden, until the girl falls 'neath my power." Morgause fingered the unusual ring on her finger, her gaze sweeping lovingly over its glistening surface.

"And then?"

Morgause let her gaze flow across the sensual curve of Rafe's parted lips. "And then I will trust to your expertise in making Santadar and his whore pay in blood for the sins of his father."

Chapter Thirteen

LEAVING the door open behind her, Tessa walked slowly into the chamber assigned to her. Her eyes swept the tiny room with its musty tapestries that had once been grand but were now threadbare where the moths had feasted upon the jewel-hued threads. Though the room was far from the pulsing center of the bustling castle, it was a respectable, aye, even a rich sanctuary for the daughter of a common sailor and far too fine for a humble player.

Yet another simple room had seemed a wonderland indeed when it was wreathed by the rosy glow that had been Rafael Santadar's love, a magical, mystical love, full of new beginnings.

Now she heard only the echoes of Rafe's farewell, and she saw nothing but an endless sweep of gray before her—days devoid of indigo eyes blazing with passion, lips far too solemn, which she had delighted in coaxing to smile.

She tugged the pearl-encrusted headdress from her hair and let it fall from numb fingers onto the bed that stood at one end of the room.

Rafael was lost to her. Lost forever.

Any faint hope she had held that he might somehow understand once his first raw fury receded had vanished when she had looked into his eyes. She had sensed that somehow, some way, Rafael Santadar would leave—slip away from the castle, from his grandfather, from her, and disappear into the sea from whence he had come.

And she could do naught—would do naught—to force him to stay.

Her gaze skimmed the table upon which her untouched meal still sat—hearty bread, a savory meat pie, and a honeyed pastry that would have delighted Tessa had she possessed any appetite. A pewter goblet stood on the silver platter beside a flask of wine.

Two hours ago, she had been about to delve into this feast, when Lord Tarrant's servant had rushed in carrying the magnificent gown and announcing that Tessa was to hasten to the throne chamber.

If she had known what the old earl had plotted, she would have defied his order, cast the finery into the servant's face, and told them both to go to the devil. And yet . . . had she done so, who would have diffused the dangerous anger that had been stirring within Warburton and within the queen?

A sigh weighed down her chest, and she raised numb fingers to a face still damp with tears.

Damn them both to hell—Rafael Santadar and his grandsire as well. They had caught her between them most handily, trapped her in a dilemma from which there was no escape.

Well, Rafe can take his cursed pride and loathe me

forever, if he be fool enough, Tessa thought. She was glad she had performed so well—glad he was safe. She wondered if he would return to Spain and find some adoring woman to give him a hundred babies. Perhaps he would be given so many blasted ships to command that he'd be half crazed with trying to keep track of them.

Hating herself for such speculations, she swept up the marionette head she had been working on hours before—a perfect image of Rafe's arrogant face. She stared down into those lovingly fashioned features, blinking back tears. "Sweet God," she said aloud, "I hope he realizes what an ass he is being, and comes back for me. Damn you, Rafael Santadar! Damn you!"

"Men can be most infuriating, can they not?"

The familiar breathy voice made Tessa wheel around, dashing the tears from her eyes. Her heart lurched as her gaze fell upon the white-garbed form in the doorway.

Morgause Warburton? Nay, Tessa thought with a ripple of panic, 'twas impossible. The lady of Warvaliant had not been present in the queen's chamber with her odious son. Tessa knew she would have seen her, sensed the webs of menace.

"M-my lady." Tessa forced the words from stiff lips, eyeing that otherworldly countenance with a wariness that brought a cunning smile to the noblewoman's lips.

"Come, child." The honey-sweet voice dripped from Morgause's lips. "You need not fear me. I assure you that what transpired between us in the tower room of Warvaliant is forgotten. Look you—the bruises from the ropes are nigh gone."

The woman glided into the room, extending her hands toward Tessa.

Tessa let her gaze sweep to the slender arms, bared as gauzy sleeves fell back, and she was horrified to see angry red marks still encircling those slender wrists.

"I— Forgive me," Tessa said with genuine regret. "I meant not to bind you so tightly."

Morgause brushed away her apologies with a benign wave of her hand. "'Tis forgotten between us two, child. Forgotten. I did not seek you out to utter recriminations."

"Then why are you here?"

"I heard about what happened between you and the queen—the puppet play you made for her. And I happened to be in the corridor when Captain Santadar came storming out."

Tessa could not stop the flash of pain from crossing her face, and it made her feel vulnerable, exposed.

"I thought . . . " Morgause hesitated an instant, then gave a soft laugh. " 'Tis little known that I had a broken heart myself when I was young. I know 'tis difficult to believe, now that age has taken what little claim to comeliness I might have had. But I suffered . . . " The words drifted to silence as the noblewoman walked over to Tessa and smoothed back a tangled lock of her dark hair. "I cannot tell you how much I suffered."

Tessa felt a shudder work through her at the woman's touch and at the queer light in her eyes, and she couldn't stop herself from drawing away from those chill fingers. Instantly she regretted it, for the unaccustomed softness in the noblewoman's eyes hardened like the thinnest layer of ice.

Tessa swallowed, trying to conceal the revulsion she felt. "I am most grateful for your concern. 'Tis kind of you. But if 'twould not trouble you, I would lief be left alone."

"Trouble me?" Morgause's mouth split in a brittle smile. "Nay, child, not at all, as long you allow me to do whatever I can to see that you are . . . comfortable." The noblewoman turned, and the scent of withered roses wafting to Tessa's nose reminded her of winter and death.

"I assure you, I am quite—"

"Quite comfortable. I know." Morgause drifted toward the bed and smoothed one hand over the soft bedclothes. "'Twill do to give you a good night's rest, I vow," she judged. "And look you. They have left you food as well."

"I'm not hungry," Tessa snapped, more harshly than she had intended. "I just want to be left alone."

"And so you shall be, poppet," the crooning tone in Morgause's voice grated across Tessa's raw nerves until she wanted to scream. "At least sip some wine to hearten yourself."

"I don't want any wine."

"Ah, but if you drink some, you will be rid of me, my sweet. I will leave you to your grief." The woman turned her back on Tessa, a bit of the glinting goblet just visible behind the shield of her skirts. Tessa thought that guzzling a whole tankard of wine would be a small price to pay for being left alone.

She heard liquid being poured, heard the clink of goblet against the neck of the flask as those white hands hovered over the platter. Morgause turned, both hands curved about the wineglass, her eyes hooded, her lips curved in a commiserating smile.

"There, child," she said, placing the cup in Tessa's hand. "Drink now, and then sleep. 'Twill spare you from grieving over your stubborn Santadar."

Tessa raised the goblet to her lips, suddenly thirsty, craving the muzziness wine would bring. Mayhap, once Morgause left, she would empty the flask and summon more from one of the servants. Mayhap she would drink herself into a stupor to forget Rafael.

She drained the liquid, its taste clinging to her tongue—sour, with a most unusual tang.

"More?"

She lifted her gaze to Morgause's eager face, her wariness of the waxen-faced noblewoman waning. "I would like that. Thank you."

There was a glimmer of happiness in Lady Warburton's face that pleased Tessa, and she did not object when the woman sank onto a stool beside her after refilling the vessel.

"There, now. Is that not better?" Morgause asked, patting Tessa's hand, and Tessa did not move away. Her hand was heavy suddenly. So heavy. "They drive women mad—the Santadar men," Morgause whispered in that sorceress's voice. "They are like a disease that eats away at our souls."

The wine brought welcome numbness to Tessa's senses. "I don't understand."

"I, too, was taken by that plague in my youth, charmed by a man as beguiling as your sea rogue. He had hair as dark as sin and a form so tempting that I would have suffered in hell for it."

Even through the webs the wine spun about her, Tessa felt unease flicker to life, and she raised her eyes to Morgause's face, which rippled in the candle-light as the room suddenly grew hot. Tessa felt beads of moisture on her brow as she stared, mesmerized, into the pale gaze of the woman before her. She had a strange image of a gauzy-winged moth being lured to a tongue of flame.

"I don't—don't understand."

"Your captain's father was the scoundrel who shattered my heart. Ruy Santadar." Those skeletal fingers swam before Tessa's eyes, as Morgause flicked back the heavy stone on her ring.

A miniature was worked there, minute, yet incredibly detailed. And the face thus portrayed was so like Rafe's own that Tessa cried out in astonishment and felt a very real stirring of fear. Her eyes flashed up to Morgause Warburton's. The woman's features blurred, then snapped into a painful clarity that drove spikes of fear deep into Tessa's belly.

"Rafe's father . . . " Tessa squeezed the words from lips that seemed suddenly too chill to move. Her tongue felt thick in her mouth; her throat closed with dread.

"Aye. He had the ill judgment to prefer Anne Renfrew to me. Anne! Pah! A milksop with honeyed words and a face as blandly beautiful as that of an angel painted on some chapel's accursed ceiling. I hated her. Hated them both. But they paid in good coin for my suffering."

Images spilled across Tessa's mind, scenes Rafe had painted on her imagination—the hideous slaying of his father and the mother he had adored, his own near death. Rafe had been but a frightened child when that horrible scene was seared into his mind forever. Surely this woman—this frail shade of a woman—could not have had anything to do with those horrors.

Tessa's gaze was drawn to the ring that glowed on the noblewoman's finger, the displaced gem winking evilly above Ruy Santadar's likeness.

"Ah, so Ruy's son has told you what befell them." A witch's voice was binding Tessa in chains she could not see, crushing her will, weighting her limbs. "'Twas a regrettable necessity, their death. What a lovely phrase. Regrettable necessity. That is what your lover termed the binding of my wrists. And now he lies somewhere with ropes biting into his flesh. I have such fragile skin. It bled, as he will bleed . . . as you will bleed."

Tessa struggled to cry out, to get someone, anyone to wrest her from the clutches of this woman—for Morgause Warburton was mad . . . mad. But a fist seemed to be crushing her throat, stilling her screams.

The wine . . . The goblet fell from her numb fingers, the dark liquid staining the rushes like blood. Sweet Jesus, the woman had poisoned her!

"Drive the fear from your eyes, my sweet," Morgause's voice dripped over her. "'Tis not poison. I am not adept at poisons, though I am learning. 'Tis but a posset to make you sleep, dream. Though when you wake, I fear 'twill smack of nightmare."

"Rafe!" Tessa choked out the name, her voice the faintest of whispers. "What . . . have you done to . . . "

"I fear we had to ensure his . . . cooperation in a rather ungentle manner. But he will be awaiting you when you awake. And then, my sweet, you will learn"—that hideous face rippled before Tessa

until it looked that of a succubus spawned in hell—
"and your accursed lover will learn what true terror
is . . . just as Anne learned."

A satanic cackle rose in the air, whirling Tessa
away into nightmares of Rafe being tortured, of
blades slashing, of a child's agonized cries. The
dream swept her into fear more horrible than any
she had ever known, but far less terrifying than the
reality that awaited her.

'Twas so dark. The night pressed down upon
Rafe, making him afraid. Beasts lived in the blackness, hungry beasts that feasted on small boys. But
he was a Santadar. A great lad of four years, far too
old to cry.

He closed his fingers about the hilt of the wooden
sword his father had bought for him at market,
his gaze shifting to where Ruy Santadar loomed,
a magnificent giant, upon a prancing stallion. Not
even the fiercest of monsters could reach Rafael
with his father so near. And his mother . . . Rafe
cuddled closer into her arms, his eyelids fluttering,
heavy with sleep. 'Twas so warm here against her,
her silky hair brushing against his cheek.

"Sleep, my little moppet," she crooned to him
gently, brushing his brow with a kiss. "The dream-
spinners await you. And such adventures they will
spin."

"I have to—help Papa guard . . . "

"Your father is the strongest of men, Rafael, and
the bravest." Her voice was sweet with love. "He
will let no harm befall us."

Rafe breathed in the soft scent of jessamine and
cinnamon that always hung about his mother, felt

the webs of sleep enfold him, but his dreams were
haunted by death's-heads and faces masked by hideous paint—monsters. He could feel their breath hot
upon his throat, see them in the shadows, feel them
touching him. Raw panic tore through him, and he
tried to scream, to warn his parents, but the night had
come alive, catching them up in razor-sharp claws.

Rafe thrashed against the terror that seemed to
be a living thing coiling itself about him. Laughter,
hellish laughter, echoed through the darkness as a
glimmering silver dagger arced toward his throat.

"Mama!" he cried, sobbing. "Help me!" But the
devil's face only loomed larger as fiery pain snaked
along Rafe's neck.

"No!" he screamed, hauling himself upright,
slamming his head into something above him. But
even as the fragments of the familiar nightmare
drifted away from him, they left him in a starker
hell still.

He tried to touch his face, to see if his eyes were
indeed open. But 'twas as though his wrists were
fused together before him, burning and numb.
Then all sense of the darkness was driven back
as he became aware of sticky, drying blood. With
a shudder of raw horror, he raised his bound hands
to his neck, but the skin there was whole and
unmarred.

No, the dream . . . 'twas but a nightmare from the
past, but his head throbbed as if the devil himself
were slamming cudgels against his skull.

What, by all the saints, had befallen him? Where
was he? He struggled to think, despite the roaring
pain, despite the rolling sensation that set his stomach to pitching.

He closed his eyes against the darkness, fighting to recall something, anything. His mind cleared a little, filling with images of a lavish palace, a lead-painted face wreathed in a nimbus of fiery hair. Elizabeth. He had been in the castle of Elizabeth Tudor. And he had been angry . . . angry and hurt. He could remember wide, dark eyes from across that huge room pleading for forgiveness above a wood-carved marionette.

Tessa . . .

Anguish ripped through him, fiercer even than the roaring in his head, that savaged sweet countenance shifting into another, far more sinister one.

A specter's face, a sorceress spinning spells from fingers white as candle wax. Morgause had promised him a ship. He had rushed down the stairs to meet her. Then something . . . someone had struck him.

He shifted against the surface he sat upon, suddenly aware of the smell of pitch and tar and the scent of seawater seeping through an ill-tended hull. He cursed himself for his idiocy in not knowing right away where he was.

He was aboard a ship, right enough, but why did ropes bite into his wrists and ankles with a savagery that drained the blood from them and made them numb?

Why the hell was he locked away in darkness, his throat parched? Was it some twisted revenge for the time he and Tessa had bound Morgause in the room at Warvaliant Castle? Had the eerie noblewoman vowed to make him pay?

He struggled against the pounding in his head, trying to think. But he had not bound the woman's birdlike wrists. It was Tessa who had done so.

Rafe's eyes flashed open, his fear for her lunging wildly in his chest, a groan of denial passing his lips as he struggled to stand. His shoulder cracked into a beam, and the force drove him to his knees.

He heard footsteps above him and looked up to where tiny cracks in the deck overhead let in slivers of light.

"Damn you, open that accursed hatch! Plague take you!"

His bellow echoed back to him, and he slammed himself back against the damp wall, frustration and terror for Tessa coursing through him in dizzying waves.

"Open it, damn you!" His cry was choked, desperate.

He started as the wooden panel above him was slammed back, crashing to the deck with a force that made the pain in his skull surge anew. A square of blazing light blinded him.

Pain speared his arms as he raised them and ground his burning eyes against his velvet sleeve. Then he raised his face and forced his eyes to focus.

Incredulity and denial bolted through Rafe, the stench of gunpowder and death assailing his memory, the soul-chilling crack of masts shattered by cannon fire raged again in his mind as he stared into the face of the man he loathed—the man who had sent Rafe's gallant crew to the depths of hell.

Encina.

With a curse of fury, Rafe hauled himself to his feet, staggering as the ship's roll mingled with the throbbing in his head and raked at his numb legs. He nearly fell again, only force of will and his own half-crazed fury keeping him upright.

"Encina, you bastard!" he shouted, straining to see through the hatch. "I'll kill you!"

"I doubt you'll kill anyone, Santadar, ever again," the inquisitor sneered. " 'Tis you who will die . . . a most gruesome death, I fear, but well deserved."

"Damn you, I'll—"

"You'll do nothing, Santadar. Nothing. You should have perished on your infernal ship, as I planned."

"Planned? Why, blast you?" Fury and confusion raged through Rafe. "Do you know how many men died that day? Innocent men! Brave men! *Why*?" Rafe shouted the question that had gnawed at his sanity in the hellish hours he had struggled to reach the English shores, the question that had haunted him with horrible guilt.

"You do not know, then?" The smug expression that crossed the inquisitor's face made Rafe bellow a curse.

"Of course, I don't know, you murdering bastard! Tell me! What grievous sin did I commit? What crime so heinous that you were willing to cast hundreds of men to the bottom of the sea to ensure that I paid for it? God damn you to bloody hell, *tell me*!"

"Look at me, Santadar," Encina rasped evilly. "Can you not see it? Feel it? From the first time you saw me, I feared that you would."

"Would what?" Rafe demanded. The glint in Encina's eyes made his skin crawl, made him shudder, as it had from the moment the inquisitor had glided onto his ship.

"I haunt your worst nightmares, shatter your

sleep. When you remember me you wake in a cold sweat, screaming." Encina smiled—a devil's smile, an evil leer that raked razor-sharp talons through Rafe's consciousness, tearing away veils of night terror to reveal a child's most hideous fears.

"Ah," Encina purred. "Now you know me, my bold captain, don't you? Are you shaking? Scream, Santadar, as you did long ago. Shriek—"

"You." White-painted features roiled within Rafe's mind, and Encina's demon eyes glared down at him. The knife slashing at Rafe's throat was grasped in that long, pale hand stained with blood.

The tortured face of his mother rose in Rafe's memory, her angelic features savaged beyond recognition, her eyes pools of agony. And he remembered his father, his broad chest slashed open, the wound gaping in a fiendish grin.

"Yes. I was most disconcerted when I boarded your ship and saw Ruy Santadar staring back at me from your face. I might have dismissed it as mere coincidence, a poor jest made by fate, except that your jerkin lay open that day, and I saw the scar."

"I'll kill you, Encina, for what you did to my father and mother. Sweet Christ, she was so gentle, and you—"

"Killed her? *Sí*. And you cannot know how sweet it was to slash the beautiful face and body of Ruy Santadar's woman. He was still alive, your father, when I stabbed her. Did you know that? He saw me do it."

With a shriek of raw pain, Rafe flung himself at the opening high above him, a futile gesture, fraught with madness.

"You bastard! Come down here, coward! Face me like a man."

Encina made a clicking sound with his tongue, shaking his head as though scolding a blustering child. "Oh, no. I prefer subtler means than fists and swords, Santadar. Had your father been reasonable, we could have settled our . . . differences civilly."

"How? With poison? Or a dagger slipped between his ribs?"

"It matters not." Encina shrugged. "Ruy was too distraught to be reasonable."

"While his wife was being stabbed? While his son's throat was slit? Oh, that would put me in the most reasonable of moods."

"No, before that, when he had the misfortune to discover that I was, er . . . shall we say, purchasing secrets from the English and selling Spanish information as well, not for the benefit of your father's cherished king, but rather to line my own pockets. 'Twas most lucrative, this barter I had arranged. You see, I had found it most annoying to have to live within the confines of my misguided vow of poverty."

"My father was going to expose you?"

"*Sí*. And now you, too, could reveal dark secrets about me, could you not? However, I doubt my peers will put any stock in testimony regarding a pious man like me—especially on the word of a prisoner I have brought before the tribunal. And soon . . . the flames will silence you forever."

"What, Encina, are you going to set fire to this ship as well?"

"Oh, no. What happened upon your *Lady of Hidden Sorrows* was the result, I fear, of a momentary panic. I have given much thought to your demise, since I learned that you again had escaped death's scythe. I fear you are proving most difficult to kill."

"Come down here, Encina, and see how hard it is to deal me death."

"But don't you see, Santadar? That is the beauty of it. This time I will not have to see to your demise myself." His austere features were washed with obscene pleasure, his lips pulled back from his teeth in unholy glee. "I regret to inform you that you are to be brought before the Inquisition, Captain Santadar."

"Are you mad, Encina? You can prove nothing against me. No one would believe your charges."

"I have taken care of that one small difficulty— and with such genius it astonishes even me."

Foreboding iced Rafe's veins, and his fists knotted as he watched the inquisitor's face.

"You have been consorting with witches, my good Rafael." Feigned sorrow flooded Encina's face.

"Like hell—"

"And to banish any doubts the Holy Office might have, I have brought along the demon temptress who ensnared you."

A fist of raw horror clenched itself about Rafe's throat and a denial was torn from his lips. Then Encina waved, and two burly Flemish sailors, reeking of rum, wrenched a pale figure into the light of the open hatchway. Even before Rafe's gaze locked upon that fall of midnight hair and those huge, oddly glazed dark eyes, he knew who lay within Encina's heinous power. And in that instant Rafe tasted the terror his father must have known when he saw the woman he loved at the mercy of a madman.

"Tessa!" he cried. The sailors pitched her through the open hatch and Rafe flung himself beneath her in an effort to break her fall.

She crashed into him, and together they fell to the deck. Dull lances seemed to pierce Rafe's body at the impact, but he was grateful to have spared her that much pain at least. 'Twas precious little, sweet God, but this was all he could do for her. And he felt again the helplessness of the child he had been, his tiny fingers clutched about the hilt of a wooden sword.

Hampered by his bound hands, Rafe struggled to turn her so he could see her face, and what was revealed to him filled him with renewed foreboding. Her eyes were dull, unseeing, her face gray, while the mouth that had always been so animated now trembled with the effort to speak. Muzzy, unintelligible words snagged upon her tongue as her fingers gripped his doublet with the frail grasp of a babe.

"Dear God, what have you done to her?" Rafe's gaze slashed up to the inquisitor, and he hated the fear that edged his voice. "Curse you, Encina!"

"Your lady, it seems, was attempting to drown her sorrows in a flask of wine after your little misunderstanding. Lady Warburton merely hastened along the sweet oblivion the wench was seeking."

"Poison? Damn you! Will she be all right?"

"'Twould hardly be wise of me to kill the woman who is to be my greatest weapon against you, Santadar."

Relief seared through Rafe, and he sucked in a

shuddering breath and looked again at the ashen face pillowed against him.

'Twas as if the very sound of his voice held the power to loose the grip of the drug upon Tessa's senses, for a choked sob rose from her lips and the haze that had dulled her eyes receded a little. Rafe struggled to press her to him, wanting to soothe her, comfort her, but leashed as he was by his bonds, he was only able to capture her hands in his own.

"Rafe . . . " She slurred his name, her voice unsteady, but filled with joy. "Sweet God, Rafe, you're alive."

Tears coursed down her cheeks, tears for him— the man who had allowed his pride to shatter her— and that certainty made his chest ache with anguish.

"Yes, wildwitch, I'm alive. And you're here now, with me. I'll take care of you."

"Take care of her?" The inquisitor's voice was like oozing poison. "Your interests would be better served if you choked the life from her now, Santadar, with your own hands. Don't you see? 'Tis she who will destroy you."

"She is naught but an innocent girl, Encina. And by your black soul, you know your superiors will believe me. You have no proof! No proof!"

"Ah, but that is where you are wrong. You see, your harlot is guilty of the most grievous of sins— torturing our good King Philip with her witchery."

"Of all the insane accusations—"

"'Tis scarce insanity, Captain Santadar. After all, 'tis known throughout the kingdom that our sovereign's joints have been paining him most grievously of late. The surgeons are having difficulty determining the cause, because it is not physical.

Maybe His Majesty lies in agony because of the pegs your sorceress whore has driven through his joints."

"You're mad, Encina. Mad," Rafe flung up at him. "Your superiors will never believe you."

"Oh, won't they, Captain?"

Rafe started to curse, to roar out his scorn at the inquisitor's threats, but the words died in his throat as an evil laugh hissed from Encina.

"What think you your words will mean, Captain, when the grand inquisitor sees this?"

Something unfurled from Encina's hands, then dangled above Rafe's head like a felon from a gibbet.

The marionette swung on its strings, its carved features strangely sinister in the light streaming through the hatchway. And in that sickening instant, Rafe knew that the cursed Encina held him and Tessa in his evil power, for from his hand hung Tessa's likeness of the Spanish king— its knobby joints speared with the spikes that would condemn her.

Chapter Fourteen

THE hatch slammed shut, enveloping the hold in darkness, but this time the inky shadows fell in a welcome veil, devoid of Encina's leering face. Rafe whispered soothing words to the still trembling Tessa, as her drug-weakened hands struggled with the ropes that bound him. Even so small a foe as those hempen cords seemed beyond her meager strength.

"I can't loosen the bonds. I can't hold on . . . " Her voice quavered.

"Hush, wildwitch, I know you can do it. Take all the time you need."

She seemed to steady herself, the ragged sound of her breathing softening. Suddenly she gave a cry of triumph. Rafe felt the bonds fall free; spikes of pain drove themselves through his hands as blood rushed into the numbed flesh. Yet despite the sickening pulsing, Rafe caught Tessa to him, crushing the softness of her against his broad chest.

"Wildwitch, when I saw you and thought they had poisoned you . . . Mother of God, I nigh went mad." He choked out the words as he felt her shudder against him. "Forgive me, Tessa, forgive me."

"For being a blasted witling . . . a stubborn oaf?" Tessa sobbed shakily into his doublet. "I would hate and despise you forever, if I weren't so glad to see you alive."

Rafe's eyes stung at her words, a ragged laugh working through him as he threaded his fingers through her hair. "Ah, wildwitch, only you would curse me to the high heavens with Encina hovering near." His lips traced the wet curve of her cheek, his arms tightening about her slender form, as though by his will alone he could shield her.

"I've been worse than a fool, to let my infernal pride come between us. To dash off like a madman into Lady Morgause's grasp. Ah, angel, wildwitch, sweet God, what have I brought you to?"

"Heaven, Rafael Santadar—and hell. And when we are free, you can take two lifetimes to make it up to me."

When we are free . . . The trust in those words made Rafe wince inside, and 'twas as if he could feel the Inquisition's dread flames reaching out toward them. Encina would never let them go now . . . now that Rafe knew the inquisitor's hideous secret. Rafe had seen the ruthlessness in the holy man's eyes. He knew that if, by some quirk of fate, the tribunal failed to condemn them, Encina himself would use any method necessary to ensure that they were silenced forever.

The vile Lucero had slaughtered Rafe's father and mother, and now, the cruel bastard possessed the perfect tool to effect Rafe's own destruction, and Tessa's as well. Rafe's eyes skimmed over her face. It was only a pale shape against the darkness, but in his imagination he could envision perfectly those fey wood-sprite features, so brave and yet so incredibly fragile.

Did she not realize the stark danger in Encina's threats? No. Surely Tessa had no idea that Lucero, with the "evidence" he held, would make his peers and then all of Spain believe them to be guilty of sorcery.

She had witnessed the ugly face of a mob gone insane before, had seen the horrors they could wreak. But now she would stand before a tribunal of judges. Rafe sensed that she would expect some small justice, hold some hope.

But she had never seen the eager crowds throng the square, hungry to watch the suffering of those who had sinned against the faith. She had never witnessed the mantle of superstition that clung about his homeland, had never seen the spectacle of the auto-da-fé.

Thank God, a voice within Rafe whispered. *Thank God.* For if she knew what was in store for her at the end of this voyage, her terror would drive her mad.

She had quieted against him, her fingers tangled in the hair that grew long at the nape of his neck, her face tucked into the curve of his shoulder. Rafe drew rein on the thoughts that raced within his brain, pressing his lips against her tear-damp lashes.

"Rafe . . . " Her voice was tentative, quavering.

"What, *mi corazón*?"

"Your mother and father . . . Encina killed them? Tried to kill you?"

Rafe's jaw clenched, his arms tightening about her. "*Sí.*"

He felt her hands glide down the corded muscles in his neck, her callused fingertips finding the arc of his scar by sense of touch.

She pressed her lips, petal soft, to that jagged line. "I'm sorry you had to find out this way . . . here."

Now, as I lie here trapped and helpless? Rafe thought. Now, when my love, my life is in the cursed butcher's grasp. Damn Encina! Damn him!

But Rafe only made a soothing sound low in his throat, brushing his knuckles in a tender path down her cheek. "Don't think about that now, wildwitch. Just rest. Sleep."

She murmured bits of her own story, but he scarce heard her as she told about the lady of Warvaliant and the drug that had swept Tessa to sleep.

For as he whispered gentle endearments to her in Spanish, his fingertips smoothing her hair, he was listening instead to the lapping of the sea beyond the ship's hull. And he knew that for the first time, the vast ocean was his enemy, trapping him for Encina, cutting off all escape until they reached Spanish shores.

But once they did, he vowed if he had to sell his soul to Encina's own devil, he would find a way to avenge his parents and save this woman in his arms, this woman who had sacrificed so much for him, who had shown him what true courage was, and love.

"Tessa." He breathed her name against the babe-soft curve of her brow. "I love you."

As he spoke, he sensed Morgause's posset claiming her again, for Tessa's voice blurred as she whispered, "'Tis about time you realized it, you stubborn oaf."

* * *

Tessa braced herself against the lurching of the closed coach, knowing that she must not— *must not*—show her fear. To do so would torture the man beside her more savagely than any device in the inquisitors' chamber of horrors. For days she had watched the lines carve themselves deeper into Rafe's face. She had seen the desperation build in those eyes that had always been so strong, so unyielding. And she had known that the anguish in those indigo depths was born, not of his own dread of the cruelties that awaited him, but of his terror for her.

"Wildwitch," he had said, "sweet God, what have I brought you to?" The torment in those words still clawed at Tessa's soul, mingling with her own private hell as she watched guilt destroy the man she loved.

Rafael was nigh crazed with the need to save her. He had raked through a thousand desperate plans as the days at sea bled into weeks. Even the brief moments of respite they had captured making love in the ship's dank hold had been tainted by Encina's shadow. The wild need within Rafe as he pleasured her, shielded her, had taunted Tessa with the certainty that Rafe was not truly making love with her, but rather was struggling to bring her surcease in the only way within his power.

"Forget, Tessa love," he had whispered when he thrust inside her, his hands and mouth devouring her as he drew upon every skill he possessed to drive her to madness in his arms. Yet afterward, when he thought she was sleeping, she would perceive his despair, and tears would sear her eyes at the sight of his pain.

She had lost her confidence that no one in Spain—not even the Inquisition—could tarnish the shining honor of the man renowned as the Phantom of the Midnight Sea. For as she watched Rafe's mounting agitation, heard his half-crazed plots as he groped for some small chance of escape, even she was forced to see the hopelessness of their plight. And that hopelessness struck terror to the center of her soul.

She closed her eyes, trying to blot out the memory of the first night she had seen Rafael Santadar—on the beach near Gnarlymeade, the air thick with the stench of burning flesh. Hagar had been dead when the flames consumed her, but there was little chance that the Inquisition would accord a sorceress the same mercy—a sorceress who had woven a spell about their king.

Tessa shook herself inwardly to stifle the wild laugh that rose in her breast. 'Twas the ugliest of jests that the puppet she had carved to lighten the fears of children would now be used to destroy not only her but the man she loved as well. Even Encina's evil power could not have touched Rafe were it not for the wood-carved figure in the loathsome inquisitor's hands.

Damn him to hell, Tessa railed, the image of Rafe's hated enemy rising again in her mind. Nay, Encina, you'll not have Rafe! No matter what horrors you work upon me, I'll not betray him. If it costs me my own life, I'll not drag him into the flames.

Tessa again looked up into Rafe's taut face, memorizing those proud features, the high slash of cheekbone, the patrician nose, the mouth that had given her such exquisite pleasure, such sweet, sweet tenderness, and the eyes that had burned with passion, aye, and with unshed tears . . . for her.

"Wildwitch."

The ragged edge in his voice snapped her from her dark musings, and she forced a stiff smile to her lips, knowing that what he needed of her was courage.

"You once told me Spain was beautiful," she said, her eyes scanning the interior of the crude coach. "When we are free, you must show it to me."

"Curse it, you know we'll never be free! Never!" Anguish tore through Rafe's voice, his head arching back against the coach wall as his face contorted with pain. "Wildwitch, sweet God, I feel so helpless. They're going to hurt you, and there is naught I can do."

Seeing his anguished face, she could imagine the horrible scenes that must be unfolding before him like some macabre tapestry, scenes of his mother's death and his father's, Rafe's gallant crew lost in the inferno his beloved ship had become. And now Encina's fingers were working Tessa into that gruesome tapestry as well, as if the fiendish inquisitor was spinning out Rafael Santadar's own private hell.

Tessa fought the tears that burned in her eyes. She would have sold her soul to have her hands free of the chains about them just long enough to touch Rafe's face, smooth away his agony.

"Whatever happens, Rafe, carry this with you," she said, her eyes bright with her love for him. "These weeks I've spent with you are worth any horror Encina has to offer."

"Tessa—" She saw tears well from beneath his eyelids, then track down his beard-stubbled cheeks.

And she knew that seeing him thus, broken, was the greatest torment she could ever know.

"I love you, Rafael Santadar." She kept her voice steady, despite the fear surging within her as she heard the driver above them bellow out a command. The equipage came to an ominous halt, and she tried to look out through the slits in the coach. The slices of light that had brightened it moments before were now blotted out by the harsh plane of a wall.

Tessa felt Rafe grow still beside her, and her eyes flashed to his features. She knew in that instant that they had reached their hellish destination.

"Rafe . . . "

She could not stop herself from whispering his name, as if 'twas some talisman that might spare them.

As she looked into his eyes, she saw the fire of renewed resolve, the savage protectiveness of a lion whose mate is threatened.

"They'll not break you because of me, wildwitch." His mouth was hard and grim. "I vow it. I'll find a way to come for you."

He strained toward her as Encina's minion wrenched wide the coach door, Rafe's lips claiming hers in a fierce, hard kiss. "I love you, wildwitch."

A cry rose in Tessa's throat as rough hands tore him away from her and hurled him from the coach. Other hands, crueler still, grasped her arms and dragged her forth, but she felt not the bruising fingers crushing her flesh, saw not the eager leers. Her gaze clung to Rafe's broad shoulders as he disappeared through the prison's dark entry.

"Look you well," Encina's evil hiss slithered over her. "For when next you see him, he'll be screaming in agony as the flames eat away at his flesh. And you will be the one who condemned him."

"Nay, Encina." Tessa met the inquisitor's gaze with a glare. "Do what you will, you will never destroy Rafael Santadar through me."

Lips snaked over straight white teeth, a glimmer of anticipation dancing like a devil in the inquisitor's dark eyes.

"We shall see the mettle of this English courage we have heard so much of, see whether you stand firm or scream, as Anne Santadar did so long ago. How much have the captain's thrusts meant to you, witch? Enough to make you suffer in silence as the *garrucha* rips your arms from their sockets? As the *potro* stretches you?"

The inquisitor flicked travel dust from his robes with one long hand. "But even if you do suppress your screams, 'twill do Santadar no good—not when I produce your mannikin of the king. Not when they see your tempting witch's face."

The Spaniard's sharp nails bit into the soft flesh of her cheek as he traced its curve. Tessa gritted her teeth, her eyes aflame with hatred.

"*Sí*, I might even be tempted myself, *wildwitch*"—Rafe's endearment was blasphemy upon Encina's lips—"were I not bound by my vows as priest."

Tessa spat into that smug devil's-face, fierce joy spearing through her at the revulsion that swept Encina's features as he drew out a lace-edged cloth and dabbed away the spittle.

"That was most unwise," he observed with a blandness that chilled Tessa's blood. "You would do well to tread lightly about those who hold your fate in their hands. Santadar is dead to you now, and no one within these walls cares what befalls you. The guards here are hardened to pain and screams; they are like the mellow music drifting up from minstrels during a feast. You are mine, witch. Mine. As is your cursed lover."

One hand gestured toward the entry, and Encina's men yanked her forward. The death-cold fingers of the Inquisition closed about Tessa's throat.

Rafe paced the confines of his cell, feeling as though he would go mad. Mad? He gave a harsh laugh. Madness would be sweet relief from the grinding misery of watching the days slip by, seeing even the slightest of the hopes he had clung to disappear. How long had it been since they had torn him away from Tessa and thrown her into a cell God alone knew where. What had they done to her in the time that had passed? What had she suffered? For him, curse it, for *him*.

He gritted his teeth against the anguish clawing within him, his fingers reaching instinctively for the glistening ring that had always dangled from the chain about his throat, but the bit of jewelry was gone; Rafael had entrusted it to a stone-faced guard with a plea to smuggle it to Don Gualterio de Bautista y Aligar, Bastion's father. The stalwart grandee was Rafe's only hope, the single weapon he held that might be able to pierce the secret prisons of the tribunal.

When that guard vanished, Rafael's fragile last hope had turned to despair. The ring was no doubt worth a fortune to a man of the guard's humble means. And in truth, Rafe could scarce blame him for hieing off with it and forgetting the man who had pressed it into his hand.

For in the dungeons of the Inquisition, 'twas easy to forget . . . forget the glow of the sun, the cream-crested sapphire waves of the sea, to forget your very name . . .

Rafe shuddered. He had heard tales of those who had never escaped the inquisitors' grasp, who were not even granted the release of death. There were whispers of men grown old within these dank walls, living skeletons cackling away in their insanity.

Would that be his fate? Tessa's? To be entombed here forever?

No, not Tessa's. Encina was too hungry to sacrifice her to the flames, too eager to cause pain for another Santadar, too eager to have his name honored for capturing King Philip's supposed tormentor. The cursed bastard would do anything in his power to bring about Tessa's death. And within these walls, Encina's power was akin to God's.

With a curse, Rafe flung himself at the heavy door, venting his frustration and fury against the thick portal. Shards of pain shot through his shoulder, and he clenched his jaw against the groan that rose to his lips—then suddenly all sound died within Rafe's throat, silenced by the harsh grating of the door swinging open.

Rafe staggered back, blinded by the light as a torch was thrust into the aperture. "Captain Rafael Santadar? Known as Phantom of the Midnight Sea?" a gruff voice demanded. The torchlight dripped orange over a flowing black mantle, but a voluminous hood concealed the man's features in shadows.

"Go to hell!" Rafe snarled, hating all who lurked within these evil walls.

"I tried." A strange, suppressed amusement in that voice sent a spear of disbelief through Rafe's body. "But I confess, *mi compañero*, that the devil would not have me."

"No . . . impossible. 'Tis impossible," Rafe gasped, one hand reaching out to steady himself against the cell wall. "They have finally driven me mad."

"There is nothing new in that, Rafael," the voice teased. "I've said you were crazed from the day I met you."

Heart racing in his chest, Rafe reached out and yanked back the man's hood. The earth seemed to crumble beneath Rafe's feet as he gaped in disbelief and wonder at a sight he had never hoped to see again—the rakehell grin of Bastion de Bautista y Aligar.

Tessa struggled to stiffen her spine, her chin jutting in defiance as she walked between the two men guiding her through the maze of corridors that wound through the prison. Not a word had they said when they unlocked her cell door, their eyes gleaming like rat's eyes beneath their shelflike brows. Their lips had been wet, glistening and eager, the stench of sweat and filth clinging to their thick bodies, their hair hanging in strings slick with oil.

Tessa fought the urge to plead with them, to beg to know where she was being taken. Images of the torture Encina had promised her raked at her courage, but she clenched her fists, the manacles cutting not half so deep into her flesh as her resolve to meet her fate with a courage befitting Rafael Santadar's woman.

Where was her bold sea phantom? Was he still tormenting himself with guilt, driving himself mad with his plot to gain her freedom? Even during the eternity she had suffered in the suffocating darkness of her cell, the most excruciating torment of all was imagining Rafe—proud, noble Rafe—enduring the skittering rats, the coarse, meager food, and the endless echoing silence.

And most unbearable of all was the certainty that she would never touch him again, never again see that achingly beautiful solemn-sweet mouth, unless it was twisted by agony.

"Santadar is dead to you . . . " She could still hear Encina's snarl.

Yet she knew that could never be, for Rafael lay deep within her heart. She remembered when he had told her the story of his mother's fierce courage as the wounded Anne had carried her bleeding son across miles of rugged terrain to get him to safety. Love had given Anne Renfrew Santadar that super-human strength, made her able to work a miracle— love for her husband, love for her son.

And love for that child, grown into a man, would steel Tessa's own courage in the ordeal to come.

The guard grumbled something she did not understand. Then the man straightened his slumped form as they neared a grand archway.

A torture chamber? she wondered with a shudder of panic. Nay. Light from magnificent windows gilded the room, and even from a distance Tessa could see astonishingly rich furnishings—gleaming and smooth, carved of teak and oak.

She struggled to shake free the webs of confusion, the interminable days of darkness and despair having dulled her senses. If this was not a torture chamber, then what was it?

The guard prodded her forward, and she stumbled into the room, her gaze sweeping tapestries and paintings of saints and martyrs—Saint Stephen, his flayed skin delicately draped over one outstretched arm; Sebastian, his flesh bristling with arrows; Catherine, bound to the torturer's wheel.

Despite their grisly fate, the countenances of the saints had been wrought with a serenity that grated on Tessa's nerves. They all were smiling, their eyes turned up to their God. Yet Tessa knew full well that God could not hear her within these walls that were supposedly his own.

"Tessa of Ravenscroft." The resonant voice made her gaze snap to a long table stretching the length of the room. Four men garbed in flowing white sat behind it. Her gaze clashed with that of Lucero Encina. The hated inquisitor looked so solemn, so holy, she would have sold her soul for an opportunity to crack her palm against his smug, evil face.

"You have been brought before the holy tribunal to answer charges of heresy," a stern, gray-haired man announced. "The heresy of witchcraft."

As Tessa let her gaze sweep the faces of her captors, she could see in their eyes that she already stood condemned.

She let a bitter laugh break from her lips and took refuge in the biting wit that had always served as her shield from fear. "Sir, if I were a witch, do you think

I would still be languishing here? I would long since
have cast a spell to spring open the locks."

All the men behind the table, save Encina, went
pale and began, in their harsh voices, to babble in
a tongue she could not understand, but she sensed
that her hasty words had frightened the men before
her.

When she glanced at Encina, his eager grin chilled
her like the kiss of death.

He rose from his seat, steepling his hands before
him as he watched her. "Strange, witch, that you
should say that. A spell to spring wide prison doors?
Perhaps you could reveal to us how your devil-
spawned powers allowed you to do just that."

"To do it? I said that if I *were* a witch, I would
have done it."

"Perhaps you do not waste your sorceress's spells
upon your own worthless life, slathering them
instead upon that of your demon lover."

Tessa felt her belligerence melting beneath that
opaque, evil gaze. Confusion battled with the odd
sensation that she was treading across a bottomless
lake sheened over with the thinnest sheet of ice.

"I have no demon lover."

"You deny having spent many nights in Captain
Rafael Santadar's company—and in his bed, mistress?" Encina goaded her. "And heed well your
answer, for I saw with my own eyes his lust for
you."

"Nay. I do not deny . . . sharing Captain Santadar's bed. But even you, Encina, cannot think him
a demon. He is a captain who warred so valiantly
for your cause but a few weeks past, a man who lost
his ship and nigh lost his leg from the wounds he

suffered in the fighting." She turned pleading eyes to the implacable faces of the other men. "Please listen to me. Rafael Santadar is known throughout your country for his honor, his courage. He has battled your foes, spilled his blood in your king's name. I swear to you that I am no witch, but I am even more certain that Rafael Santadar has never committed the dark sins with which Encina charges him. He is innocent."

"And if he is a truly innocent, honorable man, as you claim," Encina purred, "would you not agree that his most fierce desire would be to face his accusers and clear his name?"

"He will," Tessa flung at Encina, her gaze slashing again to the other white-robed men. "And when Rafael Santadar is brought before you, when you look into his eyes, you will be unable to believe this wicked man's lies."

An ugly chuckle rumbled from Encina. "I fear that will prove most difficult."

Tessa blanched, terror that Rafe might already lie dead racing through her. She bit down hard upon her lip, to stifle a cry of fear and denial. "Why, blast you?"

"Because your bold, noble captain has turned coward and fled."

Tessa felt the blood drain from her face as waves of dizziness pressed down about her. "Rafe . . . is free?" Relief shot through her; her eyes filled with tears of gratitude and joy.

"*Sí.* But then, you knew that, did you not?"

Tessa's gaze snapped back to Encina's, and she felt the jaws of a subtle trap spring closed about her. "Nay, I did not."

"Did you not say moments ago that *if you were a witch* you would weave a spell to fling wide the cell doors of this prison?"

"'Twas a jest, to show how ridiculous the charges were. Would I have stood here pleading for Rafe's life if I had known he was free?"

She shuddered at the triumphant light that glowed in Encina's eyes. She knew in that instant that she had damned herself with her own careless words, even before the evil Lucero had shown the other inquisitors Tessa's marionette of the king.

"You see, my dear brothers, how clever she is?" Encina asked. "The devil's own, bragging about her powers, trusting that we poor men of God are too dull-witted to see her trickery, to hear her laughing at us."

"You, Encina? A man of *God*?" Tessa flung out the question, desperate to drag Encina into hell along with her. "A murderer? A thief? A man who would sell his country's honor to the highest bidder? You killed Ruy Santadar!"

"Girl, you will silence yourself," the gray-haired inquisitor commanded.

"Nay, please listen. Encina confessed his crimes to Rafe when we lay imprisoned within the ship's hold. The inquisitor confessed."

"*You* should be considering your own confession, English harlot!" Another inquisitor sprang up from the table in outrage. "Do not add to your sins by attempting to soil the name of one we know to be beyond reproach!"

"Beyond reproach!"

"Silence!" The roar nigh shattered the magnificent stained-glass windows. "If you value your tongue, girl, you will keep it still, else you might well lose it."

Tessa stared into the faces of her judges, each one bearing features vastly different from the others, but each man's eyes glacial and condemning. 'Twas hopeless. It had been mad to think for even a heartbeat that this accursed tribunal would listen to her.

Encina strode from behind the table, and Tessa could smell the stench of triumph upon him. His fingers curved beneath her chin, jerking it up so that the light streaming from the window bathed her face.

"Did I not warn you, my brothers, that this woman is Satan's own angel? Look at her—this English slut, this devil's whore who stole Rafael Santadar's soul and then turned her evil against our king. She has condemned herself from her own mouth. And now I have obtained evidence that will even further damn this woman to the fate she deserves—flames! The flames!"

Tessa tried to keep the terror from her eyes, seeing in Encina's visage her own hideous death. The inquisitor stalked to the table and yanked from beneath his robes a cloth-wrapped bundle. One long hand jerked the fabric free. The other men started in their seats as wood clattered against wood, their eyes fixing upon the puppet before them. It lay on the table like a battle-flung corpse, grotesque, twisted—more damning than any mere words might be.

"Look you at this proof of her sin."

Tessa heard Encina's snarl through a haze of despair, her memory filling with an image of the silvery

tresses that had wisped about Hagar's aged countenance, the sweet innocent face that another pyre
had consumed. And Tessa felt herself letting go of
life, of hope, as her gaze focused upon the marionette she had whittled on firelit nights a lifetime
ago.

"We are men of God," Encina's evil voice rang
out. "And as such, 'tis our duty to see that this witch
suffers. She must drink of her masters' fire. Drink of
agony, torture. She must taste of hell, my brothers,
from our holy hands, before she is cast into the dark
angels' domain for all eternity."

Chapter
Fifteen

IT was far too beautiful a day for dying.

Tessa squinted against the rays of the sun that trembled like liquid gold upon the rim of the horizon. She drank deep of the tang of the sea wind, the heavy, lush scent of leafy trees. She felt the heat reflecting off the baking clay and stucco that lined the rutted streets.

Warm. The day was so warm and fresh.

In the weeks that had crawled as she sat in her stench-ridden cell, she had forgotten what it was like to fill her lungs to bursting with blossom-sweetened air. She had forgotten how bright the sky could be.

Aye, she had forgotten everything except the ruggedly hewn planes of Rafael Santadar's face, the fierce love that had shone in his deep blue eyes, and the wonder of his solemn-sweet smile. Those she had clung to, fingering the memories of their days together like a strand of precious gems, each single stone glittering with its own special magic.

Rafe's love had been her talisman, weaving about her a web of strength that even the ruthless Encina could not break, though he had tried, curse him to hell. He had tried.

Tessa flexed her fingers slowly. The muscles in her arms throbbed with pain; the joints of her shoulders ached as though some malicious gnome had thrust a red-hot poker into the sockets. The *garrucha* had proved an abomination worthy of the fiendish Encina, and the torture master had worked its wrath upon her with most delicate savagery, as the inquisitor attempted to force from her a confession implicating Rafe.

"He has escaped you. You cannot reach him!" she had cried out in her pain. Encina had only snarled that Santadar would never escape him. Never . . .

And Tessa had known with a grinding sense of doom that the inquisitor was right. Encina would not even have to bestir himself to seek Rafe out in order to capture his quarry, for her bold sea phantom would never rest until the man who had murdered his parents and sent his lady to the flames had died beneath Rafe's own sword.

The thought sent fresh pulses of dread through Tessa, and she glanced about her, as though expecting to see some sign of the tall seafarer, some glimpse of indigo eyes spitting rage as he attempted to wrench her from Encina's grasp.

'Twould be impossible, Tessa knew, for anyone to be rescued from this atrocity of pomp and splendor, this terrible majesty that was the auto-da-fé.

Yet Rafe's words echoed back at her, taunting her, tormenting her, with his fierce promise: "They'll not break you because of me, wildwitch. I'll find a way to come for you."

"Nay, Rafe." She whispered the plea, her throat

aching with unshed tears. "Even a sea phantom
could not steal through this madness, especially
with Encina's wolves circling all about me."

Her gaze flicked to the two burly guards who
had escorted her to the tribunal's chambers and
who now stood watching her with salacious eyes.
Wicked knives were sheathed at their thick waists,
daggers were thrust into their boots, and their meaty
fists flexed as though they were eager to plunge into
the fray. They were waiting, eager and alert, for
someone to try something futile, desperate. They
were hoping.

Yet even the sick light within their twisted faces
did not rack Tessa with half the horror she felt as
her eyes roved past the small courtyard in which the
"penitents" waited. Beyond it she could see the huge
dais that had been erected to afford an honored few a
better view of the spectacle. Thick stakes surrounded
by mounds of faggots dotted the earth below the dais
like festering sores. A crude street cut a path through
the houses to the place where the ceremony of death
was to take place, and that narrow, muddy ribbon of
road was thronged with the pious, come to watch
Satan's minions die.

Bile rose in Tessa's throat. How could they watch
this without retching? How could they look upon
these, the damned, the poor unfortunates who had
fallen beneath the Inquisition's fury without won-
dering what it would feel like to wait here for the
horror to begin, robed as though for a bridal bower?

A chill swept over Tessa as her eyes scanned the
other pathetic prisoners who also awaited execution.
Twelve of them there were, a motley gathering at-
testing to the far-reaching power of the Holy Office.

An aged man, his face carved with the features so typical of Spanish nobility, stood erect beside the gate, as if impatient to have the infernal business done. A boy of about sixteen stood in the man's shadow, his whole body trembling as he looked out at the crowds choking the street. A young woman with huge eyes fingered a lock of pale hair so fine it could only have come from a child. Tessa felt her chest tighten as she imagined the poor woman's babe, sobbing for the mother who would never again croon lullabies or chase away the nightmares with her kiss. And the others, too many others, with faces that blended into one mass of silent horror.

Loathing raced through Tessa as she watched the priests move among the condemned, attempting one last time to break their will and make them fall to their knees before Spain's unyielding God in the minutes before they faced death.

And what would it matter? Tessa thought bitterly. She had heard the young boy plead with the priest, repent for crimes so absurd that she would have laughed had she not been choked with horror. The boy had embraced "the true God," begged for mercy—and the Inquisition's twisted mercy had been accorded him. The priest, that smug, sanctimonious bastard, had passed an approving hand across the lad's head, promising that he would be strangled at the pyre before they lit the flames.

Tessa smoothed chill fingers down the pristine white folds of the San Benito that covered her body. The richly embroidered robe seemed to jeer at her about the horrors to come. Flames stitched in red by the hands of dainty Spanish girls writhed upward upon the snowy cloth, and hideous faces contorted with agony seemed to claw their way through the blaze that consumed them. The robe was a signal telling all who watched that this prisoner was to die racked by the full agony the flames could offer—burned alive for her sins.

Tessa shuddered, imagining the Spanish women clustered in some sunny room, their fingers flying over their work as they laughed and chattered about their husbands, their lovers, their round-cheeked children, as all the while their delicate hands plied their needles over the robes that were to garb the damned.

Those who watched were the flower of their society, but something in their heedless acceptance of human suffering horrified Tessa in a way that even the violent madness of the mob at Gnarlymeade had failed to do.

She glanced at the other robes. The flames on the boy's garment spiraled down toward the earth, like obscene tongues, proclaiming that he had repented and was to die before the fire touched his flesh.

Two captives wore the garments of penitents, white robes adorned with a huge cross. They were to prostrate themselves before the gathered masses, confess their sins, and be forgiven. They had no doubt groveled before the tribunal and acceded to all the demands of the relentless inquisitors. They would emerge from this day stained with their shame, marked forever by their crimes against the church, but alive. Alive.

And Tessa could not find it in herself to blame them for buckling to the dread tribunal's will, but she had contracted some of Rafe's sense of honor in the time she had known him—caught it like the pox or the plague. She prayed that when she felt the searing heat of the flames she would still cling to that steely courage.

" 'Tis time."

She flinched inwardly at the harsh bellow, her fingers clenching in the folds of her robe in an effort to steady their trembling. She stiffened her back and compressed her lips with resolve, then was surprised to see one of the accused, the aged Spanish nobleman, drawing nigh her. His craggy features were touched with approval, his brown eyes holding a glint of strength.

"Are you the English witch we were told of?" he asked. "The one who wove spells about the king?"

Tessa nodded.

"I overheard the guards talking about your words to this illustrious tribunal. They said you told the inquisitors that if you were a witch you would have cast a spell to unlock the prison doors." A laugh breached the Spaniard's lips, the sound strangely heartening. "If you know of any sorcery that might aid us in escaping now, 'twould not come amiss. Perhaps you could stir up a bat-wing brew and make us vanish? Or change us into birds? Falcons, perhaps. 'Twould give me great pleasure to pluck the eyes from the cursed men who condemned me. What think you, witch?"

One thick gray brow lifted, and his eyes twinkled.

"I fear my supply of bat wings is depleted," Tessa said.

"Ah. Well, then, we will just have to amuse ourselves by thinking what wondrous hauntings we shall wreak upon our accusers after we become one with the spirits of the night."

Tessa cast the man a stiff, yet grateful smile, knowing he had sought to distract her, but nothing could dull the raw panic slicing through her as she saw the wrought-iron gate swing open, felt herself being prodded forward.

"*Bruja*! English whore!"

The crowd shrieked their hatred at her, spilling upon the single enemy they had within their grasp the loathing they felt for the nation that had shamed them. Tessa gritted her teeth against her terror, half afraid that the crowd would burst into the violent frenzy that had inflamed the mob at Gnarlymeade and that these dark-eyed Spaniards would forget the pomp of the auto-da-fé and fall upon her, ripping her apart with their own hands.

She felt the old man struggle to hold his place beside her, his bent shoulders but small shield against the hatred of the crowd. And she prayed that this gallant Spanish nobleman would die swiftly this day.

"Burn her! Bride of the devil! Burn her!"

Tessa's gaze flashed to where a haughty Spanish matron cried out her hatred, the faces of those crowding the lane mingling into a vision of sheer horror.

"Vultures," the old man muttered. "Hungry for human sacrifice to their God. And they think the Aztecs are savage!"

But even the kindly Spaniard's efforts to ease her terror no longer held any power to dull the threads of hysteria weaving themselves into her courage as she fixed her gaze on the thick stakes to which they would soon be chained. Beyond them, she could see three men she recognized as her judges. They sat on a bench in the center of the platform. One face, however, was missing—that of Lucero Encina.

Was that God's one small mercy? To spare her from dying beneath her enemy's malicious, gloating gaze? Or was Encina lurking nearer the flames, the better to revel in her death throes?

She glimpsed the flickering orange and red torches that would serve to set the pyres ablaze; they glowed in iron holders near the stakes. And 'twas there that she saw him, his robes flowing about him like those of an angel born of hell. His hands were folded prayerfully before him. Would the vile inquisitor put the torch to her pyre with his own hand? Would he glory in the terror in her eyes as the dried tinder caught fire, as the flames crept up to curl their fingers about her?

Sweet God, just let it be over, Tessa pleaded silently, forcing her eyes to shift away from that evil visage, away from the dais crowded with spectators, away from the piles of wood awaiting the flames. She struggled to fill her mind instead with treasured memories, images of Hagar's face, beautiful and young, and of her father's merry grin, and it seemed as if her mother's gentle hands were reaching out to Tessa, soothing her.

Mama, help me through this, Tessa pleaded inwardly. Help me. I don't want to die.

But there was no comforting whisper even from the sea winds, no hint of gentle laughter as Hagar told her to banish her fears.

Only a bright-winged bird swept by overhead, its green plumage a splash of color against the sky. Tessa watched it winging away from the earth, a single shining beauty, and she knew in that instant how Hagar would have delighted in it.

Aye, and she would have delighted in the strong will of the child she had plucked from the sea. Tessa thrust her jaw out, stubborn resolve surging through her as she vowed she would not let fear and the ugly eagerness of her tormenters fill these last minutes of her life with evil. She drove the sound of their cries from her ears, barring any sound from entering the shell she had enveloped herself in.

Shutting her eyes, she dredged deep in her soul, drawing from some well of courage she had not known she possessed. She envisioned Rafael Santadar's beautifully carved features, remembered the wonder of his touch. She traced in her mind the scar that had marked his throat, the scar she had kissed a hundred times. She felt again the sweet, heavy weight of him as he pressed her down into the soft feather tick. And she fingered the memory of his words, his laugh, his voice, rough with passion: "I love you, wildwitch . . . "

"Peace, my daughter, for the love of God!" The deep, annoyance-laced voice startled Tessa from the welcome ease her thoughts had given her, snapping her back into the dirty lane, the whirling mass of faces thirsting for her pain. She glared at the one who had spoken—obviously more than once—in an attempt to gain her attention. It was only another infernal priest dripping in vestments, a hood drawn low over his features, a prayerbook open in his hand.

For an instant she felt a strange surge of hope and fear as her eyes fought to pierce the shadows veiling the holy man's face, but when she glimpsed a hawklike nose and a mouth too wide to be Rafe's, she sank deeper still into hopelessness.

"I want only to be left alone," she said through gritted teeth.

"No, child. Take comfort in God's word," the man urged her, thrusting the prayerbook toward her. "For the sake of your immortal soul."

"My soul is already damned, Father." Tessa let her loathing drip from her voice. "So you can take your accursed God, his word, *and* my immortal soul and—"

Tessa's words died upon her lips, silenced by shock as the priest muttered a most impious oath and rammed the book against her hip with decided force.

A bruising pain throbbed through her, and she uttered an oath of her own as anger, despair, and terror mingled in a flash of raw temper. Her hand whipped out to strike the book from the priest's sun-browned hands—when suddenly her gaze locked upon the page the man held open.

Her heart slammed against her ribs, and for an instant she could not breathe as she stared down at the device of the stag *courant*—the Renfrew crest, penned crudely on a sheet of vellum.

Rafe! Sweet God!

She turned her gaze again to the face of the priest, her confusion deepening as she stared at a pair of exasperated but amused brown eyes, and a mouth battling valiantly to keep an appropriately somber expression.

"Who . . . " Tessa began to ask, but the man raised one long finger in caution.

"I am called Father Bastion."

"Bastion?" In that fleeting instant the memory of Rafe's anguished tale of his ship's destruction flashed through Tessa's mind, and she remembered the story of his most cherished friend, the friend who had died at sea, the friend whose death had clawed lines of guilt and grief across Rafe's face.

Tessa felt the blood drain from her cheeks. A wild dizziness washed through her, and she feared she would shatter whatever plans Rafe had made by drifting into a faint. "But Bastion is dead," she breathed.

The priest's shoulders shook, and Tessa could see his face redden with the effort it took him to stifle his laughter. After a moment he managed to say in a most sober voice, "So little faith, my daughter? Do you not believe in miracles?"

"Nay." Tessa met that merry gaze, all her fear evident in her face, her terror for Rafe and for his friend nigh driving her insane. "The time is past for miracles. 'Tis too late. Look you!" Her eyes swept the crowd which was still clamoring for the destruction of the English witch as if, by burning Tessa, they could somehow glut themselves on enemy blood, though they had been robbed of Elizabeth Tudor's own.

The dais was thronged with Spanish grandees, their armed retainers milling about upon magnificent caparisoned horses, and the streets were so packed with people that there was no route for a hasty, desperate flight.

"Please," Tessa whispered. "Don't risk your life. Don't let Rafe . . . "

Her words trailed off as the crowd about them

thinned. The solemn procession began as the victims trailed into the open square.

Tessa drew a deep breath, the smell of the burning torches singeing her nostrils as she passed scarce an arm's length from Encina and heard the man's low, cruel laugh.

"Now you will die, witch." The words skated chill across Tessa's skin. "Die . . . "

She started to hurl her own bitter scorn back at Encina, but in that instant the entire crowd seemed to erupt in a crazed frenzy. Wild cries assailed Tessa's ears.

"Burning is too good for her. She is Satan's own! Let us take her! We shall avenge our soldiers!" In a crashing tide of humanity, the spectators who had lined the streets spilled into the square and thrust themselves through the meager barriers that had barred them from the execution site.

A scream rose in Tessa's throat as the mob raced toward the cluster of prisoners. It was as if she had been engulfed in an old nightmare. She was again drowning in the horror of Gnarlymeade and in her own fears. She heard the Spanish nobleman curse, saw Bastion fling his prayerbook to the ground, and felt his hands close about her arm.

But it was too late. The mob was already flooding over her. Harsh hands were tearing at her hair, her robe. She heard hoofbeats pounding toward her, heard shrieks of fury and pain. Then suddenly 'twas as if a hurricane had swept her up and flung her high.

Terror wrenched through her as she cracked hard against an object that drove the breath from her body, and she caught a glimpse of the glistening

black haunches and thick, rippling mane of a horse
now beneath her. One of the mob had dragged her
astride it, holding her in his grasp. Desperately she
struggled against those binding arms as other hands
tried to drag her into the morass of vicious faces.

"Hold still, you little hellcat!" her captor shouted
into Tessa's ear, biting deep into her terror, shattering it into a million fragments of joy, fear, stark
relief, and fury.

Her gaze slashed up as the horse reared, and
through the tangled mass of her own hair, Tessa
glimpsed the blazing indigo eyes of its rider. Rafe.

No avenging god could have held more fearsome
splendor or such stark resolve. But even if Rafe
could trample the mob of spectators, Tessa knew
he could never reach the open street beyond. The
mounted men she had seen flanking the dais were
even now charging toward them, swords drawn,
while menace even more threatening surrounded
them.

Screams of rage reverberated through the mob,
and she expected that both she and Rafe would be
ripped from the horse at any moment. The beast
bolted toward a breach in the mass of people, and
Tessa suddenly saw what looked to be a fiend from
hell barring the horse's path.

Torchlight shaded Lucero Encina's face in grotesque patterns. The inquisitor's eyes were wide and
nigh mad with hate and rage. Both of his hands
were clasped about a flaming brand, wielding it like
a satanic cudgel.

Rafe cursed as the stallion shied away from the
blazing torch. The huge beast reared and pawed the
air, nearly hurling Tessa and him from its back in

terror. And in that instant Tessa saw the inquisitor's mouth slacken with ecstasy and triumph.

Somehow Rafe managed to keep his seat on the horse's back as the thrashing animal's hoof cracked into Encina with a dull thud, sending the blazing torch tumbling from his hand.

That single second seemed to spiral out into eternity. The flaming torch streaked like blood down Encina's white robe, leaving a writhing stain of flame.

Tessa saw his eyes widen with horror as his hands clutched at the burning robe. But 'twas as if Satan himself had worked some sorcery upon those flames. Encina's rippling white robe had suddenly ignited and burst into a searing mantle of death.

Even the frenzied mob fell back for a moment, stunned by the hideous spectacle Encina had become. Inhuman shrieks split the air as the inquisitor writhed in agony, his hair aflame, his features contorted as his flesh was consumed.

Rafe wheeled the stallion away from the spectacle, urging it away from the hideous scene—the pyres, their stakes lancing the sky, the dais burdened with those hungry to watch the death of others, the inhuman mass of agony that had been Lucero Encina.

Tessa buried her face in Rafe's doublet as the inquisitor's shrieks fell still. Horror pulsed through her, mingled with a savage joy that the man who had condemned so many to such a hideous fate had himself fallen before the flames.

There was the sound of more hoofbeats, and she heard Bastion's jubilant cry. "We've bested them all, Rafael! May Encina roast on the devil's own spit!"

Tessa clung to Rafe, as he drove his horse forward at a killing pace, Bastion a few lengths behind, and she was stunned to glimpse a wondrous empty space about them.

Freedom?

It had seemed too great a miracle even to hope for, and yet in that instant it was within their grasp.

"We've made it, wildwitch. We have bested them." She heard Rafe's growl of triumph, felt him drive his heels into his horse's sides in an effort to spur it to even greater speed.

The stallion surged forward, catapulting them onward, until they lost themselves in a countryside as rugged and untamed as Tessa's own cliffs, terrain that would shield them from their pursuers for days to come.

It seemed they had ridden an eternity before Rafe drew rein, halting within the garden of a small abandoned hermitage. Tessa had long since drifted into an exhausted sleep in his arms, even Bastion's jaunty banter having faded to weary silence. But as Rafe's gaze swept the house and the wild hills surrounding it, he knew this destination had been well worth the arduous journey.

The night was dripping violet shadows down the craggy stones, enveloping all around them in a sweet haze of peace that seemed to blot out all of the horror and ugliness of the cruel world lurking beyond this rugged slope. 'Twas as if the spirit of Brother Ambrose still wandered about his beloved wildlands, welcoming any in need of haven.

As they dashed across the Spanish hills, Rafe had felt a ribbon of memory, a sense of safety, drawing him to this place where he had known such pain and such joy. 'Twas a place to rest, if only for a little while. A place to heal.

"Is she all right, *compañero*?"

Bastion's soft inquiry prompted Rafe to gaze into Tessa's ashen face, and his heart twisted at what he saw. The mad race across the countryside, mingled with the grinding terror of facing what she had thought to be her death, had left scars on her delicate, waiflike features. The skin that had been rose-blushed with health was now waxen, and her slight form, even in sleep, trembled against him with remembered fear.

Rafe could almost see the images that tormented her still. Taking great care not to disturb her, he eased himself down from his saddle and carried her inside.

"Rafe . . . " His name was scarce a breath upon her lips. "Was so . . . scared. I thought—"

"Hush, love," he soothed her, shuddering inwardly at how close to death she had come. "Did I not promise I would come for you?"

"You took . . . your bloody time."

Rafe was startled as a roar of laughter sounded close to his ear, and he turned to glare at the grinning Bastion.

"Don't rail at him, Tessa," the younger man said. "I all but had to chain him to a wall to keep him from charging into that cursed prison. I made him wait till the time was right. Patience, I fear, has never been one of Rafael's greatest virtues."

Rafe carried her inside and eased her down onto the musty bed. Gently, quickly, he made her comfortable so she could drift into sleep. But even after he knew she was at rest, he could not bring himself to ease her from his arms. He was loath to relinquish the pure pleasure of threading his fingers through her silky hair.

How long he stayed there beside her he did not know, but suddenly he was aware of his friend's eyes regarding him. Bastion's merry face was touched with a most unaccustomed solemnity.

"So," Bastion said softly, " 'twas not just another of the phantom's noble quests, this wresting of an innocent from Encina's flames. It seems you have a new heart's mistress, Rafael."

"She is going to be my wife as soon as . . . " Rafe let the words trail off, but Bastion would not be evaded.

"As soon as what, my friend?"

"As soon as I confront the bloodthirsty bitch who cast Tessa and me into Encina's hands, as soon as I find out what the hell this insanity is all about. Christ, they could have burned her, Bastion— burned her alive."

Rafe felt a warm hand close over his shoulder and tighten in a bracing squeeze, but Bastion's comforting gesture failed to penetrate the fury still throbbing through Rafe's veins nor did it dull his fierce resolve to hasten back to England.

He would return to the land that had crushed his pride, shattered his life, and then given it back to him, filled with a love more beautiful than any he had ever known.

He would go back to the grandfather he had turned his back upon.

And he would confront the woman, that haunting, eerie woman, who had entangled him and Tessa within her dark and sinister web.

Chapter
Sixteen

DAWN was dancing with the moon, trailing skirts of mauve across the Spanish sky. Rafe watched the lady of morning bewitch her lover, saw the moon's impassive face fade into the gold his lady so loved, lost once again in her brilliant rays.

He lifted his face to the breeze that wafted sultry and warm across his cheeks, listening to the burble of the rill that tumbled in cool sapphire beauty near his feet. And he wondered if any place in England could hold such sweet serenity.

His gaze shifted to the overgrown path that wound down the hillside from the hovel and disappeared in the distance. Bastion had dashed away on his dun-hued mount before the stars had faded, hieing off to arrange secret passage for Rafe and Tessa on a ship bound away from Spanish shores, a ship that would sweep Tessa out of the Inquisition's grasp, that would carry Rafe away from his homeland, perhaps forever. He closed his eyes at the pain that possibility struck through him, remembering the somber glow in his friend's dark eyes.

"Even with Encina dead, 'twould be impossible

to gain you a pardon," Bastion had warned. "The inquisitors had no idea who I was and no reason to connect me to Tessa's escape, but you, Rafael, now stand guilty of wresting from the Inquisition a woman condemned for witchcraft."

"Do you know what their evidence against her was, Bastion? A marionette she had carved—a puppet to amuse children."

"I fear the Holy Office was not amused, and they will be even less so now that they have been made to look like fools before a crowd of Spain's finest citizens. Unless you wish to widow your Tessa before you've had the pleasure of filling her with your sons, you must never return to Spain again."

Never return again . . .

It sounded like death. So permanent. So hopeless. But despite his reluctance to admit it, Rafe knew Bastion was right. It would be folly to risk his life just to wander these sun-baked hills—especially because of the woman who lay sleeping in the hut on the rise above.

So after his friend had ridden away, Rafe had stayed outside, sitting near the ruins of the herb garden Brother Ambrose had so loved, beside the stream where he had splashed as a child, and he watched, for perhaps the last time, the glory of a Spanish sunrise.

"Rafe?"

He had not heard the soft footsteps approaching, had not had time to banish from his features the melancholy that clung about him. He cursed himself inwardly, knowing from the sorrow in Tessa's voice that she had seen his sadness and sensed its cause.

"You will miss coming here. You will miss Spain.

Won't you?" she asked softly.

"I don't know why." Rafe's lips curled into a rueful smile as he plucked a tiny lavender flower and cradled it in one hard palm. "From the time I turned fourteen until now, I've spent no more than eight months upon land. I was always happier roving the waves, seeking out exotic ports, new adventures. Ambrose was dead. I knew naught of my family. There was no one for me to come back to. Spain was just *there*, like the air, wildwitch. But now that it is gone, I feel as if some part of me is dying, some part I never even knew existed."

He stopped, looking up into her great dark eyes, not wanting to shadow them with any more pain. There was a depth of understanding beneath those thick lashes that wrenched at his heart, a kind of tenderness and softness that had not been evident in the wild-eyed harridan who had tumbled from the cliff.

He raked his fingers through his hair, and his voice was unsteady as he thought of the anguish that had so changed her. "It doesn't matter, Tessa— leaving here—what with the Inquisition poisoning the land. All that matters is that you're safe. When I think what could have . . . what almost happened to you because of me . . . " A choked sound rose in his throat.

"But it *didn't* happen to me. And even if it had, 'twould not have been your fault." Rafe felt her hand drift, whisper-soft, over the wind-tossed waves of his hair. " 'Twas Encina's evil that ensnared me, Rafe, and Morgause Warburton's trickery."

"I dragged you into the midst of their plot. I was the man whom Encina wanted dead. It was my blood for which he thirsted. And Lady Morgause was trying to use me as well. She wanted me for some dark purpose of her own. Murder . . . sweet Savior, she wanted me to murder someone. She told me so when she summoned me to her tower room."

"Who was it? Whom did she want you to kill?"

A bitter laugh shook him. "I never knew, never even wondered who it was she wanted dead. I thought her plot was but some madwoman's rambling, and I dismissed it as such. Christ, I hardly spared it a thought once you freed me from Warvaliant. I was too lost in my own anguish, my own pain at discovering that I was not one with the proud Spanish, that the mother I had worshiped like a Madonna was English."

" 'Twas a horrible shock," Tessa said, "one of many you'd been forced to endure. You had just lost your ship, you thought Bastion dead, and you knew Encina had set the *Lady* ablaze. You'd been wounded and hurled up on an enemy shore. And then, when all seemed hopeless, you discovered that the blood of your worst enemies ran in your mother's veins. 'Tis no wonder you weren't thinking clearly. 'Tis a miracle that you were able to think at all."

He heard the faint rustle of Tessa's skirts as she sank down beside him, curling close to his side. Her warmth seeped into his skin, and yet he felt as though he deserved none of its sweet comfort.

"Dammit, wildwitch, don't you see? 'Twas my selfish wallowing in my own pain that nearly got you killed. I should have known that a woman like Morgause would be eager to have me silenced forever once I suspected her secret. I should have known that a man so desperate to kill me that he was willing to burn my ship would not simply rest once he discovered his will had been thwarted. If I had but dragged myself out of my self-pity long enough to consider the danger I had placed you in, none of this would have happened."

"And then you would have stalked away from Elizabeth's court and out of my life forever." The words were soft, so soft, and they twisted in Rafe's gut like a knife. "The love you have offered me is precious, Rafe. So precious 'twas worth facing Encina."

" 'Twas worth nothing, Tessa." Rafe's fists knotted at the sweet agony of her loving. "The love I gave you was a fragile, meager thing, too weak to withstand even the battering of my pride when you tried to save my life. I saw you try to spare me there in the queen's chamber. Your eyes begged for understanding and forgiveness. For what? For risking your own life in Warvaliant to save mine? For deflecting the queen's wrath from a man who snarled and roared at her like a caged lion?"

"Rafe, you—"

"No, Tessa!" Rafe turned on her, his hands delving deep into the tumbled curls at her temples, his whole body shaking with fury at his own stupidity and fear at the danger that had nigh consumed this woman he loved. "I can't listen to you spin excuses for me anymore. You watched your mother burn. *Burn*. You faced rape at Lord Neville's hands. When you might have been spared the horrors of that dungeon, you plunged in after me, to tend my wound, knowing that your actions would bring the wrath of Warburton down upon you. And after your puppet-playing in the queen's presence, you took your pride in your hands and offered it to me."

His voice thickened, his eyes sweeping every beloved plane and hollow of Tessa's face, his heart burning with her pain. "Tessa, I threw it back in your face, everything you had given me. And then, as if 'twas not enough, I took from you even more."

"I gave it to you willingly, Rafe. You took nothing."

"You're wrong, wildwitch. And I'm going to take even more. Because I can't help myself. Because you're the only thing in this madness that makes any sense anymore."

Rafe saw her eyes darken, her lips part as his hands swept down her body with desperate hunger.

"I told you before, Santadar, you've never 'taken' aught from me I didn't want to give." The sad-eyed waif shifted before his gaze into the wildwitch he had named her. He marveled at her strength, her courage, her tenderness. Marveled that, after all the pain he had dragged her through, those lustrous dark eyes still held the purest of love for him, the hottest of passion.

"I need you, Tessa." He eased her down upon a bed of flowers. "I need to feel the life in you, the fire, the forgiveness."

He kissed her, his mouth branding hers with the love he had denied her in Elizabeth Tudor's palace, with the love he had feared he would never be able to offer her again when they had ripped her from his arms outside Encina's loathsome prison.

His hands shook as he removed her clothes, his eyes closed as his mouth trekked over her body,

savoring the honeyed warmth and creamy smooth-
ness with his tongue. His hands bracketed the curve
of her hips, his fingers eager for the feel of her. Then
he froze as a sudden gasp that was not of pleasure
came from her lips.

His eyes snapped open, and he drew away, his
gaze skimming over what his mouth had just
caressed.

Bruises marred her delicate ivory skin in stomach-
wrenching blotches—dark purple, saffron, a sickening greenish blue. A huge fist seemed to slam into
his vitals as Tessa scrambled to draw the folds of
her skirt over her nakedness.

"Tessa . . . what did he do to you? Encina, that
cursed bastard!"

She would not meet his eyes, and in that moment
he knew that she had indeed faced the full fury of
the Inquisition.

"Why?" Rafe blazed. "They had all the evidence
they needed to condemn you! For God's sake, all
that kept me sane while we were trying to effect
your rescue was the certainty that they would not
use their horrors on you to gain a confession."

He caught her chin in his fingers, forcing her to
look at him, and 'twas as though some malevolent
giant had dashed his feet from under him. "Oh,
my God." He breathed the words, as a horrible
sinking sensation washed through him, bile rising
in his throat. " 'Twas me, wildwitch, wasn't it?"
he rasped. "They needed your confession to impli-
cate me."

"Nay, Rafe, I—"

He stopped her protests, laying his fingers upon
her lips, seeing the truth in that savaged angel face.

He tried to speak, but couldn't. Lunging to his feet, he stalked to a gnarled sapling on the bank of the stream and buried his face in his hands.

"Don't, Rafe, please," Tessa begged as she stood up and hastened to him. " 'Tis over. It doesn't matter."

"*It doesn't matter*?" Rafe wheeled on her, his voice a tortured shout. "Sweet God, Tessa, how can you say that? How can you? You suffered torture for me. How can I ever touch you again? How can I hold you without remembering, without hearing you scream? How can I kiss you without hating myself for the knowledge that while Encina brutalized you, I was at Bastion's *castillo*, mad with worry, plotting your escape, but safe. *Safe* while they—"

"While they stole away all chance for me ever to know happiness?" There was an edge to that wood-nymph voice, a determined light in her eyes. "You've been lashing yourself about drowning in self-pity, about casting away happiness because of your stupid pride. Yet now, when you see a few welts on my skin, your blasted honor sticks its nose in again. You can't bear knowing that I suffered these bruises for you. You can't touch me, hold me, kiss me, *after I nearly got myself killed over you?*"

"Tessa—" He tried to halt her flood of angry words, tried to cling to his own white-hot anguish and guilt, but she looked like a raging child, her chin thrust out, her face flushed scarlet.

"Damn it, Santadar, *you owe me!*" One small fist thumped against the wall of his chest. "You owe me a lifetime of kisses, the feel of your hands on me, the joy I feel when you come into my body and reach so deep it seems you touch my very soul."

"Tessa!" He cried out her name the instant before his lips crashed down upon hers, his eyes burning with anguish and wonder. The folds of cloth she had clasped about her breasts now fell from her grasp, whispering down to pool about their feet. His arms closed about her with a tenderness that belied the raging passion building within him, his shaft throbbing and swelling as she pressed herself against him.

But it was not tenderness she needed from him. She craved the quick, hot blaze that always flamed between them. He sensed it in the way her hands swept restlessly over his chest, dragging off the soft silk that had enveloped his shoulders.

"Wildwitch," he said against her lips, "I want you, too. Here. Now. But I don't . . . don't want to hurt you."

She pulled away from him, her eyes glistening in that wondrous enchantress's face. "You already have. Now heal me, my phantom. Heal me."

She drew him down onto the rumpled folds of her gown, her teeth taking nips from the bronzed flesh she had bared. Rafe's jaw clenched as her tongue skimmed over one of his ribs, then down the line of black silk that bisected the muscles of his stomach. She toyed with the dip of his navel, then pressed a kiss to the waistband of his breeches with such sweet fervor he ached of it.

Then she was easing away that last barrier between them, the soft breeze sweeping down the winding stream cool upon his fevered flesh.

He grasped her arms, wanting to draw her in to his kiss, but she shook her head, the rich cascade of her hair tumbling down in a lake of midnight silk upon his belly. Her tongue flicked out, moistening her full berry-red lips. Then she was lowering her head yet again. Rafe felt her breath, hot and damp upon the nest of hair at the apex of his thighs, and he scarce dared hope that she would bless him there with the warmth of that full, sweet mouth.

She cradled him in one hand; then her lips drifted down to taste of his hardness. The taut muscles of his stomach jumped as she encircled him, drawing him into the wet haven of her mouth, teasing him, loving him until he could bear it no longer.

"It feels so good . . . " He squeezed the words from a throat rough with pleasure. "No, love. No more, lest you unman me."

He grasped her arms, dragging her up, sweeping her over until she was pillowed upon the folds of her gown. "I love you, Tessa," he said, his knee parting her thighs as he pressed himself deep. "Sweet God, I love you."

He caught the rosy tip of her breast in his mouth, suckling and teething it as he drove himself against her, willing his love to pour deep into the woman who had suffered so much for him. And afterward, when the madness had possessed them both, he led her into the sparkling waters of the stream and pleasured her there until neither of them could stand.

Over and over he brought her to ecstasy while she drove him wild, until there was nothing left untouched between them, no bruises of body or spirit that had not been soothed by their hands, their lips, their loving.

As Rafe drew her into his arms on the streambank, allowing the heat of the now-cresting sun to dry their sated bodies, he knew that nothing and no one could ever come between them again.

As though she had read his thoughts, Tessa propped herself up on one elbow and gazed down at him with love-filled eyes. " 'Tis over now, isn't it, Rafe? All the pain, all the fear. It's over."

"Not quite, wildwitch." Regret laced his voice, but he couldn't lie to her now, even to shield her from what was to come.

"I don't understand. Do you think they might find us?"

"Here? No, love. No." He threaded his fingers through her hair, cupping the back of her head in his palm as he pulled her down against his chest. "No one can touch us here. But once we leave these shores and sail back to England—"

"England?" She pulled away from his grasp, and he hated the darting fear in her eyes. "Are you mad? We can't go back to England any more than we can stay here. Rafe, you were an enemy captive and you escaped the queen. And they no doubt think I aided you. You humiliated Her Majesty, betrayed her trust, as did I, and she'll never forgive either of us. She'll cast us into the Tower and order us executed or, at best, imprisoned for life. We have to go someplace else, perhaps to one of the ports you've been to and loved."

"We have to go back there, wildwitch. We must finish this." Rafe levered himself to a sitting position and caught her face in his hands. "Don't you see—"

"I see that you're being as stubborn as ever, and as crazed!"

"Tessa, all my life I've lived with specters—the death of my parents, not knowing who I was. Nightmares tortured me when I slept, and I'd wake, my body drenched with sweat, shaking, my mind filled with my mother's face, bloody and battered, the monster that was Encina leering at me. That ghost has been banished now, laid to rest. But now there is a new terror within me—the terror I feel for you."

"I'm fine, curse it."

"Do you think Morgause Warburton is going to forget we ever existed, Tessa? Especially when she finds out that Encina is dead and that we eluded even the might of the Inquisition? Encina said he killed my family because my father discovered that he—Encina—was embroiled in some plot with an English person, a plot so dangerous it was worth murdering an entire family—a grandee, his wife, his son."

"Encina could have been scheming with anyone—anyone, Rafe—all those years ago."

"Why, then, did he enlist Morgause's aid in capturing us in England? And how was he, *a Spanish inquisitor*, able to move about Elizabeth's palace, however stealthily? Without the aid of a woman with the power of Morgause Warburton, 'twould have been impossible. There must have been some alliance. I feel it, sense it."

"It doesn't matter, Rafe!" Desperation carved deep lines between Tessa's brows as she pleaded, her hand clutching at his arm.

"Yes, it does, Tessa. For all her oddity the woman is powerful. Rich. And she has a son who is as ruthless and brutal as she is. And we—you and I—carry with us not only the knowledge of her link to Encina but also the certainty that she is seeking to do murder as well."

"If they had as much power as the queen herself, they could never find us. We can lose ourselves."

"Where, wildwitch?" Rafe demanded, unable to yield to her even that small hope. "In some hell-spawned port town reeking of poverty and despair? In some country foreign to both of us, where we would be outcasts forever, running from shadows?"

"Aye, damn you, if 'twill keep you safe!"

"I can't abandon some other innocent to the fate of my parents. I can't flee, do nothing, while someone is murdered."

"But you don't even know who she's after."

"Would it matter? Even if it is naught but some fisherman's daughter, do I not owe her a chance at life? And what if it is someone much closer to me, some member of the English family you took such pains to reveal to me? What if it is my grandfather?"

Tessa blanched. "Nay, he is too strong. They could never touch him."

"Not even with the poison Morgause is so fond of? Or a stiletto hidden in the night? God knows the Warburtons loathed Tarrant Renfrew enough even before I set foot on English shores. And now they have an even better reason to seek vengeance on him. What if it is your precious Earl of Renfrew who lives beneath the blade of Morgause's dagger?"

Silence fell between them, heavy and fraught with anger and pain. Rafe met her gaze with a gentle firmness. "When Bastion comes, 'twill be to take us to some foreign ship bound for England. I'll take you to my grandfather, make certain you are beneath his protection. Then I will go to confront Lady Morgause and her thrice damned son, alone."

"The devil you will!" Distress streaked across the

features that had been dewed with pleasure and regret twisted inside Rafe, but he only skimmed his knuckles over her flushed face.

"All my life I've been stalked by shadows, wild-witch," he told her gently. "I'll not abandon you, and the babes you will bear for me, to a future clouded by such a dark fate, even if this venture costs me my life."

Chapter Seventeen

THE wind lashed in from the sea, battering the English coast with its fury. Rafe felt it pulse deep inside him, driving high his dread, his anger, and his stark frustration as he urged his mount at a breakneck pace over the night-shrouded countryside. Yet 'twas all he could do to keep pace with the dark-tressed virago at his side, whose billowing scarlet cloak was like a wound upon the mist-laden darkness.

Lightning shattered the sky into a score of midnight fragments, the flashes of bright light searing images of Tessa's face into Rafe's memory.

Her hair flew back from pale, taut cheeks, and her lips were still set in the expression of mutinous anger that had fallen upon them that long-ago day when they had loved by Brother Ambrose's cottage. There was in her features the same fierce determination and steely will that Rafe had seen in the visages of battle-hardened sailors.

She was going with him to Warvaliant, to Morgause, to the brutal Lord Neville, and there was naught he could do to stop her.

In the weeks that they had traveled, how many

times had he heard her vow that she would not leave him? How often had he seen in her eyes a warring glint that might have shone off the blade of a well-honed rapier?

In the end he had seemed to accede to her. He had nodded when she railed that 'twas foolhardy to pit his lone strength against the might that was Warvaliant. He had told her that they would stop at his grandfather's castle to enlist a small party of his men. And then they would continue on toward Warvaliant.

A grim smile curved his lips as he remembered those keen black eyes upon his face, the ring in her voice as she had told him that they damn well would.

He felt a shaft of longing tug at his loins as his imagination welled with images of his wildwitch in the midst of a bevy of children—daughters woven of fire and ice, sons with the bravery and inner strength that had shone in their mother. Damn, they would breed such children, he and his wildwitch. There would be naught they couldn't tame between them.

"Slow your pace, blast it, before that palfrey hurls you into the next cursed earldom!" Rafe shouted. But whether the wind carried away his words or Tessa chose to ignore them, he knew not.

He swore as he saw her drive her heels again into her mount's sides, the beast's mane lashing back against Tessa's face. Then, just as Rafe was about to spur his own mount and grab the palfrey's reins to jerk it to a halt, Tessa reined the animal to a quivering stop.

Rafe sawed back on his own mount's bridle, barely keeping the stallion from crashing into Tessa's horse.

"Look!" She gestured to where a dark giant seemed to crouch upon the horizon. Just then a flash of lightning illuminated the great hulk of Renfrew Castle.

"I see it. And 'tis a good thing we're almost there. Mayhap we'll reach it before you break your blasted neck!"

"There is a small gate to the north. We'd best enter there—stealthily. If things should go awry, we want not to drag the earl any deeper into disfavor. Pull the hood of your mantle up about your face to hide it."

Rafe felt a stab of jealousy over her concern for the old warrior. "Fine. I'll swath myself in black and we can creep in like thieves."

But even before his words were out, she was again urging her mount to a gallop. Rafe gritted his teeth, one hand yanking his hood into place as he spurred his horse to follow. In what seemed a heartbeat she had whirled up to the smaller entry. He saw her smiling down at the crabbed old soldier who was guarding the gate—an aged knight who had served Tarrant Renfrew for forty years.

Rafe drew rein, his stallion dancing upon great hooves, tossing his magnificent equine head. But the anger Rafe had felt moments before eased as he heard Tessa's voice, warm as summer rain. "Good morrow, Sir Dinadan. I have brought his lordship a most welcome guest."

The soldier scrubbed at his mist-dampened face

with one gnarled hand, peering up at them from the single eye left him after a jousting accident decades past.

"I've no doubt you'd be right welcome, Mistress Tessa, save that another guest arrived a fortnight ago, and tonight is a grand fete in her honor."

Rafe felt that single knowing eye pierce the shadows beneath his hood, and he hated the subterfuge Tessa had urged him to. There was a subtle cowardice in it, as though he had something to feel ashamed of. And perhaps he did. His escape from Elizabeth's palace had left the old earl, who had risked so much on his behalf, to face the queen's formidable wrath alone.

Rafe's fingers closed about the edge of the velvet hood, drawing it back from his face so that he could meet Dinadan's gaze squarely. "Perhaps we could await my grandfather's pleasure in a withdrawing room until after tonight's entertainment."

"Nay, you witling!" He heard the knight mutter an oath. "Cover yourself! Look at the banner above."

Rafe shielded his eyes against the mist, trying to pierce the darkness with his gaze. Then suddenly another bolt of silver split the sky, and he saw the flag fluttering high above them in the wind.

The royal banner.

Foreboding drove itself into Rafe's belly, and he heard Tessa's gasp of distress.

The queen . . .

Rafe had planned to confront her as well, once he had dealt with the threat from the Warburtons. He had planned to surrender himself to Elizabeth Tudor in the hope of gaining some small measure of mercy that might in turn afford Tessa and him a chance for some kind of life here on the queen's shores. But not yet. He could not face Elizabeth now, before he knew Tessa to be safe from Morgause's treachery and Neville's cruelty.

His fingers groped for his hood, and he heard Tessa's harsh whisper. "Sir Dinadan, if there is somewhere we might wait in secret?"

"I don't know, mistress. The place is crawling with royal servants and such. There have been whispers again about some knave making an attempt on Her Majesty's life, and it seems the whole kingdom has turned out to shield her."

"There have been whispers about an attempt against Her Majesty?"

"Bah! Don't trouble yourself about it. Our Gloriana has the sense to pay them no heed. But because of the celebration, the castle is bursting with guards, courtiers, and every man and woman of note within a hundred miles."

The old guard guffawed. "Every man of note, that is, except that devil Warburton. The earl said if that dog showed his face hereabouts, he'd send him to his Maker, queen or no queen. And I guess his lordship must have believed it, because—"

"Who goes there?" The gruff voice made Rafe start in his saddle, as all eyes swept a figure striding out of the darkness. Royal livery dripped in lavish elegance from the man's broad shoulders as his weasellike visage was illuminated by the night's flashes of light.

Rafe felt his stomach plunge to his toes, knew he should wheel his mount and spur it away from the castle, away from the queen's waiting justice. Yet at that moment, Dinadan reached out and caught the reins, giving a hushed warning as he nodded toward three other guards following on the heels of the first. " 'Tis too late. You'll have to brazen it out, boy."

Rafe's gaze clashed with the knight's, but he loosened his grip on the reins as Dinadan swaggered up to the queen's man. " 'Tis Sir Dinadan Graystoke, guardian of this gate. If you are guarding Her Majesty, you'd best find more fruitful ground than here."

Rafe held his breath, knowing the old soldier was hoping to deflect the royal guards' attention from him in an effort to buy him time to slip away. But the scarlet-draped chest of the queen's servant swelled with importance, and Rafe could see the man's mouth harden in a grim, smug smile. "And these other two?" he demanded. "Who are they?"

Rafe heard Tessa start to stammer, feared she would blunder into some falsehood that would bury them even deeper in the queen's distrust. And in that instant he knew what he must do.

"I am Captain Rafael Santadar." The hard edge of command rang in his voice, and he met the royal servant's glare with a level one of his own. "I am grandson to the Earl of Renfrew and heir to this castle."

"Rafe, nay—" Tessa's protest was lost in the weasel-faced guard's surprised oath.

"You're the Spaniard, the one who fled the queen's presence."

"I *escaped* from enemy hands," Rafe corrected. "Now I am returned to surrender myself to your queen. I demand to be taken to her at once."

"You *demand*?" the guard sputtered.

"Do you dare defy the future Earl of Renfrew?" Rafe glimpsed Tessa's stunned white face and was surprised at the steely determination in his voice as he claimed the heritage he had scorned.

"I—" the guard began.

"Think well, you popinjay." Dinadan's voice was rough with pride. "You are talking to Lord Tarrant's heir."

"*Lord Tarrant's heir* is a fugitive from the Crown," the guard replied.

Rafe arched his brow and said with acid arrogance, "One who has information Her Majesty will find most disconcerting."

"Her Majesty is otherwise engaged."

"Now, man. She will see me now." As Rafe swung down from his restive mount, the magnificence that had made men cower from the Phantom of the Midnight Sea radiated from every line of his body. "Or are you willing to take the responsibility for withholding information vital to the good of her state and mayhap to her very survival?"

"What can you possibly know, Spaniard?"

" 'Tis for the queen's ears only. I'll say no more until I stand in the royal presence."

He turned his back on the guard and swept Tessa from the palfrey's back. As she slid down against the plane of his chest, he felt in her the thrumming of her dread.

"Rafe, nay. We can't go before the queen. We're not ready."

Rafe peered down into that delicate face that had been seething with mutiny and he was touched by the fear for him in those wide dark eyes.

He took her face gently between his hard palms, skimming his thumb over the warm velvet of her full lower lip. "When you are out on the sea and a storm blows wild, you are never prepared either, wildwitch," he said softly. "But you have to face it anyway."

He clasped her chill fingers in his and drew them through the crook of his arm. Then they turned toward the massive castle to confront the full fury of what awaited within.

The queen of England was a maelstrom of color, light, and ruthless power as she sat enthroned at the head of the vast carved table in the great hall of Renfrew Castle. Scores of courtiers garbed in their finest lined both sides of the huge sweep of wood, their own daunting magnificence overshadowed completely by the woman who was Gloriana, England's beloved Virgin Queen.

With Tessa at his side, Rafe strode down the length of the chamber, feeling as though the blade of an ax already hovered over his naked throat. For had there been any steel within the gazes of those who crammed the room to bursting, Rafael Santadar knew that he would already be dead.

His gaze swept past them all to where the noble Earl of Renfrew sat at Elizabeth Tudor's side. The craggy features of his grandfather, already so time-worn, were now creased with the fresh pain Rafe knew he had brought the old man.

Yet 'twas the sight of the woman who sat at the queen's other hand that made Rafe's chest tighten with wariness. For there, all but lost within the glittering majesty that was the queen, Morgause

Warburton sat, her pale eyes huge in her colorless face, her hands shaking as though she were viewing two corpses come alive.

She pressed her fingers to her bosom, and it was as if that flick of her hand had somehow broken the spell Rafe's entrance had cast over the room. The chamber suddenly erupted in a buzz of anger and indignation, and several of the posturing young nobles leapt to their feet.

Rafe's muscles snapped taut, and he half expected some knave to fall upon him with sword or dagger. But at that moment the earl lunged from his chair, the stony strength of a score of battles lying about his broad shoulders like a mantle.

"Sit down, you cursed fools, before I banish all of you from my table!" Had a sense of impending doom not hung so heavy over the chamber, Rafe would have burst into laughter at the haste with which the striplings dropped into their seats, felled like trees beneath that iron-honed will.

Rafe met the old earl's stare.

"We were not aware that we would be accorded the pleasure of your grandson's company this night, Lord Tarrant." Elizabeth Tudor's voice was steel on ice, musical, yet ringing with the unyielding, regal tones of a monarch displeased. "Had we been forewarned, mayhap we would have ordered shackles and chains to be served along with the meat pasties."

Rafe saw the earl's jaw clench, felt Tessa's fingers tighten on his arm, but before either of them could act, he stepped away from Tessa's side, strode toward the queen, and said, "Mayhap 'twould have been more meet to summon up a shroud, Your Majesty."

"A shroud?" The queen's eyes hardened further. "Mayhap, milord Spaniard, you are hungry for vengeance against us, hungry to regain the honor of your king?"

Rafe held out hands empty of weapons. "There may have been a time when I would have been willing—no, eager—to do so. I would have done all within honorable means to gain a victory for Spain. But never, even in the midst of the total destruction that followed the armada's defeat, would I have struck down a defenseless woman."

"You deem the queen of England naught but a *defenseless woman*, Captain Santadar?" Elizabeth ran beringed fingers over the gem-starred base of her golden goblet. "We fear you mightily underestimate us. We hold the power of the finest army ever to march upon these shores. And now our navy has proved itself worthy of like acclaim."

"An army is small shield against a traitor, Your Majesty. And an assassin cares not if Neptune's own trident fights upon your side."

"An assassin? Traitor?" Elizabeth shoved the goblet to one side, signaling for more wine. Yet her eyes never left Rafe's. "Those are serious allegations, Captain Santadar. Especially from the lips of a man who but a short time past was among the invasion fleet sent to steal away our throne."

"Your Majesty, if you would but listen," Tessa cut in, earnest and pleading.

"This is between Captain Santadar and us, girl. You will let him tighten the noose about his own proud neck if he so chooses."

"In truth, 'tis not only between the two of us."

Rafe's gaze shifted to the woman beside the queen. "There is another."

Morgause Warburton paled further, a rapid pulse beating beneath the fragile layer of skin at her throat. Her fingers played in agitation over the ornate rim of the queen's magnificent goblet.

"Your Majesty," she interrupted smoothly, "surely state matters can wait until after we've finished our feast. An hour or two cannot make a vast difference in the Crown's affairs."

"I fear it could make a great difference in the Crown's affairs, Lady Warburton," Rafe said. "It could well determine whether or not your queen will continue to sit upon her throne."

As Morgause's pen-stroke-thin brows arched in something akin to alarm, the dart of terror in her pale eyes confirmed Rafe's mounting suspicion.

"And what could you know of English affairs," Morgause demanded scornfully, "a cowardly Spaniard who ran from the queen's presence?"

"And into the grasp of a Spanish spy, a man who spent a lifetime gleaning English secrets from a source buried within the queen's own nobility."

Morgause winced, her eyes taking on the dangerous glint of a trapped animal. "Her Majesty will not listen to such ramblings from a cursed Spaniard."

"A cursed Spaniard who refused to drown himself in blood for your benefit, Lady Morgause?" Rafe said. "Even when you tempted him with tales of how he could redeem himself after the defeat of the armada, how he could save his honor after suffering humiliation at Drake's hands? Like a sweetmeat you dangled your intrigue before me, tempting me."

A nervous laugh tripped from Morgause's lips. " 'Tis pure folly, this. Madness. Your accusations are so ridiculous no one will be witless enough to believe you. I had no link to Spain or to Encina. I—"

"*Encina*?" Rafe spat the name, infusing it with loathing and scorn. "Strange. He was the man who claimed to hold England's secrets in the palm of his hand. Yet I have not spoken his name this night. How came you to know of him, milady? Tell us." He saw the woman stand up and take a step back, the queen's goblet wavering as Morgause's fingers left its engraved rim.

"But of course you babbled his name." There was a wildness in the woman's voice as her gaze darted to the queen. "You spoke of the Spaniard!"

"The one who dragged me from the queen's own palace? Threw Tessa and me into the hold of a ship, and dragged us before the Inquisition because we knew—"

"Must we suffer the ravings of this Spanish pig?" Morgause shrilled, grasping the base of her own wine-filled vessel. "He has already proved himself a coward and a liar as well, duping all within this castle into thinking him an honorable heir to the house of Renfrew."

"Too honorable to do murder for you, my lady." Rafe planted knotted fists upon his hips, his harsh gaze giving Lady Warburton no quarter.

"Enough! Both of you!" Elizabeth snapped. "I weary of your quarreling. Accusations, Captain Santadar, are most dangerous. We have little patience with them when they are unfounded."

The long, ruby-ringed fingers reached out to curve about the shimmering goblet, the canny eyes contemplating the dark red liquid within. And Rafe realized that there was a steely warning in her words. His memory stirred with the stories he had heard of the queen's mother, the witch Boleyn, tales of how King Henry's proud Anne had fallen beneath the ax because of questionable testimony.

"Your Majesty, my accusations are not unfounded, I vow—"

She waved him to silence then lifted the goblet and slowly swirled its contents. "What cause have we to believe the bellowing of a Spaniard against the word of a peeress of our realm?"

Rafe gritted his teeth in frustration. His eyes slashed to Morgause, the light of victory in the woman's ghostly eyes filling him with barely leashed fury. Her pale, childlike fingers fluttered against her gown of night-black velvet, as though weaving some dark sorcery while the odd ring glinted upon her hand.

The ring!

His gaze flashed up just as Elizabeth Tudor touched the rim of her goblet to her lips.

"No!" His hand shot out and closed about the queen's wrist. A gasp of outrage sprang from the monarch. A dozen men erupted from their chairs, and the hiss of weapons being torn free of scabbards echoed among the cries of alarm.

Even Tessa had lunged forward, her eyes huge in her face.

"Poison!" Rafe's heart thudded against his ribs as the queen's fingers clenched beneath his grasp. "Your Majesty," he said. "The wine is poisoned."

The queen's eyes pierced Rafe's and yet, despite the aura of dignity that still clung to the monarch,

Rafe felt the slightest of tremors in the fingers beneath his.

"That is the most absurd of all your allegations, Captain. Everything is tasted before it touches our lips."

"Lady Warburton slipped the potion into your wine from a compartment concealed in the emerald she wears on her finger. She showed it to me when I was prisoner at Warvaliant, when she was attempting to lure me into dealing death to someone in her name. But never did I suspect, Your Majesty, that it was you."

Elizabeth turned on the lady of Warvaliant, all eyes in the room bearing down upon Morgause's waxen face, and it seemed the hostile glares, fury, and suspicion would crush her.

"What say you, my lady?" Elizabeth questioned. "Shall we call in the castle hounds, have them sip this wine that holds the truth?"

Morgause's gaze flicked to the wine. " 'Twill not be necessary to waste such a fine vintage on the beasts. You wish the truth, Your Majesty?" Morgause tipped the queen's goblet up and drank deeply.

"Sweet Christ!" Rafe grabbed for the vessel and knocked it away, but Morgause had already drained the dark liquid.

The whole room seemed frozen in a shattering silence, all faces turned toward the lady whose eyes blazed with madness.

"Why this plot of murder? Why end it in your own?—" Rafe couldn't stop the question as he stared at her icy face, the muscles stiff as the poison ate deep inside her. His fists knotted as Morgause staggered around the table toward him and clasped the fabric of his doublet in her chill fingers.

"For the same reason you sailed with your accursed armada! For the same reason you fought Drake— to bring . . . bring the true faith back to England."

Rafe's hands swept out and closed about her bone-thin upper arms to steady her, but her knees buckled. He eased her down gently onto the rush mats on the stone floor.

"A surgeon! Someone hail a surgeon," Rafe shouted, ripping open the close-fitting ruff about Morgause's scrawny throat in an effort to ease her ragged breathing.

"But my methods," he heard the woman rasp, "weren't honorable enough or noble enough for you, just as I was not beautiful enough to hold you—Ruy . . . "

Her fingers curved up over his cheek, the nails biting into his beard-roughened skin as he felt the spasms twisting her small frame.

"I loved you. I loved . . . "

The hand grasping at him was racked by the tremors that quaked through her frail body. Suddenly Morgause Warburton stiffened as though some agony had ripped through her. Then she sagged, limp, in Rafe's arms, her opaque eyes rolling upward beneath open lids.

Dead. She was dead, but on her face there lurked a smile that would haunt Rafe for eternity, not the chill madwoman's smile that had made his skin crawl in Warvaliant's turret chamber, but rather a smile touched with softness, the smile of a maiden running to meet her lover.

Rafe heard the babble of voices rise all about him as the courtiers crowded around, but in that moment 'twas as if he and Morgause were the only people in the world.

He took the noblewoman's hand and had started to lay it on her breast when his gaze snagged upon the miniature that was half exposed by the open emerald ring—a likeness of his father. Rafe stared at it, feeling as if he were peering into an enchanted mirror, viewing a scene of love and hate from a generation past.

He heard a furor as someone shoved through the maze of velvet- and satin-garbed figures—a broad-faced surgeon hastening through those assembled.

"Is there sickness? Has someone—"

"Someone has died, sir." Rafe released the lady of Warvaliant's hand and rose slowly to his feet.

"And mayhap someone has been reborn." 'Twas the queen's voice, low and laced with gratitude.

Rafe regarded the monarch who now stood in regal splendor beside him. "Reborn?"

"Aye. Rafael Santadar, heir to the Earl of Renfrew. A valued subject who was lost to us when he was but a child, but who has been given back to us—if it should please him to remain upon our shores."

There was a tightness in Rafe's voice he had not expected as he faced the woman who ruled all of England—Tarrant Renfrew's beloved captive princess who had become the greatest queen ever to sit on a throne.

Rafe tried to speak but couldn't. He felt Tessa's fingers soft and warm upon his arm and glanced into eyes dark with love and tentative hope.

"You have saved our life, Captain Santadar," the

queen said softly. "Let us give you a gift of life as well, a life with this Tessa who stands fortunate enough to hold your proud heart."

Rafe looked up into that regal, aging face that had known so much sorrow, held such strength.

Someone has been reborn . . .

He glanced at his grandfather, the noble Lord Tarrant, and at the wood-sprite features of the woman he loved.

And then the heir Renfrew slowly sank to one knee in silent tribute to his queen.

Chapter
Eighteen

RAFE arched his neck against the weariness grinding down upon him, trying to banish the haze that seemed to muddle his mind. Five hours it had been since he was swept from Tessa's side and locked in a stifling chamber with his silent grandfather, Elizabeth Tudor, and her most trusted advisers. They had raked through every wisp of information Rafe had possessed concerning Morgause Warburton's plot, trying vainly to rip away the mystery that still shrouded the noblewoman's attempt at regicide.

But in the end there had been only a heavy sense of regret and impatience in the queen's sharp eyes as she had paced to a simple depiction of the Temptation of Christ worked in fine tapestry. She had shaken her head, like a mother wearied by recalcitrant children, and the words she had spoken clung even now to Rafe's memory: "Religion! Why cannot they all leave one another in peace? Catholic, Protestant, Puritan—let each one go to the devil in his own way."

There had been wistfulness and wisdom in her sentiment, and her words had filled Rafe's mind with remembered scenes of flames, crosses, and white-robed judges who worked atrocities in the name of God. The auto-da-fé held its own special horror, and yet those who embraced the faith of the new church were in truth little better, wanting only to send different people to their death for the same insane reasons.

And people like Lady Morgause were ready to do anything, commit any crime, to enthrone upon the altar their own version of the deity all Christians worshiped.

Was she now dancing with her own accursed devils in some hell woven of flame? Rafe shook off the thought, trying to drive away the clinging sense of horror her death had given him. No. There was no sense in trying to understand Lady Morgause's madness, even though Elizabeth's councillors and the solemn earl were still attempting to do so in that small chamber.

They had dismissed Rafe when their discussion turned to the ramifications the murder attempt would have on the state. Rafe had left the chamber relieved, yet restless, and now he wandered at leisure through the quiet halls.

It was so long since he had felt this inner stillness. He reveled in it, loving the freedom he felt to rove about the stone edifice his mother had so loved.

'Twas over.

Two lives had been struck through with horror, but the evil wreathed about the lady of Warvaliant had at last faded away. Rafe lifted a single taper from a sconce upon the wall and carried it with him as he made his way into a deserted sector of the castle.

He was not surprised to find himself drawn to the gallery in which he had first accepted the fact that he was of English blood. The room had been the site of excruciating anguish. His pride and his sense of honor had been snatched from beneath him there that long-ago day.

Yet now, as he stared up at the portrait of the mother he had loved, he felt only a strange contentment. And he wanted somehow to tell the dimpled girl-child in the painting that at last all was well. He longed to share with her the sense of peace stirring within him.

Even the lingering shadow of Lord Neville had been banished. A contingent of armed men, under the command of the dauntless Sir Dinadan, had ridden for Warvaliant to place the nobleman under arrest for his part in the conspiracy to end Elizabeth's life.

Rafe's lips twisted grimly at the memory of the man who had tried to brutalize Tessa. Yet though Rafe hated the cruel lord, he much doubted the Englishman had any knowledge of the devilment his mother and Encina had been plotting. Regardless, Tudor justice would strike swiftly, thoroughly, and as devastatingly as Rafe's own sword would have done.

Rafe shrugged inwardly. In truth, it mattered not to him that Neville Warburton might be forced to pay for a crime he did not commit, for the man had been guilty of a score of atrocities that had gone unpunished. Warburton's suffering now would atone for those wrongs.

Rafe rubbed the back of his aching neck with his fingers. He had slipped into this long corridor to avoid the commotion of the countless courtiers who still lingered in the distant great hall, but it seemed that even here he could find no solitude, for as he looked upon the sweet face in the portrait, he heard someone approaching. No doubt 'twas one of his grandfather's servants coming to set the chamber ablaze with candles or to see if he was a house-breaker come to steal away the plates.

"I need no more candles," Rafe said without look-ing back. " 'Tis light enough."

"I always thought so, too, whenever I came here to bask in the light of Anne's smile." Tarrant Renfrew's voice was low and heavy. Slowly Rafe turned to face the man who had shown little trace of his true emo-tions in the uproarious hours since Rafe had entered the great hall.

In the time that had passed, he had not had a chance to speak privately with his grandfather, and he knew not how the earl felt about the grandson who had abandoned him. The mighty Earl of Renfrew had shared in the gratitude of Elizabeth and her powerful courtiers for Rafe saving the queen's life, and yet Rafe had no idea how Tarrant Renfrew, the man, felt as he was confronted once again with the grandson who had hurled the earl's proud lineage away as though it were something to be ashamed of.

He stared at Tarrant Renfrew, knowing that he would scarce blame the earl if he chose to slam the gates of the castle upon him and Tessa and turn his back on those who had hurt him.

But despite the lines carved into the earl's face, despite the toll the past weeks had taken upon the strong glint in those indigo eyes, Rafe saw within

Tarrant Renfrew a tentative rejoicing, hidden behind a brittle facade of pride.

The earl cleared his throat, looking distinctly uncomfortable garbed in court finery, and Rafe had the sudden perception that the old man would be far more at ease balanced on the prow of a ship with the sea winds whipping his face.

"Grandfather." Rafe wanted to ask the older man's forgiveness, but the plea for understanding was like acid on his tongue. "There was no time to warn you before Tessa and I burst into the hall. No time to ask your forgiveness for my flight from the queen's palace. No time to ask your forgiveness for not having the courage or the decency to tell you good-bye. But I want . . . want you to know that—"

"That you wish your escape could have been otherwise? That you wished to confront me with your plan, but dared not?" There was a kinship in those eyes so like Rafe's own that touched him with hope. "You would hardly have made an effective escape, Rafael, if your grandfather had locked you in your room like a fractious lad. And I would have. I wanted you to stay in England at any cost. I wanted you to *be* an English Renfrew and to stand at my side."

"You were incredibly generous," Rafe admitted. "Accepting a stranger into your life."

"*Accepting*?" The earl's laugh was rough, yet heartening. "Do you not mean *demanding*? I demanded that you surrender yourself on my terms and become a loving grandson with the wave of a hand. People do not give their hearts that way, and I of all people should have known that."

" 'Twas just that I was still raw from the disaster that struck my ship."

"Aye. And even after all these years, I was still hurting from the loss of my Anne. It was because of your mother—the way I loved her, missed her—that I all but crushed you in my eagerness to give you a place in my heart."

Tarrant's face was touched with a wistful sorrow. "She was everything to me, everything a father could have wished for in a daughter. Other men were hungry for sons, heirs, to fight at their sides, to bring honor to the family name. Sons—King Henry even did murder to gain them . . . But Anne was enough for me. From the first day I looked upon her little face, I loved her with a fierceness that frightened me."

"Your lady wife wanted no other children?" Rafe asked, sensing the old man's need to discuss his past with the one person who shared his blood, to talk about it without meeting surly resistance or outright belligerence.

The earl shook his head, a wistful smile pulling at his lips. "Alison was not . . . er, inclined to take joy in the marriage bed. The only thing she feared even more was childbed."

"But she wed you, an earl, who she must have known would need sons to inherit his title."

"We were forced to marry when we were but children, the ambitions of our parents outweighing any needs of our own. We were ill suited from the first— she so timid, and I stalking about with my fierce temper and wild ways. I tried to be gentle, but 'tis not in my nature. She feared me, feared everything, from the shadows in the castle buttery to the falcons in the

mews. Even Anne seemed to frighten her. Alison
cloistered herself in her room with her prayers and
what priests I could smuggle in to give her comfort."

The earl paced toward Rafe, stopping beneath the
portrait of his daughter, and the warrior's scarred
fingers reached up to caress the gilded frame. "She
was mine. Anne. From the very first. Willful, wild,
yet tempered with such winning kindness and sparkling wit that everyone who knew her fell in love
with her. She was forever taking in injured nestlings
and fussing over the skinned knees of the servants'
babes. Those who were hurting in body or in spirit seemed to sense the healing power within her,
and they came to her, to let her ease their pain, to
bathe themselves in the light of her smile. It seemed
only natural that Morgause Bledford should do the
same."

"Lady Warburton?"

"Aye. Her parents died when she was but six, and
her brothers and their wives wanted naught to do
with the girl. She was neglected, ignored, unloved.
A strange child, even then. But it mattered not to
Anne."

"Anne and Morgause were close, then?"

"Yes. When they came to court their friendship
was a jest among the beaux. They called Morgause
'Sweet Anne's Shadow,' because the two were never far apart. Yet it was more than friendship on
Morgause's part. 'Twas a pathetic mimickry. She
imitated Anne's laugh, Anne's ways. Even the garments she wore were pale copies of Anne's. Morgause was a wistful child, and even I felt pity for
her—until Ruy Santadar strode into your mother's
life."

Tarrant's brow furrowed, and Rafe could see the aching light in his eyes as he regarded the likeness of his daughter. "Morgause wanted Ruy. She tried every sort of trickery to entrap him. But he, like so many others, had fallen beneath the spell of Anne's love. He wanted to wed Anne, and Anne . . . I've never seen a woman so in love. Ruy wanted to take her to Spain, make a life for her, and I thought that Anne would be safe there from Morgause's plots. I thought her but a foolish woman who would forget about Anne and Ruy once they disappeared from her life. I was a fool."

Tarrant strode to the window and looked out across his lands. "After Anne died, I was mad with grief. I wanted to attack Warvaliant and accuse Morgause of taking part in Anne's murder. But that was a ludicrous idea. By then the woman was wed to Warburton and had just been delivered of a son. She seemed to have forgotten about Anne and Ruy." Tarrant ran his fingers back through his riotous waves of graying hair as he berated himself. "How could I have failed to see how crazed she was regarding Santadar, how gluttonous for vengeance? Christ, I could have forbidden Anne from ever seeing Ruy again. I could have refused to let her marry him . . . "

Rafe turned his gaze again to the portrait, the hazy memories he held of the woman portrayed there rushing through him with a stronger clarity than ever before. He smiled, a sad smile touched with understanding. "Even if you had handed my mother a sorceress's crystal and shown her all that would befall her if she went away with my father, I am certain she would have married him anyway.

I believe she loved him from the first moment he kissed her until the end. To her the joy would have seemed well worth the suffering."

"And has your suffering been worth it as well?" Renfrew asked. The grief had faded from the old man's gaze, and Rafe saw in his face a kind of surrender.

"My suffering?"

"I saw the girl striding into the chamber at your side. Saw the way you looked at her before you were swept off to talk to Walsingham and the rest. Her eyes reminded me of Anne's when she stood at Ruy's side. They held all that was good, brave, pure. And strength, aye, there was enough love and strength in that child's face to keep you warm for the rest of your life."

"She has promised to stand beside me, whatever my life might be." Rafe watched his grandfather's face, searching for the disapproval he had seen weeks earlier. But he saw only resignation and a spark of respect.

"I made a muddle of it when last you were here, lad. I tried to arrange your life as I saw fit. If you'll consent to stay, I'll not do so again."

"Grandfather, I'm going to wed Tessa, make her my wife." Rafe met the earl's gaze levelly, wanting no veils between them. "Were I to be crowned king on the morrow, my intentions toward Tessa would not change."

"I much doubt you'll e'er be offered a monarch's crown, lad. But the golden circlet of an earl will be yours one day. I raged at you when first you told me you wanted to take Tessa to wife, and in truth the girl lacks the skills and graces necessary for a chatelaine. But on second thought, mayhap she has qualities more important than courtly manners and an understanding of how to run a vast castle." Tarrant's face creased with an aged guilt.

"My Alison was bred of generations of nobles, but within these walls she always had the look of a frightened tiring-maid. Your Tessa was every inch the countess when she entered the great hall at your side. You said she was willing to stand beside you, whatever your life might be."

The earl stepped back, slipping free a velvet pouch that hung at his waist. He spilled the contents of the bag into Rafe's palm, the light glinting upon the ring Rafe had treasured. "You might give this to her, if you wish. Ask her if she'd like to be a countess." A grin curved Tarrant's lips. "May God preserve us all!"

Rafe stood, silent, in the arched doorway, his gaze treasuring the sight of Tessa silhouetted against the jeweled tones of a tapestry depicting the return of Odysseus. She bent to some hidden task, industrious as any Penelope, unaware of his presence as the heat from the brazier turned her smooth cheeks a warm red, an adorable crease marring her brow. Her nose crinkled in concentration, her fingers deftly wielding some object in her hand, while her body— that ripe wood-nymph body that had driven him to madness—was veiled from his sight by only the wispiest of nightrails.

Her full breasts pushed impudently against the soft fabric, the aureoles' tempting shadows hinted at by the glow of candlelight. Her lips were stained so red he wanted to nip at them to see if they tasted like the berries they resembled.

Sweet. She was so sweet, his Tessa. Like a winsome fairy—until she changed into the wildwitch who had stolen his heart. And she was his now. Forever. His.

The awesome wonder of it made his heart thud hard against his ribs, made his arms ache to hold her. But he only stood there watching her, wanting to hold this moment of magical contentment for as long as he was able.

"Hellfire and damnation!" Her oath startled him from his musing as something fell from her hand and clattered to the floor. She lunged to her feet, popping her thumb into her mouth and sucking on it, but not before Rafe glimpsed a drop of crimson staining the folds of her nightrail.

"Tessa?" Her name was a question as he hastened to her side. "Did you hurt yourself, love?"

She fair jumped from her skin, her eyes blazing, accusatory, as she thrust something behind her with her other hand, and there was naught of the winsome wood sprite in her face. Instead, she had the look of the sea just before a storm, entrancing, alluring, irresistible.

"What the devil are you doing here? Why did you not warn me?"

"That I was coming to my own bedchamber? I thought you were waiting for me. In fact, I cherished some strange hope that you might be relieved to see me freed of the lion's den." Rafe allowed himself a smile as he drew her injured hand into his own, rubbing the palm in seductive circles as he examined the tiny cut. "I thought that you—*we* might spend what little remains of the night celebrating the fact that I managed to keep my head this day—quite literally."

" 'Tis fair a miracle, the way you went stalking in there like a witling! 'Tis just good fortune Lady Warburton was attempting to poison the queen, else—"

"Good fortune?" Rafe gave a shout of laughter, loving the way Tessa's face washed red with temper. "You'd best not let anyone else hear you say that, or we'll be taken up for treason."

Tessa's eyes flashed to the door, but there was no fear in them. "Think you there is anyone skulking about?"

"If there is, I will summon them in at once, demand they aid me in discovering what secret plot my betrothed has been about in my chamber."

"Plot?"

He nodded, feigning solemnity. "With my own eyes I saw you hide something behind you when I entered the room." Her lips were set in the mutinous line he loved, and yet she looked almost shy— and seeing his Tessa thus sent desire racing through his blood.

" 'Tis none of your affair, Santadar," she warned. "If I had wanted you to see it, I would scarce have taken the trouble to hide it."

"If you had *not* wanted me to see it, you would scarce have brought it into my room." He raised her hand to his lips, kissing the tips of her fingers, tasting them with his tongue. "Now relinquish your treasure, my pretty"—his voice was deep and husky—"else I demonstrate how ruthless rovers upon the sea make their captives spill secrets."

Tessa caught her breath as his lips sought out the shadowy curve of her throat, teasing the sensitive flesh with a playfulness she had never seen in the bold sea hero she had come to love. She pulled away from him, glimpsing the twinkle of merriment in his eyes, and despite the unaccustomed shyness wisping over her, she could not muster any expression except a grin to match Rafe's own.

"All right, you merciless brigand. All right. I surrender. But 'twill be the only time you'll ever bend me to your will." She stomped over to the chair and drew something from the rushes behind it.

And then there was no more amusement in her face, no more laughter. She felt suddenly vulnerable and incredibly foolish.

"Here." She all but jammed a circular piece of wood into the hard plane of Rafe's stomach, then wheeled away, unable to watch his face as he saw what she had labored upon.

Silence seemed to press like lead upon Tessa's chest as she waited for Rafe to say something, anything. But at last she could stand the silence no longer. "Well? You were so anxious to see it. It serves you right to have your eyes thus offended."

"Offended?"

"Aye. 'Tis ludicrous, this carving. But I've never done anything like it before. The chin is not stubborn enough, and the nose doesn't hold enough arrogance. And the lips are the most ill worked of all. No matter how hard I tried, I couldn't carve tenderness, temper, and the hot sweep of passion upon them all at the same time. 'Tis your own fault for having such difficult features. I would have used it for kindling, but—"

"This is how you see me?"

Tessa thought he was baiting her again, teasing, but as she wheeled upon him to snap out a sharp rejoinder, what she saw stole the biting words from her lips.

He was staring down at the disk of wood she had been carving upon, but his eyes were glowing, not with humor, but rather with a kind of awe. The long, bronzed fingers that had caressed her body with such feverish need now traced the image she had wrought of him.

In the wood carving, waves crashed in wild abandon, storm-tossed about the figure of a woman racing into the sea, into the arms of a man who was rising from the waves like some sea god come alive. She had sculpted the silky darkness of Rafe's hair blown by the wind and had struggled to carve the beautifully hewn planes of Rafe's face, but though she had done her best, she felt she had failed to capture the strength, the tenderness, and the fiery passion that had consumed her.

"I began it before we left for court, when I thought you would sail off to Spain one day and leave me. I wanted something to keep, something to remind me of the day my sea phantom came for me, just— just as my father always promised he would."

"Tessa"—Rafe's hand was unsteady—"I can never be the man you've carved upon this wood. I can never fulfill all the wonderful dreams you've captured here. 'Tis beautiful. So beautiful. It makes me afraid I'll somehow fail you."

"Nay." Tessa's heart swelled with joy at his praise for the carving that had been for her a labor of love. "You could never fail me, Rafael Santadar. You are

more beautiful than any man I might have imagined.
And your love fills me until there is no more room
for fantasies of sea gods and phantoms. No room
for aught except a Spaniard with a foul temper and
far too much pride and eyes as blue as a sun-struck
wave."

"Tessa." He groaned her name, catching her to
him, and Tessa gloried in the feel of him, so hard, so
hot, so hungry, as his lips closed upon hers. "Tessa,
I need to ask you one more question, before we cel-
ebrate."

"Question?" She could scarce speak, scarce think
as his hands wove magic upon her breasts and but-
tocks.

"Mm-hmm, would you suffer being a countess?"

She stiffened with surprise, shoving at his chest
with her palms. "A what?"

"A countess." She could feel his laughter soft
against her as he nudged aside her nightrail, his
lips seeking out the crest of one rosy breast. "Just
think, you could spend all your days ordering people about, and when you fell into a temper the whole
castle would be forced to listen to you rail."

A soft cry burst from Tessa's lips as Rafe's mouth
caught the hardened nub he had been teasing with
his tongue, suckling it for an instant, then releasing it.

Tessa bit her lip to stifle a groan of need and
resolved to treat Rafe to the same subtle torture.

"But then I would have to wed an earl, and you
. . . you wanted naught to do with being one."

"Ah, but I changed my mind after my grandfather
and I discussed the . . . er . . . responsibilities that
would be mine. You see, it seems that earls are duty

bound to father hordes of children—sons, daughters, heirs. 'Tis a most wearing task, but one I think I could suffer if my future countess had skin as sweet as new cream and lips that tasted of honey, and breasts so full they filled my hands."

She heard a ragged moan work through him as her fingers began to skim down his flat stomach, the sound banishing any hint of teasing from her as she lost herself in the joy of this tender, loving man.

"Rafe, are you sure? I don't need to be a countess. I don't need a castle or land. If you are hungry for the sea, we can sail away on a ship."

He kissed her, fierce and hard, with all the love he felt for her. "Ah, wildwitch, do you not see? Loving you is more adventure than I ever dreamed of. I need no other mistress, not even the sea. You are tempest enough for me, wildwitch. I love you . . . love you."

His lips closed upon hers, tender, so tender, and her bold sea phantom swept her into a world of wild imaginings, of dreams that would last forever.